CINDY M. AMOS

RECONCILED FROM HEARTACHE
By Cindy M. Amos

Horizons of Hidden Promise Book 2

Copyright © 2021 by Cindy M. Amos
Published by Forget Me Not Romances, an imprint of Winged Publications

This book is a work of fiction. Names, characters, places, and incidents are the product of the author's imagination and are used fictitiously. Any resemblance to actual events, locales, or persons, living or dead, is coincidental.

All rights reserved including the right to reproduce this book or portions thereof in any form whatsoever – except short passages for reviews – without express permission.

ISBN: 978-1-952661-69-3

*Blessed are those who cherish justice,
who are guided by virtue at every turn.
Psalm 106:3*

Chapter 1

Aley Halstead maneuvered the agency truck down the narrow tree-lined lane headed into the heart of rural nowhere. Crosswise for this particular client's visit, she'd have to bluff her way through and cut the inspection short. From rumors around the conservation office, this new landowner lacked any ranching experience at all. The assignment fell to her as low person in the hierarchy at the Emporia office. To quell her exasperation, she checked her hair in the mirror.

The tree canopy gave way to the open prairie as the land rose toward an unimpressive hill. Lyon County had its share of grandeur as a chink in the Flint Hills, safeguarding what remained of the midcontinent's tallgrass prairie. She loved the grass-covered slopes, chopped occasionally by limestone outcrops that bore the hard chert which lent the formation its flinty name. She felt less inclined toward the all-male office staff with whom she currently worked.

A modest farmhouse appeared to the right, so she eased the truck forward and began to assess the dated ranching operation. Signs of dereliction glared at every turn, especially the sagging outbuildings. Built in sturdy cottage style, the little residence still possessed an air of primness. A simple coat of white paint would perk up the exterior with a brushstroke. Upon second glance, she hoped to avoid falling through the porch planks when she knocked on the front door.

She parked the truck out in the open, not knowing which direction they would head out to assess the current pasture conditions. Her plan to make suggestions for management improvements depended on whether the land qualified for any federal programs for added enhancements. As she slid from the cab, she chuckled at being regarded as a heartless regulator. Despising that tough-guy approach, she would cling to her determination to make a difference for natural resources. After all, Christian stewardship included range management. Here in Kansas, it represented the only kind of conservation work available. *So stuck in Lyon County.* But maybe not for long. A turkey vulture circled overhead casting a shadow on the ground.

In steps, a hollow thud resonated from a nearby grain silo. She halted, thinking she may have caught the resident rancher out doing chores. The next thump came accompanied by a protesting growl. She headed south to investigate what kind of creature might be cornered by an innocuous storage bin. A guilty ladder soon caught her attention, fallen to one side.

"God, please," a man shouted. "Let me out of here." Another thud chased the plea.

Aley tucked her notepad into her shirt pocket and tried to tamp down the teasing grin that his predicament had birthed. Mr. Know Nothing would now become fodder for her first improvement recommendation, as soon as she unlatched him from the imprisoning situation at hand. "Mr. Warren? Is that you in there?"

Something shifted inside the metal cylinder and produced a scraping sound. "Yes, it's me. I've been trapped in here for hours. Please, can you release the door from the outside?"

She put both hands on the rust-encrusted lever and hung some weight on the far end, forcing it to comply. A grating scrape indicated progress as the latch dropped down until it clicked free. Shoved from inside, the rough-edged door almost scraped her cheek as it swung open in haste. With little time to react, she managed to free her hands as a man's torso came lunging through the opening to clamp her in a breath-stealing embrace.

"Thank you, Lord," the rancher muttered through her hair.

A prisoner, Aley refused to react to his touch even the slightest bit. She held her hands in the air, not knowing what to do. She'd never become part of the land assessment before. This represented new ground—and it held a certain tactile element despite the corrugated metal edge cutting into her midsection. The whole scene clearly extended beyond department policy.

"I'm so thirsty. Please, could you help me out of here?" He pulled back and looked at her from close range, his gaze still wild from the entrapment episode.

Only when he rested his hands on the opening did she notice his fingertips. Raw and bloody, they spoke of longsuffering and dire attempts at self-rescue. Moved with a tinge of compassion, a lump formed in her throat. "Stand aside, Mr. Warren. I'll drop several of these landscape timbers into the granary, so you can use them for steps."

He blinked as if not understanding. "Call me Hake."

She stood and lifted the first wood block. Once hoisted to the door, she allowed him to take hold. "I'm Aley Halstead from the Natural Resources Department. We have an appointment this morning to see if your land qualifies for our EQIP program."

His mouth hung open for a few awkward seconds. In recovery, he snatched the block and settled it by his feet. When he appeared back in the doorway, he gave her a searching look. "Not Al Halstead like the phone message implied?"

She gave him a temperate smile and let it fade. "That's a little trick the staff enjoys playing on me back at the conservation office. It's a real men's club…except for me. Let me get you one more block, and then I think we can try clearing the doorway." She scrambled for the wooden chock to make good on the promise. Still off-balance from the hug, she didn't know what to make of this guy. She plunked the block on the door's edge and held it for the transfer.

"Guess I'm going to be a wreck for your tour. Maybe I should just reschedule." He took possession of the block and lowered it onto the other. When he stood on the stack, it teetered.

Aley reached through the opening and caught his shoulders for steadying. "No need to reschedule since I'm already out here. What if we take a half-hour break to turn into fully functional human beings again? I think those fingertips of yours might need some first aid."

He hovered over the rim before lifting one leg to escape. "Well, if you're offering, then I'm accepting." Despite his wounded state, a tiny grin tugged at his cheek.

With his boyish good looks ramping up in such proximity, Aley had no way out. She gave his shoulders a tug and brought him through the opening. Airborne for only seconds, the added weight drove her straight to the ground. Though guarded by his shoulder at the last second, the tumble still knocked the air from her lungs.

Hake rolled to one side, his arms splayed in the spring-green grass. "How was that for making a strong first impression, Ms. Halstead?"

She drew a deep breath and contemplated how honest to be. "Regulators don't usually receive hugs on these determination site visits." She inhaled more spring freshness into her lungs. "I'm still not sure whether to classify you as an errant climatic force or a hidden natural resource I've stumbled upon." She turned and looked at him over the blades of grass.

"Sounds like I win either way," he replied, seemingly content to be the object of her inspection. "I have bandages in the hall closet."

"Good, you're going to need them." With that, she rolled onto her knees and headed for the truck. Nothing official in the cab would remedy this introductory rescue predicament. Today, she would have to rewrite the policy book, something she'd longed to do for some time. For some reason, that prospect lifted dread off her shoulders. She had blue skies overhead and green grass under her feet. *Dare I ask for anything more?*

~

Hake smoothed his hair back and sorted through half a dozen ways to save face in this strained situation, so the attractive conservation rep might view him in a more favorable light. The truck lurched through a collapsed culvert while they headed to a remote pasture that seemed more rock collection than grazing land. He'd acquired the entire acreage dirt-cheap by market standards, but cheap could equate to long-range expensive when improvements leaked a hole in the owner's bank account. He'd have to spread out the forthcoming enhancement plan, even if that meant the comely officer would visit less often, a sorry happenstance.

She turned toward him, her eyes sparkling. "I see the former owner let the trees invade this rear pasture. Our EQIP program offers financial assistance to fight against hardwood encroachment to allow the grass to maintain dominance. With the spread so extensive, I'm convinced that condition alone would qualify your land for the program. You can hire out the clearing work, or do it yourself. Both practices are acceptable."

"Okay, if there's financial assistance to make sure the work gets done, I'm going to like doing business with your department." Somehow, the confession lowered his apprehension. "I might do some of both, but I'd hire out clearing the larger trees, for sure. I have a different day job, so I might strive to keep my limbs intact for that citified work." He added a folksy tone to the admission to keep the exchange light.

She chuckled. "No one would ever guess that you ranched by occupation, Hake. Still, hobby ranching holds considerable merit. As a landowner, you have quite the opportunity to bring your land back to the best condition possible. I admire that goal."

"That's my Christian obligation—to be a good steward," he replied. When she nodded, he decided to take it a step further. "I do everything as unto the Lord. That value permeates every corner of my life. Believe it or not, there are some less clumsy domains in which I thrive."

That garnered a throaty feminine laugh as the truck slowed to a halt. "That's great news. Let's start right here. I'd like to trace the pasture's edge down to that drainage below. We can talk about how much of that riparian buffer of trees along the creek you might want to retain."

"Trees along the creek are okay—but not ones in the pasture?" He exited the cab, scratching his head. There would be more than riparian buffers to learn about—like rusty grain silos that liked to gobble unsuspecting men for breakfast. Momentarily dazed, he stood off the front grill trying to gear up for the walk.

In seconds, Aley nudged him with her shoulder. "Hey, are you up for this part?"

"Guess we're about to find out."

"I'll set a leisurely pace and talk about what I see. That way you can learn which hardwoods to watch for, the types threatening to encroach on the pasture."

He held her gaze a few seconds and stepped down-slope toward the tree line with some reluctance. "So how about you? Have you always been the outdoorsy type?"

She picked a bright green leaf from a solitary tree as

they passed. "Called out as a tomboy—you're exactly right. This is American elm, what some regard as a trash tree. See how the leaf looks like the logo on an ice cream carton? That's a quick way to remember this one."

He ran his bandaged fingertips over the jagged-edged leaf. "You know, there just might be some hope for me yet. I already know a cedar tree when I see one."

She shook her head. "That line over there is all Osage orange, sometimes called hedge trees. Even after you girdle them, the wood remains so hard, the tree will stand for another decade or more. Some like using the heartwood to make furniture. The grain has an interesting orange tint, but the name really comes from the balls that grow as grapefruit-sized seed pods."

"They're colored orange then?" He flexed his brow to heighten the inquiry.

She chuckled and picked at a shrub barely leafing out. "No, they're actually lime green and crenulated, you know, crinkled like the surface of your brain."

"If I had a brain," he replied under his breath. Wiping his overgrown hair out of his field of vision, he sensed a need to overcome feelings of inadequacy on the ranch if he held a sliver of a chance to make a go of it. "Okay, what kind of bush did you pick?"

A little smile warmed her expression. "Well, I tried not to pick at it too much, so you might have more gooseberries left to make into pies and jams."

Ready for more revelation, he intended to make it personal. "Do you like making jams and such from what Mother Nature provides?"

"Yes, I enjoy living off the land like that. I'd like to garden, but I don't have a yard right now. I live in an apartment in Emporia, but I did have planter boxes on the porch last summer to grow tomatoes."

"Aha, worthy aspirations trapped in boxes. That doesn't sound totally satisfying for someone who has such an obvious connection to the land." He gave her a quick glimpse to see how the probing comment landed.

Aley walked down into a gully, her feet sliding on the crumbly rocks lining the slope. "You don't want this shrub in the pasture. It's rough-leafed dogwood." She strummed her hand across several thin bare-wood stems. "Get rid of it while it's small and easier to clip through."

"I'm going to need some strong loppers," he replied, rubbing his hands together. The sight of his bandaged fingertips reiterated that he lacked the proper handle on that challenge.

She squared around to him once he'd joined her at the lower elevation. After she held his full attention, she smiled. Then it faded all too fast. "About those worthy aspirations trapped in boxes—I'm on the verge of doing something to remedy that. In all fairness, you should know. I'll get your enrollment started for the program and put your enhancements in place, but another conservation officer will likely walk you through the process. I'm looking to transfer out of the Lyon County office to much greener pastures. You'll do fine, as long as you stay motivated."

The gully suddenly lacked air, as the detrimental news broke the possibility for a personal tie before he could even hint toward such collusion. The next agent wouldn't have soft hazel eyes framed by curvy lashes and long hair the color of frosted tree bark. As she walked on dribbling leaves from her hand, he stood frozen by the dogwood, feeling equally discarded.

What kind of management plan would transform him from less of a trash tree, at least in the eyes of the current enticing regime? He stumbled across the loose flint rocks, searching for a way out of the impasse that had opened between them. A sense of longing quickened his pace. *Lord help, I'm trapped in another grain bin.* Oh, how he hated operating from the panicked end of the response spectrum, yet another rookie predicament to escape.

Chapter 2

Hake poured the hot brew from his makeshift coffee bar and let his gaze roam the law office. Spartan at best, at least he'd mounted his framed diplomas to lend authority to the workspace. So far, last week's advertisement for a free first consultation had generated only a trickle of walk-in traffic. He slid his healing fingertips through the handle of the coffee mug, enjoying the heat radiating through the ceramic.

The door latch sounded behind him, announcing his first client of the day. Too early for his eleven o'clock appointment, he turned to discover who sought his services. When a well-dressed woman halted in the doorway, he couldn't have been more surprised.

She gasped audibly. "Hake? *This* is your day job?"

A feminine version of Aley Halstead stood in front of him, but he couldn't find the first words to acknowledge it. The curves once hidden by her conservation officer uniform now called for full attention, to his immediate liking. At a loss, he shoved the mug toward her. "Coffee?"

Her lips parted to continue the incredulous exchange. "Really? You're a lawyer?"

"Really and truly, I am." He motioned toward the row of diplomas and had to smile when she promptly checked them out for authenticity. "With all the rights and privileges thereunto appertaining…or some such wordage as that. Aley, please let me pour you a cup of coffee."

She straightened her spine and stepped back to inspect him. "Yes, thank you. Sugar only. I've come for a consultation regarding a real estate transaction. I saw your ad for a free visit and thought it might benefit me to gain more clarity before I act. So, here I am."

After pouring the coffee with care, he grabbed a sugar packet and motioned toward the guest chair nearby. He sat the mug on a napkin along the front edge of his desk and hesitated before taking his seat. "This is where I typically say *good morning*, though this visit doesn't quite fall in the realm of typical. Good morning to you, nonetheless."

She tugged her fitted skirt down and reached over to sweeten up the coffee.

Hake shrugged and stepped around the desk, trying to regain a modicum of genteel professionalism. He sat and pulled up against the desk blotter, where he noticed the bundle tucked under her arm for the first time. "So, how may I help you today?"

Her chest rose and fell with a breath, though her expression remained distant. After a few tense seconds, she proffered a leather-bound document, bracing it against the desk. "I'm here to seek advice about selling off some family land. I've never done anything like this. Quite frankly, I don't know how it goes. Right now, call selling a distant consideration, but after I move away, it seems strained for me to maintain possession." Her bottom lip trembled the slightest bit at the admission.

"A land deed? May I examine this?" He gestured toward the document and waited for her curt nod before he made contact. "They don't make titles like this anymore, Miss Halstead. What a gem." He drew the bundle closer for inspection and unfastened the closure. Using kid glove treatment, he expanded the leather-bound folder and took a look at the cover page. "Would you look at that? The date reads eighteen ninety." He shook his head, beaming his admiration.

The client seemed to warm a bit. "Herbert J. Rusher was my great uncle's grandfather. The Rusher clan merged with the Halsteads a couple of generations ago. I inherited the tract from my grandparents. It no longer has a functional house on the land." She looked at the mug.

"Two hundred and forty acres, that's a sizable pasture. And, knowing the owner, it's likely in pristine condition, which will attract a top dollar if and when placed on auction." He sat back and studied her complex expression. Some matter hadn't become fully evident, as she had a premature case of seller's regret. "Yet, you have cause for hesitation—as you seem unsettled. Want to get that out in the open, so I can offer you the best legal advice possible?"

Her gaze shifted across the room, until it finally alighted on him. "I'm fighting to work beyond feeling like I'm some kind of double agent—saying that I care for the land in one breath while selling off my own heritage plot to the highest bidder." She stopped long enough to sigh. "On a bad day, the holding flat-out strikes me as a constraining liability, having so much land hanging like a millstone around my neck."

He pressed the leather cover back into its historic folds, but didn't fasten the binder. Sympathetic to her lack of decisiveness, he leaned toward her. "Such a pity, good coffee going to waste like that." The need to wander struck him full force, so he conceded. He gave a fleeting smile and pushed back from the desk. His restlessness would lend Aley a few moments to collect her demeanor—or perhaps *he* needed the collecting.

The view out onto Merchant Street proved optimal neutral territory. He heard the faint scrape of the mug off the desktop and let that tiny satisfaction tint his mindset. Thinking to be more transparent, he turned the conversation. "Making my first consultation free allows me the option to render an initial opinion in the take-it-or-leave-it category. Nothing ventured and nothing gained, so to speak. Many clients find that preliminary guidance sufficient enough to assume a new tactical direction or let the legal route gain traction, as necessary. With that preface, may I offer you some up-front advice?"

Her eyelids fluttered closed as she sipped the coffee, her lips curving against the ceramic mug like a caress. When she opened her eyes, no trace of resistance remained. She swallowed and nodded. "I came here today for honest advice, so yes, please do."

He opened his palms toward her to show he had no hidden agenda. To close the distance between them, he approached the corner of the desk and sat on it casually. "First, I'm impressed by your land deed. It's both handsome and historical at the same time. Maybe that's what makes it a good talisman for representing the ranch property. In hindsight, your relatives put their backbreaking, hard-earned money into buying this particular piece of prairie. Their home—not yours—but the deed passes down to you where, on a bad day, it feels like a millstone. That could be a byproduct of your wanting to leave the immediate area. Now, you could keep leasing the grass as an absentee landowner to continue making steady income, or you could sell."

"That's what it comes down to—do I keep it or *not*? I'm the one who has to make that final decision." She put the mug down and stood. The plush Oriental rug soon became her pacing track. "I've rehashed this quandary a thousand times and never gain any new insight."

"Well, we haven't spoken about the good day yet."

She stopped short and flexed her brow. "The good day?"

"Yes, the other side of the spectrum when owning the tract doesn't seem like a burden. I'm talking about when it seems like an honor, a bestowment, or even a treasured keepsake to own and care for family heritage lands for yet another generation."

Her eyes grew wide as she regarded him with her full attention. Her hands slipped onto her hips. "The Good Lord knows, yes. Land ownership is an honor. For my job, I probably say that at least once a day in some form or fashion. Are you saying I'm not taking that to heart? Maybe I have a blind spot here." One hand drifted up her blouse buttons as if to add a guard.

Drawn by her sincerity, he stood and stepped closer. "Aley, let me be a doctor for a few seconds instead of legal counsel. You have a first-class case of sellers regret, only you're experiencing it prematurely. You're obviously unsettled, which is no way to enter into something as legal and binding as a real estate transaction. Look, buyers with deep pockets are out there waiting to get their hands on quality tracts of grass. Such opportunities are moneymakers here in the Flint Hills with the promise of steady grazing income. Unless you're desperate to have a large lump sum in short order, I have to advise against selling the land. That's my honest professional opinion, which I think matches the doubt I read in your eyes."

She blew out a long breath as her frame grew less rigid. "Yes, it matches, at least for now. I just needed to hear another levelheaded person say it, that's all."

He peered over his brow, commanding all his boyish charm. "Hey, if that's a cloaked compliment, I'll take it. Now, do you have time to sit with me and finish your coffee? I have a string of thought-provoking questions to ask you. For instance, are you going to a job interview dressed like that? You sure aren't going into the field, not with those spiked heels."

She laughed, trying to cover her mouth with the back of her hand. Her gaze warmed and illuminated her face. "Okay, I have time for coffee...and a few of your questions."

"I won you over with my overt charisma, didn't I?" In

seconds, he had the second guest chair pulled square to face hers and settled in for a welcomed collaboration.

"I'll be honest. You won me over with this coffee."

He wove his fingers together and leaned toward her. "You really plan to go in for a job interview today, don't you?"

Her lips hovered over the rim of the mug. "Yes, your intuition is right, I'm interviewing early this afternoon. The natural resources office in Morris County may have a position come open as early as next month." She paused to sip, her pink lips contrasting with the white mug. "It would be a lateral move, but quite the necessary one, I assure you."

He winked in concession. "One's immediate sphere of influence is so important. I'm sure you tried to shine your light in a dark, rough place for the Lyon County office. No matter that they called you Al and pulled all manner of gender privilege on you. If you've done all you can to rectify matters toward equality, a lateral move makes sense, as long as the cost of living and housing availability at the new location don't factor in."

"Council Grove has some amenities—and lots of history."

He nodded to concede the point. "But it's smaller than Emporia and has less shopping."

"You're not going to mention Walmart and Bluestem to try and dissuade me, are you?" A slight hint of a grin surfaced, making her look all the more attractive.

"I avoid Wally World and I'm clueless what this Bluestem option entails, but I most certainly am sitting here trying to dissuade you, Ms. Halstead. You're the most interesting woman I've met in quite some time, but you always seem to be walking out the door."

She stood up, giving him a complicated look. "Can I shatter that fade-away image? If you have a spare forty-five minutes, I can tour you through Bluestem—a rancher's heaven."

Heartened, he leapt to his feet. "I have an hour and forty-five minutes, in fact. May I throw myself at the mercy of my guide for a favorable verdict?"

She reached for the deed and tucked it under her arm. "If you can leave the courtroom theatrics behind, I'll be glad to drive you over."

"Okay, I'm with you—and I couldn't be more pleased." He toasted her with his mug, taking the last cool draught of coffee to quell his nervous energy—or possibly to refuel it.

~

"That's the one, definitely the one." Aley hitched her brow, but stopped the wink before it could happen. When Hake had suggested a cowboy hat, she had no idea he'd follow through with buying one. In truth, he looked like a movie star in a spaghetti western with a modern-day mercantile for a backdrop. The tour of Bluestem had already paid a few extra dividends. Maybe she'd forgotten how to laugh lately.

"Okay. I guess I can get used to the faux turquoise brad clamping the band together. That's more style than I thought a humble Kansas rancher might need." He pulled the brim lower and scanned the shelf's horizon, ending at her. He squinted as if trying to look the part.

The cowboy hat overrode the starched oxford shirt to make him seem more approachable. "That's your new persona, Hake. I may have to start calling you Hank instead."

He shifted closer, his masculine gaze in full examination of her facial features. The hat brim stopped mere inches from her forehead. "Tell me I don't look like a hayseed."

When a wry smile tucked into his smooth-shaven cheek, Aley got a bit distracted. Shopping didn't usually hold this kind of allure, even at Bluestem. She played with her blouse collar and realigned her necklace. It felt warm for some reason. "No, you don't look country in the least, but the hat will come in handy, if you're serious about ranching on the side."

His gaze dropped to her lips once or twice during the explanation. "I'm buying this hat. It fits well. Plus, I'll appreciate the portable shade by June. Let's swing by the parts counter on our way to the register. I want to see how they operate back there."

"They stock everything a rancher might need in the way of spare parts for machinery." She stepped out of range, but decided to bait him to follow. "Plus, they have free popcorn on Saturdays. That's to offset the sting of your bill." She pressed her lips together in a restrained grin and led to the rear of the store.

The acrid stench of fertilizer came and went as they passed an aisle with bulk bags of nitrogen mixes. Displays of flower seeds decorated the end-caps. She fingered the filigree cross that flourished a note card assortment, pausing to let Hake catch up.

Ahead at the parts counter, a muscular man raised his voice. "Don't promise me one thing and then give me another. I have to get that sprayer fixed this week. Get a manager out here, right this minute."

Aley glanced over and recognized a staff member from the county's noxious weed department. She always avoided that guy like the plague because of his reputation as a lady's man around town. To diffuse his possible notice of her dressy attire, she reached back for Hake and relaxed a bit when he readily accepted her hand.

Reassured, she headed for the far end of the counter where large catalogs laid open for looking up proper fits for specific models of machinery. She touched the dog-eared page. The paper seemed to ground her. "This reference is used for ordering the right part. It pays to know your model number, whether tractor, mower, or implement."

"I need to paint the house this spring." He squared his shoulders and blocked the rest of the counter. "Do you think they rent a sprayer here?"

"No, but I'll show you the equipment rental place when we drive back to your office. It's right up the road."

He peered over his shoulder, his gaze returning after he'd given the array of parallel shelves a scan. "Let's head out, unless you have something else you're looking for."

"No, I'm good. We need to protect our time anyway." She led to the front of the store and slid into a short line beside a display of old-fashioned bulk candy. The aroma of molasses compelled her attention to linger. She fingered a bag of white and pink coconut squares.

Hake nudged the small of her back with a knuckle. "Pick one out and toss it in with the hat. We'll split the contents."

Unsure, she turned to look at him. "But I don't know what kind of candy you like."

"Try me."

The candy selection now took on the aura of a compatibility test. Aley squirmed under the pressure, dodging choices that had excessive dyes in the coating. She finally spied her grandmother's favorite treat and grabbed the front bag of white-centered caramels.

His chin raked her shoulder as the clerk motioned them forward. "Confection perfection," he whispered, laying the hat on the counter beside the candy.

Her heart beat in staccato at his proximity, she so stepped away, feigning interest in a nearby bulletin board filled with event posters and homemade sales flyers. She read a sheet announcing the reopening of the farmers' market by the first of May, a short-lived joy until she remembered her desire to move away. Maybe everything about Emporia didn't register as bad. She fought that recognition until they were back in the car, heading for Merchant Street.

Hake unsealed the cellophane bag and began dividing the wrapped candies. "I guess you don't have time for lunch today."

Regretting that his tone sounded so wistful in private company, she thought to throw out a nugget of hope. "Not today, but how about a rain-check? Let me get this interview behind me."

"Right. News flash—an attractive young woman spotted backing out yet another door."

She pressed on the turn signal and pointed out the equipment rental company flanking his side of the road. Unsettled by his comment, she saw Hake pop a caramel into his mouth. The combination made her wonder what his candy-enhanced lips might taste like. Her neck grew warm at the idea, a fleeting sensation.

She cleared her throat to snap the spell. "I'd appreciate your prayers around one o'clock when the interview begins. Even though I know I'm qualified, there always seems to be a quagmire of trepidation right at first. I'm not fond of having to pitch myself so directly, but that's what a job interview is all about. At least that's what I keep telling myself."

"Wow, that should test my faith, right? Praying for the exact thing I hope won't happen." His spoke with gooey undertones as he struggled to isolate the caramel wad in his cheek.

"Okay, how about taking the middle ground and praying for God's perfect will to be done?" She arched her brow and gave him a not-so-demur glance.

He nodded, working to clear his mouth. "Speaking of middle ground, my ranch in Bushong is probably near the navigable midpoint between Emporia and Council Grove. Even if you wouldn't be my conservation agent with the new job, you'd still be relatively close by."

His rational progression sent a tingle of interest down her arms. An amicable compromise, maybe it meant not every personal interest in Emporia would have to be terminated upon a more distant hire. The realization lightened her mood. Spotting the teal awning over his office window, she slowed the car and pulled toward the curb.

He put the finishing marks on a candy wrapper note and held it toward her. His message bore only the essentials. *Lunch with Hake* followed a hastily-scrawled phone number. He popped the door open and turned for a parting comment. Tucking his chin, he fingered one of the caramels left on the console as the hat dangled in his fingertips. "I'm probably not the best at waiting too long for the redemption period on such a personal rain-check."

She gave him a slow smile, but this time couldn't keep the wink from happening. "I'll call soon, I promise." As if to endorse the pledge, she picked up a candy and held the wrapper in her teeth, spinning it to loosen the seal.

Hake stood on the sidewalk and put the cowboy hat on, bending to give her a farewell salute. The twinkle in his eyes spoke volumes. By all indications, he wanted her to call.

She accelerated from the curb, headed north to Council Grove. An odd elastic sensation seemed to tether the car, like an invisible pushpin now somehow anchored her to the tiny law office. She eyed the leather-bound land title as the caramel slid into her mouth. *More questions, yet no answers.* For some crazy reason, she decided to track the odometer reading to Bushong as she drove her way out of a hopeless work situation.

CINDY M. AMOS

Chapter 3

Hake chewed the inside of his cheek as he followed the road signs for the noxious weed department. Ever in pursuit of his next advertising angle to increase business, he'd stumbled upon a new class action lawsuit against the maker of Rid-A-Weed, a widely used herbicide. The mental alarm it had set off made his skin crawl. As best he could tell, no one in Kansas had addressed the matter, so fostering it could have major potential for increasing his business.

Not one to go off half-cocked, he needed to know more. Who better to ask than the men handling the most herbicides in their line of work? He checked the clock on the dash display before cutting off the engine. Thursday held the remarkable designation of his first dinner with Aley, a date he wouldn't screw up with some ill-timed research complication. He grabbed the legal pad for recording details and shoved open the car door.

Despite the drabness of the industrial parking lot in the foreground, the mid-April day had warmed to a comfortable temperature. Several cottonwood trees by the building had new leaves. He drew a deep breath and wondered where Aley's work might have taken her today. Spotting an employee through the glass-paneled door, he turned the knob and entered the office. The smell of sickly-sweet chemicals overwhelmed his senses, making him vow to be quick.

A muscular man with unkempt black hair turned and gave him the once-over. "Can I help you with something?"

"Just information, thank you. I'm Hake Warren, the new lawyer in town. I'm researching a case that has just come to my attention. It's centered around the widespread use of Rid-A-Weed. Are you familiar with this particular herbicide?"

The man laughed. "Geez, are you kidding? Rid-A-Weed is like aspirin—we prescribe it for almost anything. It's a lawn-and-garden-variety herbicide that works in four days to kill most any plant. It's non-selective. If you want some, you can pick it up at Walmart. We only carry the stronger stuff here, but our chemicals require prior certification for the operator to be licensed for application." He pressed a knee into a cardboard case marked Tordon and straightened.

Hake made a hasty note on Rid-A-Weed's common usage and its potent killing efficacy. More questions surfaced. "Say you're using the stuff, do you typically wear gloves or a protective mask of any kind to avoid direct contact with the chemicals?"

The man leaned over a cluttered desk toward him. "Listen, buddy. There's no avoiding contact with this stuff. We use it day-in and day-out. The Kansas wind doesn't make that kind of spraying work a picnic either, believe me. I get chemical burns all the time—a hazard of the job. Still, you don't see my hair falling out, right? Somebody's making a big deal out of nothing, most likely." He picked up a box knife and slit through the tape on another box of Tordon.

"The glyphosate in Rid-A-Weed has been recently linked with a type of cancer called non-Hodgkins lymphoma. I plan to help locals who have been exposed to the herbicide apply for financial help that may be available to offset the cost of medical treatment. That's making a big deal out of something to me. Thanks for your time today, and for answering my questions."

The man grunted his response, turning his back to restart his work.

Hake strode toward the door, ready to be out of the stench of concentrated chemicals. As he opened the door, he thought to have the last word with the testy worker. "Still, it seems like a small gesture to slip on a pair of rubber gloves to protect your hands. You know what they say about an ounce of prevention, right?"

The man straightened, his jaw clenched tight. "Yeah—it's worth a pound of mind-your-own-business." He stepped into the rear storage area out of sight.

Hake let the April breeze blow away the residual cynicism of a narrow mind. Tordon would likely make the carcinogenic list next, and all the non-glove wearers would end up meeting a nice oncologist to start their multi-phased battle for life. The need to intervene for the unaware Rid-A-Weed users intensified deep inside, a telltale clue he now aimed his professional intentions down the right track.

~

The golden pendant lamps made the buffet seem more formal, but Aley knew shifting the lunch raincheck to dinner had been the right move. She rubbed her knuckles against the tucked pleat of her bodice where a tight seam generated a negligible itch. When Hake stepped closer balancing a plate and a glass of tea, she met his gaze with a questioning look. "Want to pick the seat? I'm lost in here."

"Sure, it's the lighting. Follow me, lost damsel, and I shall deliver you to a safe port." His mood seemed to lighten in the role of deliverer as he led the way to a rear room full of booths. He veered left and soon had a small nook-for-two selected near the corner.

She placed her full plate onto the table and waited for him to do the same. "I need to go back for something to drink. Want anything?"

"Only to come along. I'm headed for the salad bar next.

I ran out of lettuce over the weekend, so I'm overdue." He placed a hand on the small of her back and nodded toward the front room.

"This was an excellent idea, so thank you. I hope Thursday worked for your schedule, as I couldn't wait until the weekend." She looked over her shoulder at him to see how close he had followed. Fortunately, he hovered shadow-close.

"As it just so happens, I had plans to eat on Thursday, so it works well for me," he replied with a smirk. "To dine with a beautiful woman, however, that's yet another matter." He leaned across her shoulder. "You look amazing tonight. Let me get that said with utmost sincerity."

"Thank you, Hake. I hope you had a pleasant day at the office."

He shook his head. "I'm onto something…substantive. I'll share some of it later. Right now, I want to be distracted by copious amounts of food and a pair of dazzling hazel eyes across the booth from me." He gave a quirky smile and surveyed the salad bar. "Can I bring you anything from the spinach shack?"

She rested a finger on the side of her mouth. "How about half a boiled egg?"

"Will do. See you in a short minute. Don't say grace without me." He detoured and headed straight for a mound of mixed greens.

Feeling more alive than she had in months, Aley vowed not to let business derail pleasure tonight. Once at the drink bar, she dropped a lemon slice in her glass and filled it with dark-brewed tea. Likely caffeinated, it would keep her up well past midnight. Maybe she could replay some of the evening and enjoy her handsome companion like a postgame highlight reel. Floating on air, she made the trip back to the booth without a spill. She unrolled the silverware while waiting for his return.

In no time, Hake arrived with his salad plate, bent from

the waist, and presented the dish to her. The boiled egg sitting atop of the mound got restless with all his movement and began rolling downhill. One bounce on the plate rim sent it on a collision course with the tabletop.

Aley released the silverware and cupped her hands to trap the renegade garnish. In seconds, she cradled the egg like a toddling child. She politely plunked it beside her cooked spinach and reached for her napkin.

Hake slid into the booth opposite her, shaking his head. "Awesome display of dexterity there, Ms. Halstead. I delivered a curveball, but you had home plate well covered."

"Please let me say grace, in case God isn't in a baseball mood this evening." She wiped her palm a second time and extended her hand over the table.

Hake clasped her hand with a light touch, but his gaze landed with magnetic weight.

Suddenly self-conscious, Aley clamped her eyelids closed and took a deep breath. A combination of grateful words issued from her mouth, though they were hardly the ones at the forefront of her mind. Hake duly distracted her. After saying amen, she tried to regain her poise. "Pardon me for being seriously hungry tonight. It's already been a trying week."

He picked up a carrot stick and waved it in the air. "Work—be gone." With that tease, he polished off the carrot.

Aley stabbed her fork through the egg, sliced it, and picked up some limp spinach along with the half. She gestured at him before bringing the mouthful in striking range. "To our good health." With that release, she proceeded to demolish a plateful of delectable food. The crunchy fried onions atop her garlic mashed potatoes fell under attack next.

After making a dent in his salad, Hake set the plate aside to go after his hot entre. Tender slices of roast beef found the center of a tall roll. He bit the makeshift sandwich sideways as if tackling a taco.

"Clever approach," she managed between bites.

He nodded and chewed with obvious contentment. After sipping his tea, he leaned in to deliver a smile. "Hey, we both got corn. I think that's a good sign."

"Another litmus test? I'm not on trial as a potential match, am I?"

He took a forkful of lengthy green beans instead of responding. Below the table, his shoes touched hers and gave a little foot hug that came off pretty cozy.

She tried not to signal her pleasure, but it became downright impossible when he gave her a sideways glance. Though she'd promised herself not to flirt, she did give him a long look through the curve of her lashes. The corn seemed safer territory, even if they enjoyed compatibility there. Corn tasted delectably sweet, and right now, sweet held enticing appeal.

~

Hake propped his chin into his palms, elbows on the table. Three used plates teetered in a pile to his right, but his focus returned to the lovely woman sharing the booth. "I'm not rushing into this in some cavalier fashion, but I think local cancer patients deserve tapping into this fund set aside for Rid-A-Weed users."

"Know what you should do? Go over to Newman Regional Medical Center and meet the oncologist treating these patients. He might even funnel some referrals your way, or at least let you put up a flyer for legal assistance where affected family members could see it." Aley played with the saltshaker, spinning it in quarter turns.

"That's an excellent idea, especially since I'm new in town and don't know any medical professionals. It wouldn't take much effort to put a flyer together, since I've already designed the newspaper ads. What else would you recommend? I don't want to come across like an ambulance chaser with these product liability cases. From what I've seen, ranchers and lawn care workers might be the most overexposed section of the working public."

She lowered her gaze and the saltshaker soon stood idle. "I'm a little worried about my brother Reece's level of exposure, in all honesty. Because the backpack sprayer unit is too heavy for me, he always takes on the spraying when we're conducting our weed control."

Family represented a new realm of interest, one Hake felt a draw toward. "You have a brother in town? If so, I'd really like to meet him."

She looked around the restaurant and then leaned closer. "Okay, that's a lead in to our next topic of conversation. Time is getting away from us, after all."

He gave his watch a glance. "It's not even eight o'clock."

She shook her head. "Seasonal time, I mean. Take heart, I'm working on your range management plan. Still, there are portions that need addressing prior to the start of growing season. That's why I'm calling in reinforcements on your behalf." She paused and gave him a shy smile. "Can I sweet talk you into burning that rear pasture this weekend? A timely fire will isolate those hardwoods to the creek area and rid them from the grassland. Plus, fire stimulates grass which grows back thick and lush for enhanced grazing. Burning's a common practice."

He whistled, overwhelmed with such a potentially devastating element. "Oh, I don't know about that. I'm a gringo at range management as it is. Don't put fire in my hands and expect me to be responsible." He held his forehead, trying to think if he had a conflict in his schedule to throw out there as a stronger excuse. Too bad nothing came to mind.

Aley kicked at his shoe. "You want to meet Reece, don't you? Well, I asked him if he'd be willing to help me with the burn at your ranch on Saturday morning, and he's available. You'd be our assistant, but we'd make sure safety essentials were in place. How about it? Mid-April is prime time for controlled burns, so you're landing inside the window of opportunity."

Highly familiar with that particular portal, he read the sparkle in her eyes as willingness to partner with him to get the burn done. That companionable flame he wouldn't put a wet blanket over, no matter the risk. A link to Sunday came to mind, so he tossed it onto the table. "My only calendar item this weekend is the celebration of Palm Sunday. I dearly love the Lord's triumphant procession into Jerusalem, as he gets his kingly due for a brief duration, anyway. So far, I haven't found a church that I've clicked with yet. If I capitulate for the burn Saturday, can I finagle an invitation to *your* church on Sunday?"

She folded her hands and tapped the saltshaker toward his side of the table. "Okay, that's such an easy negotiation to undertake—unless there's a side I'm not readily seeing. You'd get that rear pasture burned off, and I'd get an escort for church. Maybe I'd even wash the soot off my face, so you wouldn't be embarrassed to sit beside a field hand in the Lord's house."

"The embarrassment factor will be all mine during the burn, I assure you." In a bold move, he reached over and took her hand in his. "Thank you for offering your free time on my behalf. I'll be sure to express that to Reece on Saturday, too." Somewhere nearby, dropped dishes clattered to the floor.

She tilted her head to a coy angle. "You're most welcome. Sometimes Reece can come across bossy, but that's because the fire moves quickly. You can't afford to let it get away from you. I'm looking forward to seeing how well you work in with Team Halstead."

He rubbed his thumb across the top of her hand at the personal reference. "And you thought picking caramels was high pressure. I'm sweating bullets, but willing to assist."

"That's great, because the landowner is required to

make the call ahead of time for the burn permit. Wind conditions have to be right, but the fire department anticipates every rancher in the county will be calling within the next two weeks. Still, they like to know who's putting fire out on the grass in case anyone ends up needing suppression help, so we'll follow protocol."

"My anxiety over Saturday just ratcheted up another level."

"Nonsense. You'll shadow me, so I can tell you why we're doing things. That way, I'll keep you informed while you're keeping me safe from harm." She gave his hand a squeeze.

"Thanks for not saying I'm merely shadowing you like a rookie. I'll help carry buckets of water, how's that?"

Her eyes sparkled as a luminous smile took prominence on her face. "That you will, Mr. Lawyer-off-duty. You're going to get the hang of this ranching thing, no worries. Reece also wants to find out who you've lined up to rent your grass. He has some cattlemen buddies eager to sign a lease if your acreage remains available. Grazing season starts May first."

"I have lots of availability at your disposal. Right now, I'd really like to get out of this restaurant and stretch my legs. Any suggestions?"

Aley withdrew her hand. "Since most of the parks close at dusk, we'll have to wait for the days to get longer to explore one. Have you spent any time at Emporia State? Their campus is well-lit which makes for a great stroll."

He slid from the bench seat. "Sounds perfect." He took the bill in hand and offered her his elbow. As she stood and came beside him, he had a surge of unregulated pleasure. "Thank you for such scintillating company tonight."

"My delight."

They bumped shoulders in tight formation as he headed for the checkout counter. When he reached for his wallet, she broke off and angled down the hall to the restrooms. He absently paid the bill, reflecting on his good fortune to have such superior company. Hopefully, their friendship wouldn't all go up in smoke Saturday. He'd guard against that with more than a bucket of water. *Burn on, little flame.* If ignition could be played against suppression, he knew on which side of the fence he stood. Hopefully, no one would get burned.

~

Aley gave Hake a few extra moments to pet Corky, the bronze statue of Emporia State's mascot, on the head. The spot he chose to rub shined like copper with frequent contact, even under the warm yellow lights filtering from overhead. "So, do you think a hornet has more debonair appeal than an Ichabod mascot?"

He laughed, giving the animated character one final polish. "You definitely have that right. Though Washburn's intent may have been to depict a dashing young man in coattails, most people think of Ichabod as a headless horseman, thanks to Washington Irving."

"They train teachers here for employment all over the state and beyond. It's quite the academic heritage. Plus, their link to William Allen White perpetuates a focus on journalism."

"I didn't realize the National Teachers Museum existed on campus until I drove by the sign last week. There's so much more to take in. I sure hope I don't lose my talented tour guide to Council Grove's Santa Fe Trail." He returned and shot her a questioning look.

The night breeze riffled through newly unfurled leaves of several stately sycamore trees nearby, making the evening sound like satin. It certainly held a soothing sensation with Hake looking at her like that. She wouldn't let the future's jagged-edged unknowns rob her of such luxury. "I only see the wonderment of tonight." Her soft tone held an invitation.

He closed the distance between them, and then leaned in to plant a slow kiss on her forehead. They stayed close like that, dancing with the sycamores under a night breeze that wouldn't reveal its destination. *Here for now.* Despite the lack of committal, the juncture held such comfort, she remained under its influence for an extended moment, a liquid duration held in place by one man's arresting arms.

Chapter 4

Hake sat across from a weary man, his desk the ultimate example of widespread neglect. When he leaned forward his suit jacket pulled tight against his shoulder blades. "Thank you for seeing me today, Dr. Atkins. I know you're busy, what with the weekend approaching."

He flicked his wrist as if to knock the comment away. "We're busy every day. That's the role of a regional hospital—full staff for around-the-clock service. You get used to the pace after a while. I have two days off this weekend, and I plan to take advantage of them." He stroked the thin hair off his graying temples.

"Well, I'm setting part of my ranch on fire with the help of my conservation officer Saturday, so I'm hoping not to generate any business for your emergency room staffers." Hake laughed and instantly began to feel more comfortable when the good doctor joined him. "Let me get right down to what I've come to discuss, to respect your time. I've discovered that a commonly used herbicide called Rid-A-Weed has been linked with non-Hodgkins lymphoma. Settlements with the manufacturer have been processed through the legal system riding a class action lawsuit. No one is representing consumers in Kansas yet, so I thought to pursue notification locally to gain financial compensation for qualified victims."

"Lymphomas are prevalent right now, I assure you. Not all of those folks were spraying weeds to cause it, though. I guess you've given some thought as to how to sort through claims to find the valid ones."

"Well, occupation or chronic exposure will be prime indicators, I believe. After checking with the noxious weed department, I think direct contact is a key. The guy I talked with doesn't ever wear gloves, yet he claimed to get chemical burns all the time. That kind of cumulative exposure cannot be good for anyone's skin." Hake leaned back and drew a long breath.

Dr. Atkins shook his head. "I suppose a more important criterion for your prospective clients is that they have been diagnosed with non-Hodgkins lymphoma."

"Yes, besides NHL there's large B-cell, mantle cell, follicular, and T-cell lymphomas. All qualify for compensation under the Rid-A-Weed settlement. I need your help with referrals based on such confirmed diagnoses. I'd build a case from there and help each client file the necessary claim for compensation. Does that sound reasonable?"

"If there's financial help out there for these exposure victims, I'll be happy to make referrals. You bet. That's a step forward in my opinion."

Hake gave him a sincere look. "That's a step toward justice—which is what I'm all about." He opened his portfolio and extracted his flyer. "Here's the preliminary draft of a sign I'd like to post explaining how victims can contact me to get the process started."

The oncologist took the colored print-out and studied the message. He soon glanced back up over his glasses. "I think you're supposed to use that little trademark symbol when you mention a product by name like that."

Hake slid forward in his seat with a nod. "The manufacturer has more to worry about than a slur on their copyright. Part of the lawsuit involves their failure to warn users about risks, or even mention the basic need to wear protective gear. That kind of misrepresentation has been going on for decades. I don't mind being one of the forces bringing compensation to those now suffering the consequences."

"I like your gumption, young man. We have our 'To Your Health' wellness newsletter that goes out every month to former hospital patients. I'd suggest we run this like a quarter-page ad and provide your contact information. I'd probably include a short list of lymphoma symptoms, especially the skin manifestations. Folks who've been handling chemicals will put two and two together on this, rest assured."

"Thank you, Dr. Atkins. I'll run a feature in the Gazette and schedule a forum at the library soon to get the word out. If you're writing out a list of common symptoms, I might need to know that, too. Not that I'm going to play doctor in the process, but awareness will lend me some credibility." Hake stood and closed the portfolio. "I can't thank you enough for your help."

The physician stood and offered his hand. "Looks like we're on the same side here."

"I appreciate your support." Hake shook his hand and nodded at the flyer. "You have my contact information there, so call or e-mail me as needed."

"Not only that, but you have compelled me to clean out my chemical shelf in the garage. I probably have a jug of Rid-A-Weed just like the next guy. Good grief, what an insidious threat in the form of a lowly herbicide."

"That's the backhanded side of exposure, sir. Unsuspecting goes with unguarded. If nothing more, we'll get the word out, which can only lead to more caution when using potentially harmful chemicals." As he turned for the door, a young woman in nursing scrubs halted before entering.

Hake hastened out to free the doctor, but didn't miss the

attentive look from the woman as he passed. Having accomplished everything he'd intended, he didn't give the matter a second thought. He had an attractive woman coming to his ranch in the morning. That would light a fire on the horizon between them—quite literally—which would be his next challenge to master.

~

Aley squirmed, trying to dodge direct eye contact by looking out of the window. Her boss had the largest office in the building, complete with an administrative assistant's suite. His section had the makings of a first-rate fire hazard with wall-to-wall file storage. The heat had definitely increased in here, but she didn't know why.

"I can hardly believe you failed to confide in me regarding your unrest, Ms. Halstead. No, I had to get a phone call from the Council Grove office that you're a candidate for an opening there. That about blindsided me—which isn't the way I like to spend my Friday afternoons." He turned from hovering over his desk and began to pace along the rear wall.

She fought past the shock of learning the process had advanced, but never meant her lateral move to seem like a backstab. "Mr. Norman, please know that this isn't personal. I'm looking at an opportunity for growth, that's all. I'll be in a new area of the Flint Hills. It presents a new challenge and constant discovery, all at the same time."

"What about staying in one place and building some seniority? That used to be touted as a career strategy back in my early career."

"Yes, sir. I recognize that. I will still be accruing benefits as a conservation service employee—just not in this office." Her last phrase came out with a bit of an edge to it. Still, she had spoken the truth.

His brow hitched. "I simply don't get it. I've always approved every training session you requested. Is there some limitation you're experiencing here that I might not be aware of, Ms. Halstead?" He approached the corner of his desk closest to the window.

Aley froze, refusing to even breathe. A portal seemed to be opening to her. She didn't want to flinch and miss it. "I'm...a minority here. Some days it's more painfully obvious than others. For the last three site visits I've made, the landowners expected *Al* not *Aley*. There's a lot of disrespect around here. That includes recurring female bashing, and it's always within earshot of my station. Plus, I've found little receptivity to my ideas for streamlining procedures. Old school seems to rule this office, which is why I stay out in the field as much as possible."

Her boss appeared duly caught off guard. His face contorted as he worked his mouth into a pucker and slowly released it. After pacing a length or two behind the desk, he wheeled around to address the matter. "I've always stressed cooperation in this office. When I thought the guys might be laying it on too thick, I took them aside and spoke a mild word of correction to them. I never thought it would be magnified out of proportion."

"Well, when you're at the center of it, the proportion can be overwhelming. I'm trying to do a professional job here. The gender clash makes it uncomfortable for me. I looked at the Council Grove job as an opportunity to accomplish the work I'm devoted to, with a mixed-gender staff to support me. I would appreciate a strong recommendation for the position, Mr. Norman. I hope you can recommend me based on my professional performance."

As he battled to stifle his reaction, he took a seat at the desk. "I'm beyond thinking about giving you a positive recommendation...because I've already sent my highest commendation on your behalf. Ron Lightner received it with similar praise, saying it was only a matter of filing paperwork to have the transfer approved. You should know something by next week."

A flicker of hope lit in her chest. Trying to downplay

the sudden surge of happiness, she turned to stare out of the window. A fox squirrel leapt from a limb and ran across the parking lot. She would scurry like that, and search for fulfillment elsewhere. "Thank you, Mr. Norman. I hope filling the job vacancy won't pose any major problems for you."

"No, I've got applicants on hold, believe it or not. Most of them are male, but that won't factor in on my decision. As long as the work is getting done, I guess I'm gender-blind."

"Yes, sir. You might be, at that. Have a nice weekend." She exited the room with utter relief. Back at her workstation, she resisted the urge to pack up her supplies. Maybe next week would be better timing. A glance at the calendar reminded her time continued to flow like a river. She lifted the page to glimpse at the artwork for May and found it positively captivating.

~

Hake knew Friday evening held nothing but loneliness and drudgery. With Aley and Reece coming in the morning, he had to accomplish some major cleanup at the farmhouse. The need to make a positive first impression on her brother served as part of his motivation. Aley would see firsthand the interior of the house with its charming built-in nooks and craftsman trims. No need to let his clutter detract from those fine features. Her opinion mattered.

After glancing over to confirm he'd dutifully cleaned the coffee bar for the weekend break, the office door clicked open. A young woman with teased-up hair stepped inside, clutching her purse to her midsection. Dread clamped down on his typically open-minded demeanor, a real handicap. Instead of standing, he beckoned her further inside. The late hour would likely not be his only regret, as the excessive makeup wearer took his guest chair.

"I'm Hake Warren, Attorney at Law. How may I help you today?"

"My name is Danielle Tillison. I saw your ad and came

for some free advice. Maybe my troubles border on being legal. I'm not sure."

"Okay. Can you start with the part that may be legal? We can go from there, as my advisements tend to be general to guide you if further action seems appropriate." Hake jotted down her name on a notepad and then leaned away from the desk to gain distance from what might be coming next. Trouble always walked in late, at least that's what his favorite law professor claimed. He was in no mood to test the hypothesis so near the closing hour.

"I think my live-in boyfriend might be…messing with my head." She turned and refused to look in his direction while her neck reddened. "Here's the closest thing to legal, as most of his mysterious little acts like hiding my keys are meant to be a psychological poke—to keep me in line." She pulled out a crumpled paper from her purse. "This is my latest credit card bill. I found two charges on here for purchases that I didn't make, both for a hundred dollars."

Hake motioned for the document and momentarily had it in hand. Assessing the spending pattern, most of her purchases clustered around the weekend. Two charges broke the pattern and fell midweek. Not surprising, they were both for one hundred dollars. He added the dates under her name and recorded the charges. Seeing a thread of credibility, he delved with caution. "What about the amount? Not many purchases total out to even dollars, unless he's buying gift cards."

"When we disagree, he likes to end it by saying he's one hundred percent right. There have been more than a few bumps in the road between us lately. I figured that would smooth out with him graduating in May, so I told myself to just wait it out. Then I found the extra charges—which I can't afford—and it felt like DJ was turning some invisible thumbscrews on me."

"I hope this makes you relax a bit, as you're not responsible for any charges you didn't authorize. Simply contact your credit card company, point out the date and amount of the charges, and request they be dismissed. They have a security division to investigate fraudulent charges, so eventually you may have to answer more questions, such as who might have access to your card without your knowledge or consent." He leaned forward and stared at her. "At that time, you would need to be as forthcoming and honest as possible."

She squirmed in the chair and then crossed her legs. "Criminy. Some parts of this relationship are incredibly good, and then there's this half-hidden bothersome part. The funny thing is—he's totally aware that I know he's doing it, yet he keeps doing it just the same."

"That behavior sounds passive-aggressive to me—but I'm not here to play psychologist. I'm trained as a lawyer. Outside of the legal bonds of marriage, you have nothing tying you to this gentleman. If confrontation of this issue cannot lead to full resolution, then I suggest you re-evaluate your live-in relationship. You can legally decline the charges, so that's my best advice for immediate action, Ms. Tillison." A smile flickered to chase the advice and, hopefully, dismiss the walk-in client.

She planted her feet flat on the floor, grabbed the bill, and stood up. "At least I won't go in debt this pay period trying to cover an extra two hundred dollars in charges. I'll make that call right away, Mr. Warren. Thank you for your guidance. Maybe I should think like a fox and hide my purse from him." She smirked and straightened her crumpled shirttail.

With determined passivity, Hake held his seat. "Typically, in a game of cunning, Ms. Tillison, you can *run* but you cannot *hide*. Trust is the platform for any lasting relationship. If you move in any direction, I suggest you head toward trust."

She turned to leave, took several steps, and then seemed to think better of it. A playful expression soon transformed her face. "Like I said before, some parts of this relationship are incredibly good." With a wink, she walked to the door, scraping her high heels along the way.

Hake held his breath until she disappeared from view onto Merchant Street. He tore off the note, jotted "DJ" onto the corner, and then slipped it into the file documenting free inquiries. "Talk about courting disaster," he admitted under his breath. Determined to break formation and head to Bushong, he strode to the front door and threw the lock. "Kitchen cleanup, here I come."

Aley flashed to mind. As a reward for mop duty, he'd fire off a friendly text to her later. Hopefully, she'd be in the mood to talk fire. *Enjoy the burn.* He couldn't think of a more perfect way for kindling a relationship. This would be a hot return to his property, and not her last.

Chapter 5

Not that she had to pick sides, but Aley chose to hover near Reece to lend support for his volunteer involvement. They stood in a tiny yet efficient kitchen that sparkled. While Reece talked on about the influence of wind direction, she let her gaze wander over the small cottage. Updated to function with more open space, she detected that a dining room wall had been removed in a previous remodel. The narrow-planked original flooring of the living room stopped at the threshold, where wider oak flooring took over. At least the stain matched.

"Aley?" Hake gestured toward her in an attempt to gain her attention. "How do you feel about that? Reece suggested that he establish the black line, while you and I prep the flanks. Then he'll start the head fire and let it rip."

"Great plan. We'll stand by for suppression of any spot-over fires, but Reece will have the ATV with the water tank if we need backup. Hake, do you have an all-terrain vehicle, by any chance? That would make for less legwork, but either way works fine."

"Yes, I have one. Let me back it out while Reece unloads his ATV."

Reece headed for the front door like a man on a mission. "Go ahead and haul out the water buckets you mentioned."

Once the door slammed, Aley stepped closer to Hake. "Reece wants to be efficient with his time, though it doesn't pay to hurry fire. His wife is seven months pregnant, so he devotes his weekends to being home with her. The daddy-do list has been fairly involved, but he finally got the crib assembled."

"Wow, my gratitude for his time just doubled. Thanks for letting me know. Follow me to the barnyard and help me load the water buckets when I back out the Jeep."

She followed him to the back door and nudged his shoulder by accident when he paused to retrieve a set of keys hanging from a series of cup hooks. The plaque above it read, "Go Forth in Strength." They would definitely need that wisdom today.

Hake skipped down a trio of concrete steps that lacked any handrail. "Stay by the clothesline over by the rosebush. I have to back out blind, because the parking spot in the barn is super tight."

More than happy to oblige, she stepped toward a cluster of sizable rosebushes that had begun to leaf out in the warming weather. Interested to know what color they might be, she diverted her attention to the water buckets close by the house's foundation. When a gunshot blasted at close range, her knees buckled and she soon found the ground, her elbows tucked over her head for protection.

A clunker Jeep appeared from the barn, backing in her direction. Hake hopped out and scrambled to get her back on her feet. His expression of concern spoke volumes.

Her legs still jittery, Aley rose at his insistent tug, her feet spread for balance. "What in the world just happened? Are we under cannon fire?"

"Meet Old Backfiring Betsy—the other woman in my life," he quipped, escorting her around to the passenger side. "Maybe the engine needs a tweak, but she sure is handy for getting around out here."

"I'll be the ultimate judge of that. Reece has my

suppression tools. Let's lead him to the rear pasture and let him figure out the best location for a black line."

"First, we'll grab the buckets. I have a feeling this is going to become a sloppy mess."

"It helps to have containers with lids. If you check your speed, we should be fine."

"Okay, I'll save my Rat Pack moves for later." He flashed a teasing grin in her direction and backed toward the bucket stash. The Jeep halted with a jerk.

"That kind of jackrabbit starting and stopping will cost you precious water." She slid out to help him load. When the swing-gate came off in his hands, she tried not to act surprised. Throwing her hip against it, she helped him align the sprocket for reattaching.

Hake grunted with the first heave of a full bucket. "Maybe I'm too optimistic here."

"Yeah, let's pour off some water. Aim for two-thirds full." A horn sounded from the front drive. "That's Reece. He's impatient to start. I'll pour and let you load."

"Got it." His hands met hers for the first transfer and they soon had six buckets loaded. Hake retook the driver's seat and reached for the key. "Cover your ears—just in case."

As soon as she had clamped her palms over her ears, a deafening bang sounded from the vehicle. Aley bit back a sarcastic comment as the jalopy showed some gumption and eased into a steady clip. *Maybe this isn't so bad after all.*

"We're Lewis and Clark today." Hake manhandled the steering wheel and turned down the lane leading to the pasture. He threw Reece a wave and rested his arm on the door frame. "No portaging of canoes for us, though. We'll burn our way through to a western passage."

Catching his spirit of adventure, Aley laughed and took in the tranquil scenery up ahead. The tree canopy to the west would be their endpoint, spring green and slightly flammable. "We have to respect your nearest neighbor. He depends on that tree cover for his hunting leases. I prefer those landowners who manage for grass."

"Preference duly noted," Hake replied. He flipped up his hat brim to waggle his brow.

Aley braced against the metal dashboard as they dipped into a pothole. Water splashed to punctuate the hazard. "Dear Lord, please keep Hake, Reece, and me safe while burning, amen."

"I appreciate that prayer of protection…because I don't have a clue to what I'm doing."

When he tapped his chest with both hands, she reached over to take the wheel. "Stay by me, Hake. With controlled burning, you have to read the land and the fire at the same time."

"I'm working on my…discernment," he replied. Taking command, his right hand clamped the steering wheel, capturing hers.

The play in the steering mechanism made for quite the cozy sensation as they navigated toward their quest. Aley forgot about Reece until the ATV centered in her side-view mirror. While he unleashed his pyromaniac act along the pasture's upper end, she'd school Hake on the finer objectives of burning from the harmless flank. With anticipation building, she fiddled with the radio knob and got rewarded with some loud country crooning. The trip out became a joy ride, one she didn't want to end.

~

While the black line's fire had been a short-lived affair, Hake snapped to full awareness when the main fire tore into the pasture grasses with heady abandon. Even from where he stood on the western edge, the flames leapt taller than a man's height. The loud crackle generated by the fire's consumption of the straw-like grass surprised him.

In the distance, Aley carried a water-laden bucket along the top of a rocky outcrop. He slid his fingers through the handle and picked up another bucket, determined to follow her. Occasionally, a plume of smoke would obscure the main fire on their side, which meant Reece had it clear on the opposite flank.

The ease of the ATV patrolling the far side helped to offset his tension. If not for the fire's destructive potential, the elemental battle between fodder and flame would seem more exhilarating from this close. He exhaled and switched the heavy bucket to his other hand.

Aley signaled halt with both palms toward him. "Hake?"

He stopped on a dime and sat the bucket down. In his transit, he'd passed the fire line, but it wouldn't take long for the flames to catch up. What had appeared to be a windless morning now seemed whipped with atmospheric unrest. *What gives?* The grass fire had generated its own localized weather, no small feat. Across the pasture, the ATV passed at a steady clip, a capable sentinel. He checked on Aley about the time she signaled for another bucket.

He backtracked with his nose tucked into his sleeve to dodge the billowing smoke. The crackling laughter of the fire unnerved him. A circling vortex of flames consumed the bunch grass by the pasture's edge. When he found embers behind the fire line trying to inch into the rocky outcrop, he stomped out its creeping advance. Realizing the shovel would be more effective for that type of battle, he vowed to bring the tool back along with the second bucket.

Once he's spotted the Jeep, he made a beeline for the open swing-gate. He scooped up the shovel and clamped Aley's rake against it. Working side-by-side, the suppression task wouldn't seem so tedious, though the pasture looked infinitely long from where he stood. After balancing the hand tools, he grabbed the bucket and soon felt the pull of its weight on his shoulder muscles. He needed to do more of this physical exertion to get in shape for growing season, lots more.

The return trip brought his pulse rate down a notch.

Already a quarter done, the burning took on a methodical cadence. Hake pushed his stride to close the distance between them. This time as he passed the advancing fire line, he didn't have a free hand to filter out the smoke. He held his breath until he punched through the smoke plume. Not twenty yards off, Aley stood waiting for his delivery. He held up the tools and sat the bucket down on a level rock.

Aley moved toward him and pointed down the incline below where he'd just passed. A stand of grass invited the fire down into the rocky outcrop. Knowing they had agreed to keep this slope free of fire as a break for the riparian woodland down below, he spotted trouble in the making. Without hesitation, he tossed her the rake and began to slide the shovel over the fire's wayward edge, smothering its advance. Though the technique worked well, he needed to move faster with the application—and pronto.

"Shift down here," Aley shouted. She raked against the fire and managed to toss it back onto a burned-out area. "We can't let it get down slope—or the woods will catch on fire."

Running on instinct, he retraced his steps and retrieved a bucket. He started downhill to hand over the water so Aley could wet the ground ahead of the fire, but the imbalance of added weight made his footing unsure. He slipped and spilled some precious water. Stiffening his stride, he delivered the bucket and went to work dragging his shovel.

Every time he hurried, the flames licked back to life. Buried in an avalanche of panicked thoughts, he barely spied Aley as she made her way behind him, headed for the next bucket down the line. By the time she returned, he needed to have this lobe of the fire extinguished so they could advance. In a moment of enlightenment, he pulled out his phone and sent Reece the S-O-S message. With the three of them working the edge, they stood a much better chance.

In half a minute, Aley approached the fire from down below, having already made her descent. She poured a thin line of water just beyond the fire and circled the perimeter.

She covered quite a bit of ground, and then ran back to retrieve her rake.

Hake stood and took a deep breath to recharge. Without further threat, the advancing main fire had remained in the tall grass. After another minute of fighting this escaped portion, he'd run ahead and maintain the flank as planned. Leaning on the shovel, he redirected his gaze to strategize his next angle of attack. When he looked across the rocky outcrop, he spotted Aley with the first bucket he'd set out, trying to come down the rocky rubble to drench the lengthening side fire.

Taking the shortest route to her, he stepped back into the ashes of the main pasture and started to trot. Around the far corner, the ATV appeared to lend them an added advantage. Relieved in the moment, he used the shovel as a walking stick and began the rocky descent.

Aley stepped around a large limestone rock. The bucket struck the boulder and tipped, splashing water everywhere. Off balance, Aley took a longer step causing the rubble to loosen under her feet. Unable to stabilize, she began to lunge straight into the creeping fire.

Above her, Hake launched a breathless countermove, leaving his feet for a tackle on a goal-line stand. The bucket came loose and doused their bone-jarring collision. He heard the air rush from her lungs as he clutched her and held on for the bumpy landing. Though he rolled his shoulder and padded the fall, the rocks below proved highly unkind. Pain ripped across his upper back as Aley moaned onto his chest. He rolled further downhill until all momentum ceased. Seeing stars, he loosened his hold.

The next few seconds dimmed in his recognition of the situation, until the metal tines of Reece's fire rake stabbed the ground in front of his face. Aley's hat rolled into view next, blood-stained and sooty. That brought the moment into sharper focus.

Reece sent Aley to the ATV and bent to offer a muscular

arm. "Stand up and help me get this outbreak under control, Hake."

He seized the helpful gesture and rose to his feet, trying to silence a thousand complaining nerve endings. Somehow, a shovel made it into his hands, and he began to fight the fire with wild abandon. More personal now, he would be the victor and not let this riparian woodland go up in smoke. Aley had that creek-side feature protected on his management plan, so he'd work toward that goal, so help him God.

Half a minute later, the ATV puttered along the fence line. Aley passed by, spraying a line of water at the base of the fence in a tank-emptying last-ditch effort. The crown of her head now bore the blue bandana that had graced her neck earlier.

Inspired by her persistence, Hake increased his pace. He growled at the flanking fire as it continued sliding down the slope. By his quick appraisal, the size of the side fire had doubled.

Reece worked on the opposite side, manning Aley's rake. He found the bucket of water she'd dropped off and hoisted it above the fire line. Like an artist, he sketched the outline with a dousing seal, making the fire hiss in objection. In immediate reaction, the smoke worsened.

His chest heaving, Hake slid down the slope, dragging his shovel. He spotted the bucket Aley had emptied earlier. Right when he wondered if the water had made any difference, the creeping fire sputtered and stopped short in that area. Reading the gain, he stepped back and watched the fire's elemental response to the water line. They'd sure needed an ace-in-the-hole and now they had one. He strode to Reece's aid just as his water bucket ran out. A slide of his shovel managed to snuff out the rest.

"I hate spot-over fires," Reece said, his breathing labored.

Hake placed a commiserating hand on his shoulder. The

crackle of the main fire had hushed to barely audible. The ATV's engine rumble guaranteed that Aley stood sentinel on the fire's orderly advance from down below. A faint ping sounded almost like fairy music.

Reece reached for his back pocket and stared at his phone. When he looked up, his stare had glazed over. "It's Candice...her contractions started."

"Go on home and leave this to us," Hake insisted.

Reece tore out of his grip in a trot toward the ATV. In steps, he stopped and turned around. "What about Aley?"

Hake didn't have to think twice about that option. "Leave her with me. I'll get her home safely. Better not leave me alone with the fire still burning."

Reece nodded and resumed his trot. Aley soon responded and drove toward him. In a quick exchange, Reece took control of the ATV, leaving Aley the rake. He zoomed by with a quick wave farewell.

Hake gave the rocky slope one final check to confirm they'd suppressed the side fire. Shovel in hand, he walked the pasture's edge to catch up with Aley. As he approached, he watched her maneuver along the upper slope, mesmerized by her movement. Every ache and smoke-laced inhalation became metered by a greater sense of shared purpose. They stood on his land, working it together. He'd never seen a more beautiful orchestration in his life.

After closing the gap between them, he stepped up and touched her arm as she raked. "When we get back to the house, I'll take care of those cuts on your forehead."

She looked up at him, her eyes misted with emotion. "I'm worried about Reece's baby." A single tear overflowed the corner of her eye and cut a track down her sooty cheek.

Hake tried to catch it with his knuckle and smudged the whole works even more. He wrapped his arms around her and watched the pasture over her shoulder, her frame trembling under his touch. With the world ablaze, he leaned on the shovel for support.

"Let's take it to God, Aley. Dear Lord, please stop Candice's early contractions and let Reece enjoy a peaceful day at home with his growing family. We trust you with all things delicate, because even the cattle on a thousand hills are yours. I ask you to grow this grass back so I can feed a few of them." He took Aley's sob as the benediction as they walked over a knoll toward the blackened finish line.

~

The aroma of sizzling bacon quelled the dull throb of her headache. Aley sat stark-still at the small table, waiting for Hake to serve breakfast for lunch. Thankful that Reece had tossed out her duffle bag, she now enjoyed the worn-soft collar of her favorite chambray shirt. After she'd washed her face in the bathroom sink, Hake had insisted on dabbing first aid cream on her cuts. At least the numbing effect had calmed down the red-hot pain radiating from her forehead. Now, if she could eat something, perhaps the headache would vanish, too.

Hake squatted by her chair and delivered a glass of orange juice to the table. "Has your head trauma calmed down any?" His tone sounded cushioned with concern.

She smiled enough to crinkle the corner of her eyes, though a nod remained out of the question. "Yes," she whispered. "Much better."

"Our scrambled eggs are almost done. I'll put the toast in next. Would you like honey or strawberry jam?"

She blinked and gave him a protracted look. "You're spoiling me, Hake. I'll have what you have to make it easy."

"I'm not spoiling…you're in recovery. We had quite the workout on the back forty, so we have to take it easy for the rest of the day." He patted her hand and stood to finish cooking.

For a cynical split second, Aley tried to figure out if Hake's actions were couched in covering some cloaked ulterior motive, but when he started whistling a praise song, that line of reasoning shattered. Besides, the bacon smelled heavenly. She could hardly wait to eat at this cozy little table by the window. From her perch, the prairie seemed to stretch out forever.

~

Though it felt like gaining an advantage, Hake couldn't forfeit the chance to shower and rinse the smoke out of his hair. With Aley napping on his lumpy sofa, he had a few minutes to spare for self-improvement. He'd get to the lunch dishes later, but feared the clatter in the sink would awaken her. After slipping the clean T-shirt over his wet hair, he headed up the hallway.

"Stop—that burns." Aley's voice shook with apprehension.

Hake rounded the doorway to the living room and glanced at the front door, wondering who might have come in. The porch stood empty.

She twisted against the back cushion. "Too much fire...stay back." Her knees tucked to her midsection as if avoiding something harmful.

Unwilling to let her continue such fitful sleep, Hake knelt by her head and stroked her hair. "Hey, Aley. It's okay. The fire burned out earlier. Everything's safe." After receiving a simpering sob for a response, he tugged at her shoulder, compelled to end the stormy nap.

Her eyelids rose like slow-drawn curtains. Two hazel eyes peered at him, lacking any focus. Moments passed without any clarity. "Guess I was dreaming," she whispered. "The fire had me trapped—"

"Not from what I saw today," he replied with a shake of his head. Her eyes captivated him, almost as green as the shrubs along the creek. Spackled with gold spokes, they looked gem-like at this close range. Strong magnetism pulled him toward her, though he tried to stiffen his spine against it. "I saw a master of her domain exact her prescribed management on a needy landscape. You weren't trapped at all—except for the few futile moments I had you pinned on the rocky slope. Sorry I hit you so hard, by the way. I was aiming for out of harm's way."

Her lips pressed together and then eased into a slight smile. "I honestly didn't know what had hit me. Guess I focused on not spilling the bucket."

He inched closer to feed his fascination. Even with her forehead bandaged, Aley's face struck him as lovely, framed by thick brown hair that lightened in direct sun. Warmth radiated where he touched her shoulder. "I couldn't risk letting you get burned in the spot-over flare-up. Say you'll forgive me for manhandling the moment."

Her eyes fluttered closed and blinked open again. "Well, since you're so cooperative in pursuing your conservation plan before it's even been issued, I can forgive the body tackle."

He traced his thumb over her brow to deliver his admiration in a simple touch. "What if you weren't my conservation officer for a few precious minutes? Could I hold you?"

Instead of granting audible permission, she slipped her arm around his neck. Her eyes held the next invitation, focused and intent on the subject at hand.

He slid one hand into her loose hair and wrapped her in a feather-light hug with the other. When she nestled into the crook of his neck, he tightened his hold. Smoky hair and tantalizing woman filled his senses. If it hadn't been for the sturdy sofa, his quaking knees would have dropped him flat on the floor.

"Thank you for being here, Hake. It's so…unexpected." Her bottom lip raked the curve of his jaw with the innocent disclosure.

He chuckled and pressed the bridge of his nose into her shoulder to squelch the urge to kiss her. *Hold back, pyro.* On the verge of go or stay, he wouldn't muddy the waters of her pending decisions by ill-sparked affection. "I might need a rain-check for full expression, and just say you're welcome for now." He settled for kissing the three bandages on her forehead, a tactile compromise. "Be healed," he whispered, hoping to vanquish any trace of hurt.

Chapter 6

From the moment she'd met him outside the double doors, Aley could sense Hake's wide-eyed reaction to her contemporary-style church. Not many places of worship boasted a tin roof that sloped asymmetrically like a ski jump's ramp. Confident in her favorite lavender dress, she tucked her arm under his and led him into the building.

"Different kind of structure," he muttered under his breath.

"Same God, though. Welcome to Sunrise Community Church. We'd better get seated. Reece said he'd hold a spot for us." She led up the aisle as a group of elderly women chatted in hushed tones by the stairwell to the balcony. An usher offered the printed bulletin, so she grabbed one without relinquishing her guest.

Hake gestured for the bulletin and took possession. "Did everything settle down for Reece's wife yesterday?"

She leaned in as though she had to guard the mystery. "False labor—her first bout. Everything's fine." She dusted her whispery tone with a look of intrigue while clearing the last hurdle, the talkative music leader. "Hey, Reece. Hake's here."

Her brother stood up and shook his hand, a smile lighting up his face. "Sorry I had to leave you guys with all the mop-up yesterday. Hake, please meet my dear wife, Candice."

Hake leaned in to shake her hand. "Glad to hear your distress was a passing thing."

Candice blushed and waved him away. "Caution—first-timer who doesn't know the ropes of full-fledged maternity," she teased. "Still, it felt good to have Reece back home, so thank you for taking care of Aley for him."

Someone strummed a guitar and it amplified over the sound system. Aley gestured Reece down the pew. "I'll take the aisle, Hake, in case the ushers grow hostile collecting the offering."

His brow hitched until he caught the kidding look on her face. After leaving enough room for her to sit, he eased onto the pew and leaned back. His gaze swept the platform and stopped at the cross hanging over the pulpit. "Same God," he repeated, seeming pleased.

Aley brushed her shoulder against his. "Sing if you want to. We usually have four or five worship songs to start the service."

He ducked to share her collusion. "I'll only sing if I know the songs. Otherwise, I need to hear them first to get the rhythm right."

She nodded and tugged at the bulletin, thinking to give it a glance. Hake played hard to relinquish until she tugged at it again. She didn't miss the quirky twitch of his upper lip. Well, that certainly made for an interesting embellishment to her worship experience. To offset his effect, she checked on the year-to-date giving total. Good, they remained ahead of budget.

The full team of worship leaders took the stage. Within seconds, words to the first song flashed up on the screen in a well-timed prompt. Adam, the lead male singer, broke the silence with his rich rendering of an impromptu praise. The guitar accompaniment began in earnest, soon joined by a faint, but steady drumbeat. The congregation stood when beckoned.

Aley sang from the first note, having decided not to let Hake's presence make any difference in her ability to worship God. He needed to experience her in a variety of settings. This particular one held less pain and more heart than yesterday's endeavor. She hoped the service would come across as genuine for him. A new resident should feel included when it came to church. Once she heard him singing along, her apprehension dropped a notch or two.

The second song reflected more of a hunger for God. The worship leaders didn't hesitate to reach skyward with their heartfelt quest to stave their urging for a Savior. Today, she'd keep it conservative and not gesture, playing to Hake's comfort. They needed more of a chance to know each other, all things considered. She finished the song in a near whisper, hushed yet meaning every word.

Hake began the third song with more volume. At the mention of blessings along the road of life, he seemed quite familiar. By the time the song ended, he held up an open palm in free expression of praise.

Aley began the prayerful final song with no sense of trepidation about the man by her side. Instead, her focus latched onto an everlasting God whose hand of favor had opened in her direction. She glanced at Hake and received a quick smile as the song headed into the rhythmic chorus. Victory could come in many forms. Today, she sensed winning from high to low.

~

"These things are addictive." Hake hoisted the breaded onion ring onto the tip of his index finger to better illustrate the perfection of his claim.

Aley wiggled closer beside him in the booth and took an opportunistic bite, leaving a gaping hole in the token sample. She hummed her approval and reached for her drink.

A feminine giggle bubbled up across the table. "You have to watch her," Candice said. "Extra fieldwork always fuels her appetite."

"Look who's talking," Reece interjected, his hands planted around his burger. "Little Miss I'm-eating-for-two. Beware the hungry woman, baby or no baby." He muffled the sentiment with a huge bite, making excess catsup drip onto his basket of fries.

Hake enjoyed the good-natured volley. "How long have you two been married?"

"For three years," Candice replied. "I had to work on Reece for a while before I thought he could handle fatherhood." She chomped at a long french fry and squinted at him.

His mouth still full, Reece nodded in agreement.

"I caught Candice's bouquet at the wedding reception, but quickly wanted to toss it right back," Aley quipped. "I needed to focus on graduating from college back then, and prospective husbands weren't part of that process."

Reece reached for his drink. "She's more relaxed now, especially with the move to Council Grove just around the bend."

Hake gave her a questioning look. Maybe the topic could be approached in familiar company, so it didn't seem as threatening. "Have you heard anything definite?"

She played with a splat of catsup on her hamburger wrapper. "My boss called me in late Friday and said the offer should be made this coming week. He gave me his highest recommendation. What a surprise."

Reece waved off her sarcasm. "He better have. You do more fieldwork than their top two agents combined. Besides, the Morris County office needs your productivity."

Aley drew a red X with a fry. "It's a smaller office, yet they have more conservation contracts. I think they're more active in recruiting participants. My skills match up well with that kind of enthusiasm." She ate the french fry while looking at Reece.

"That's because you have a go-get 'em attitude, Aley,"

Candice added. "God wouldn't put you there without a good reason."

Hake bit his hamburger, letting the mellow beef flavor assuage his trepidation about her relocation. Candice's statement rang true. God had a reason for it, if the transfer went through.

"That settles it," Aley agreed. "I'll trust God either way. Hake, can I sweet-talk you into sharing another onion ring? You're right, they *are* addictive."

"Never get tired of hearing her say you're right," Reece said, gesturing with his burger. Another wedge of it disappeared with an overstuffed bite.

Despite the lurking threat of Aley's job relocation, Hake began to enjoy the impromptu lunch gathering. He selected the next sample of deep-fried cooking and let his bait dangle.

Aley gave a throaty laugh and made a lunge for it.

He shouldn't have gravitated toward the encounter so much, but found her irresistible. Her mirth painted him lavender, a hue he'd never been before. Sharing church had driven the sensation further home. After surrendering the rest of the onion ring to her basket, he launched an attack on his lunch, hopeful to stave the other hunger rising inside.

"Anybody interested in watching the Royals game this afternoon?" Reece asked.

Hake hadn't turned his television on in a week. He glanced up when a couple walked past and recognized the woman with the credit card problem. The dark-featured man trailing her looked familiar, but he couldn't place him at the moment. No doubt who was paying that bill.

"You forgot we're painting the bookshelf that will hold the changing station," Candice replied. "I can't have those vapors in the house, so you're working out in the garage."

Hake stole a glance at Aley where he found an angelic smile. He bit two fries at once, waiting for the balanced resolution. Being a twosome struck him as foreign territory.

"Okay," Reece conceded in a flat tone. "It's preseason,

anyway."

Aley shifted in her seat. "I think we might explore Peter Pan Park before Hake returns to his beloved Bushong."

"Sure, I'm game," he replied. "Forever young, right? What's wrong with that?"

"Exactly what I've been saying," Reece added. With that, his burger did a disappearing act, a sleight of hand that soon required an extra napkin, which his wife tossed at him.

In no hurry to return to the lonesome ranch, Hake put the finishing touches on his lunch. The park sounded enchanting. Tinkerbelle might even show up and dust some magic on the path.

~

Aley strolled close enough to the lake to see the refreshing spring green of the tree canopies reflect in its surface. What a relief to stretch her legs on a manicured acreage that didn't demand her constant assessment. The park setting held an idyllic quality, with expansive stretches of grass flanking up from the lake, shaded by the occasional tree. She spied a charming new pavilion on the distant shore and aimed for it at a leisure pace.

Hake trotted up from behind. "This disc golf course is amazing. I may have to come back and try my hand at conquering these eighteen holes."

"Great idea. It's tranquil out here—except for the playground area. Maybe that would help you collect your thoughts after a stressful day." She shaded her brow with one hand so he could read the sincerity in her eyes.

Hake nodded. "When that chemical lawsuit ad gets attention, the pace will pick up around the office. I put in a rush order for the claim forms, so they should get delivered Monday by close of business. I can't believe how receptive the medical community has been. I already have a luncheon speaking engagement at an out-patient clinic next week, thanks to Dr. Atkins."

"We're both doing important work." She extended her

arms and gestured across the sweeping landscape. "I read a modern paraphrase of Scripture that claimed the land has its own righteousness—one fashioned by God, the Creator. Do you believe that's possible?"

Hake stuffed his hands into his pockets and caught up a step to walk beside her. Contemplative, he gave the park grounds a lengthy look. "I think the righteousness of Jesus Christ is meant for humankind, because it reflects a condition of the soul. Maybe the land has more a state of rightness than actual righteousness."

Aley watched the midday sunlight glimmer off the distant waters. A breeze stirred the hardwood trees nearby, whose leathery leaves rustled in response. "Your word matches the Genesis account of Creation better, as God saw the day's work and considered it good."

"Well, good was the last thing on my mind when I saw my ranch for the first time, let me assure you. The last owner had overgrazed the pastures until the grass had been grubbed down to stubs. That was late October. Between my first and second site visit, the first frost hit, taking the scenery from bad to worse. If it hadn't been for the price drop and an aggressive sales agent, I probably would have kept looking elsewhere."

Aley placed a hand on his arm. "What a shame that would have been for that tract. You're going to be a great land manager and bring it back to glory. The worst spot will be the best, wait and see. You watch that rear pasture come back and then remember my prediction."

He trapped her hand in his and leaned closer. "You're beautiful when you get all fired up about the land. I have to admit being mesmerized by your silhouette as you walked the flank of the fire yesterday. In my estimation, you're as genuine a steward as they come."

She sensed the blush heating her neck under his intense inspection. "You graciously forgot to mention the scraped forehead disfigurement."

"Which is not even noticeable today because you're healing." He began to swing her arm.

The blush grew to something more widespread and magnetic. She needed a diversion. "Let's head for the pavilion up ahead. Maybe we can spot some fish in the lake."

"I see a stone house through the trees on the far bank. Do you know any history?"

"All the stone structures in the park were original WPA work projects following World War II. The park is over a hundred years old—another heritage gift of William Allen White."

Hake nodded. "I read the historical plaque about the untimely death of his teenage daughter Mary, hence the child that lives on forever in Peter Pan fashion."

"Now and then, it helps to take the clock's pressure off the situation and live deeper. That's what makes his commemoration of her death able to transcend time." She shrugged and skirted a stand of shrubs that didn't appear native. The landscape crew had likely added some color with the addition.

Wordless, Hake followed a step behind. Once they approached the pavilion, he stepped onto the wooden floor and drew her up with him. "I'm all for suspending time, especially in such a lovely setting accompanied by a captivating woman." He strolled toward the outer railing and scanned the scenery.

Still hand in hand, Aley nestled up beside him. From the lake's center, a pair of mallard ducks spooked and flew away with a slight vocal protest. The treescape wreathed sapphire waters and set them apart from the crisp blue sky. A stair-step cirrus cloud appeared to lead straight to heaven's gate.

"So picturesque here," Hake whispered as he turned toward her. His eyes glimmered with keen interest as he traced her jaw with a warm knuckle.

Off guard, her stream of logical thought froze. The blush returned, heating more than her neck. When her chest tightened, a mild protest caught in her throat. Sure this type of affection should wait until after her job decision had settled, her head and her heart began to wage war.

"Suspend time with me, Aley." Hake's whispery tone melted into a hovering presence. He studied her face for a fleeting instant before he brushed his lips across hers.

Water shadows danced on his cheekbone, until she closed her eyes and allowed time to slip away. Only her hip on the railing and his embrace held her on earth, the barest tether ever. His glancing blow alighted again to more of a lingering presence, one that confused suppression with ignition until she couldn't find the seam.

Transported, she placed a hand on his chest and felt the hammering of his heart. Somehow, that pounding rhythm replaced the sweeping second hand of a clock and became a more immediate gauge of her state of being. What a wondrous dimension, where affection conquered time.

Hake broke off and pulled her into a cozy hug. As the breeze blew, he nuzzled into her hair. "I've wanted to do that for a while," he whispered, "and it felt more incredible than I imagined."

She angled her face to look at him. "I don't recognize this romantic landscape, though it seems quite promising."

"Yes—a horizon of hidden promise. Walk it with me, Aley." His hushed tone proved compelling.

This time when his kiss returned, she fortified for the exploration. With the option to postpone now declined, she recommitted her energy to the bridge being built. His words echoed in her mind, though the tactile pace seemed unlike a walk. She caught a glimpse of the wispy stairway to heaven before shutting out everything except the man holding her close.

Chapter 7

An unbroken melody of spring floated right into his bedroom, awakening Hake to a charge he'd long ignored. The robins exchanged loud calls, prompting him to slide out from under the sheets. From the crack between the curtains, dawn had barely broken across the land. He stuffed his legs into his jeans to head out to his destiny—inspection of the back forty.

After a minimal amount of preparation, he fisted the key ring and strode toward the barn. A tabby cat ran from the doorway of the lean-to off the north side. A sliver of delight shot through his anticipation. Maybe he'd pick up some cat food on his next trip to Bluestem. The cozy sensation of having a pet offset Old Betsy's typical salute as the Jeep roared to life.

Today, he wouldn't play the lawyer who happened to live on a rural acreage. After yesterday, he woke up a changed man. Finally, he could sense key pieces of his life falling into place. It began at church, extended with the camaraderie of their lunch foursome, and ended with Aley by the lake. Awakened, the rancher had work to do, and then he could yield to his day job.

He assessed the fence line of the northern pasture as he drove its full length. A four-strand fence stood strong and tight, a relief since Reece had the cattlemen coming to unload in less than two weeks. Considering the added income, he vowed to pour every dollar back into the ranch for upkeep and improvement. That included anything Aley had sketched out in his conservation plan. In for the long haul, he embraced the responsibility with determined vigor.

He guided the Jeep through the open gate and veered left to parallel the riparian woodland as it bordered the pasture down below. The fire had left a clean sweep of charred vegetation across a vast spread, almost fifty acres of nothing but ash. Three vultures flushed and took wing, banking for cover in the woodlands. He slowed to spare a packrat that shot across the lane in escape. "Sorry if you need to rebuild, little guy," he quipped as he drove past.

On the distant flank, he spotted the bulge in the ashen outline where the spot-over fire had given them a temporary challenge. The agony of their hasty collision flashed to mind, firing off a chain reaction of contemplative evaluation. He needed to be more delicate with Aley—much more delicate. As the reactive thought played out, he pressed the back of his hand over his mouth to hold the memory of her kiss in place. From there, the early morning capitulated to prayer as the protective black line ahead blended with the sooty residue of the ravaging prescribed fire, forming an indiscernible merger.

~

With the conservation plan hot off her printer, Aley reached for the office door handle, hoping her timing would be fortuitous. So different than the first visit, she opened the barrister's heavy door with confidence and stepped into the reception area. Greeted by the aroma of coffee, she scanned the room but couldn't find the handsome occupant.

A door clicked open down the hall and Hake appeared, toweling off his face. His shocked expression soon transitioned to one of pleasant surprise. After tossing the towel back into the side room, he gave her his full attention.

"Oh, wow. To what do I owe this unexpected pleasure?" He buttoned his oxford shirt and settled his collar into place as he approached.

"I'm making a site visit to go over a landowner's new conservation plan, if he has the time to spare this morning." She splayed through the pages with her fingers to make land management appear more enticing.

"Perfect, as I don't usually get any walk-in traffic until after ten-thirty or so. Beyond an express delivery of those Rid-A-Weed settlement claim forms, nothing's on the calendar for today. Please, take a seat. Can I pour you a cup of coffee?" He gestured at the brewing station.

Her confidence began to play into something more personal at the realization they were building a history of togetherness. "Yes, please, in my usual cup."

The familiar reference generated a slight smile. Humming, he turned away to make good on the offer. Two cups clinked together at the coffee bar.

Aley took the guest chair and rearranged his file organizer to allow room for laying out the paperwork along the edge of his massive desk. When Hake approached and settled into the other guest chair, his proximity lent her comfort. She'd have to curb that fetching influence to get this professional task undertaken, but the cozy confines of his office came as a reward for her diligence to finish the report.

Hake pushed the mug onto the desk. With a flick of his wrist, he left a sugar packet at its base. "So, where should we start?"

"I'm excited to have you enroll in our CSP—Conservation Stewardship Program. This pays the rancher a federal subsidy for accomplishing designated wildlife enhancement acts during the course of the grazing season. The best part is, you get to select your set of enhancements, so we work together to match the land with the best improvements possible."

"I'm stoked for that kind of thing. In fact, I've already been out this morning, seeing what I needed to do next on that rear pasture. It almost made me late getting to work here."

She chuckled and reached for the sugar packet. "Which is why you're shaving in the restroom of your law office. Hmm, I admire that modified time allotment."

He smiled and reached for his cup resting on the desk blotter. "The birdsong along the creek amazed me this morning. It's like I heard it for the first time."

His revelation birthed a flush of heat up her neck, as she sensed having a direct link to the cause. Grateful her work could span the gap and lend credence for their time together during the workday, she tapped the report cover and then dumped sugar granules into the black brew. "Go ahead and take a look. I've printed out four promising enhancement descriptions from our website. You can choose two or three of those to undertake this period."

"How long is that commitment? I need to know what I'm getting into up front." He took possession of the report and slowly leafed through the pages.

"This contract lasts for five years. Not that we have to decide things on the spot, but I'd be proud to enroll you before my tenure in Lyon County ends."

His gaze shot up from the paperwork, a molten fire of attention. "That would be my preference, also. With that groundwork in place, I'd have positive direction to accomplish the tasks." He returned his attention to the report. Soon, he flipped between two particular pages.

"What do you like, Hake? Does something strike you as worthwhile?" She swirled the coffee and took her first sip. The java was fortifying—and plenty hot.

"Well, I have two spring-fed water tanks. Looks like I could do this retrofit of a wildlife escape ladder in each tank without too much difficulty. That wouldn't have to be my main enhancement, but I'd like credit for it before I implement the addition."

"Yes, I agree that's a strong secondary enhancement we could add to the others. To make it even easier, I had Reece fashion a prototype model for display purposes, as this option is fairly new. I already have several ladders in storage, if you want to sweet talk me into using mine."

"Have I mentioned how radiant you're looking this morning? You must have enjoyed a highly restorative day of rest yesterday." His chuckle truncated with a noisy sip of coffee.

"Goodness me. I expected a highly educated man to be a bit more complicated than that." Her teasing tone made it personal. The warmth of her mug seemed to radiate up her arm to affect the rest of her body as the office seemed suddenly snug.

Hake leaned toward her, his elbows resting on his knees. His fingers interlaced around his coffee cup, lending him a symmetric centeredness. "Now for the truth, all this land management is lighting a fire under me that I never knew existed. It's transforming me into a man I don't even recognize in the mirror, but a thrill nonetheless. That you're the one who ushered it in…well, that's a different kind of special. Help me understand all these options, Aley. I want that land to be all it can be, not penalized because some know-nothing lawyer thought he found a bargain."

In all her working career, Aley had never witnessed such sincerity. Dreamt it maybe, but not experienced the earnestness. She answered with an incredulous shake of her head. "Hake, that penalty period ended the day you closed on the property. I have every intention of helping you tailor your management plan to its best interest. Let me emphasize that we're talking about long-term improvements. I'll start that process as your professional contact, and after that, I can volunteer to help implement enhancements at your mere invitation."

Something began to swim around in his gaze that had

more than a touch of affection to it. He slid one hand off the mug and extended it toward her. "Here's your open invitation. Not that Bushong will happen to be right on your way—making drop-in visits unlikely—but still know that you're invited out anytime."

She reached her hand to clasp his, not expecting the mug's warmth to have transferred through the touch. With a current of connectivity overwhelming her good senses, she held his hand longer than prudent. "Ha. There's the personal interplay that's giving my professionalism a run for its money this morning. Want to continue together? Or would you like to figure out these other enhancements by yourself?"

He released her and reached for the report. "Alone? Not by a long shot. Please, lead me through the quagmire of indecision. The wildlife ladder is definitely in. Go ahead and thank Reece for my two samples."

"I most certainly will. If you're going to keep a handle on proper stocking rates to prevent overgrazing, maybe you should take an honest look at annual monitoring with grazing exclusion cages. That way, if things get out of balance and there are too many cattle on the land, the grass literally tells you to ease back. What do you think about that monitoring option?"

"Yeah, I saw that page. If I'm going to have that dialogue with my grass, I need to learn how to identify who's talking to me. Right now, the grass mix is a generic blend to me."

"Point well taken. I'll have to teach you how to ID your grass types. It helps to have the seed heads on, like in the fall. That's when you take the readings—after grazing season ends."

Hake ran a hand through his hair, leaving his bangs with a wind-whipped effect. He blew out a breath. "Oh, I don't know. This seems over my head at first inclination. How many cages would it take, if I go with this option?"

"Here's my suggestion, shown on the aerial photograph of your ranch." She flipped the report forward several pages and gave him a few seconds to take in the graphic. "Your pastures have cross-fences, so the cattlemen will rotate the herd. To make sure they balance out that practice, you'll install a cage on each side. I've indicated them in pairs with this symbol." She touched the one closest to his thumb. "That gives you six cages to monitor."

Hake traced over the photograph with his index finger, going from one paired set to the next. After he'd completed the circuit, he glanced up at her. "I'll sign up for this one— if you'll help me at the end of grazing season this first year. I'm out of my element here, with the quantification of grazing pressure."

"I'll help you," she replied, not meaning it to sound so cozy. When his finger stroked across hers, it sealed a promissory pact. Her last enrollment came on butterfly wings, which seemed to match the flutter in her stomach, an odd outcome for proper land management.

~

Hake slid half a dozen settlement claim forms into the upright file organizer on his desktop. The invigorating perk of having Aley close by faded with each passing minute. Well past one o'clock, the day flattened a bit when she walked out of his office. Since then, he'd read through the draft conservation plan twice. The level of commitment made him grow increasingly swamped with a feeling of incompetence.

As he smoothed back his hair, the front door squeaked open. A sliver of natural light shot past a short figure negotiating the entrance. Soon, a petite gray-haired woman stood before him, her eyes unblinking like a frightened bird. "Is this the law office fighting the makers of Rid-A-Weed?" She moved her purse in front and pressed it against her chest.

Apprehension thickened the space between them. Hake rose without speaking, the hair on the back of his neck prickled at the sight of her defenselessness. He cleared his throat to no avail.

"Well, Dr. Atkins sent me over to talk to you about my Eldon, God rest his soul. I buried him two months ago tomorrow, but still have to make payments for his funeral." She tamped the purse on the guest chair and stared at him with clear gray eyes.

"Welcome to my law office, ma'am. I'm Hake Warren, the one Dr. Atkins told you about. I'm so sorry to hear about your husband. Please accept my condolences." He gestured toward the chair and retook his seat once she'd settled into hers. "I'm representing victims exposed to the chemical herbicide Rid-A-Weed, as the manufacturer has been found negligent to adequately protect the product's users. We have to establish that link between your Eldon and the product, so tell me about your husband's line of work."

"There's no doubt in my mind, Mr. Warren. Eldon worked for the city's recreation department for nearly forty years—mowing, planting, and trimming. You name the outdoor task and Eldon did it. He practically kept up Peter Pan Park as a one-person crew."

Hake reined in the smile that tried to emerge at the mention of that particular spot. "Well, I owe him a debt of personal gratitude then. That park's as idyllic as they come. I suppose using chemicals fell as a standard part of his job?"

"Yes, I should know, because I had to wash it out of his uniforms every week." She leaned forward. "His forearms stayed eaten up with the chemical burns. Never wore gloves until it was too late. He struggled through his battle with lymphoma for six miserable years."

Hake reached for the claim form, certain Dr. Atkins had done the medical check for him. "This is a product liability case, and I will be your legal advocate in filing your claim—if you want to move forward."

"I sure do. I've been around a while, Mr. Warren. I know these matters of paperwork take some time, but if I can get any compensation for Eldon's suffering, that would ease the financial burden on me. So I have to pursue it. Doc Atkins thought it best."

He picked up his pen to start recording the claim. Embarrassment soon heated his neck. He had failed to ask her name from the outset, so he couldn't even fill out the first blank. What an unceremonious beginning for his latest crusade for justice. *Rookie blunder.* He shook it off and locked his gaze in hers. "I'm going to have to delve into your life a bit, so I hope we can be honest with one another."

"Delve away, young man. I have an answer for every blank on that paper...and then some." She squared her shoulders and leaned back. "Start with my name. I'm Roberta Wilms. You can call me Bert like all my friends do." She nodded as if to set it in stone.

"Thank you, Bert. You're the first client that I've led down this notable road, so let's be patient with each other." He cocked a tiny smile in her direction, and for the first time, her expression softened. "You don't pay me ahead of time, by the way. The manufacturer covers my fee along with your settlement once your claim gets paid out."

"That's what they call a win-win situation, isn't it, Mr. Warren?" She opened her purse and produced a worn wallet, where she extracted a bent insurance card. "I'm ready for all your questions and have my back-up records when I need them. Fire away, and let's get this train a-going toward justice."

"Now firing up the engine." As he printed out the claimant's name, he sensed an unstoppable sweep of momentum lift him higher. Moments like this made him love his job—but there needed to be many more of them to keep a fully loaded train moving down the tracks. Every man needed to earn his daily bread, even an upstart lawyer who played the role of rancher at dawn and dusk.

Chapter 8

Thursdays had somehow become their unofficial date day, but Aley chose not to question the process. She balanced the crock pot of baked beans and strolled around the farmhouse toward the aroma of grilling beef. Right when she had a cheery greeting on the tip of her tongue, Hake held a finger to his lips and nodded toward the barn.

A slender tabby cat took a tentative step away from the wooden structure on a prowl that looked a lot like crossing glass chards. It halted midstep, wary and ready to scram, its haunches set to flex at any moment. The animal appeared wild.

Testing for domesticity, Aley crouched and tried to appear unthreatening. "Here, kitty kitty," she coaxed in a sing-song voice. "What a sweet kitty cat." The feline twitched one ear and tore out on a run in the opposite direction, headed for the lean-to door.

"There's my barn cat—and I'm terribly proud of having one—wild and all." Hake waved the grill tool through the air. "Hey, you look nice this afternoon."

She twirled halfway around so her skirt flounced above her knees. "Thank you. I brought the beans, as promised." She gave a quick curtsy and set the pot down on the back steps. "Does your cat have a name?" When the grill spattered to claim his attention, she strolled closer.

He fisted a spray bottle and shot back at the flames. Soon the flare-up disappeared under the grate. "No, I call it barn cat. I've been feeding it some dry food since Tuesday, over by that wheel."

Aley glanced by the lean-to and spotted a small blue dish set in the dirt. "Hmmm, looks like someone has a soft spot. Still, the cat deserves a name, so I'll call her Honey."

Hake arched an eyebrow as he flipped the first hamburger. "A stray cat earns a term of endearment—even before I do?"

He seemed so boyishly innocent, she had to chuckle at his objection. Maybe that fueled her flirty side, as she moved close enough to feel the grill's heat. Just short of brushing his sleeve, she turned to face him and gave him a toying look. "Well, what would the owner of a loosely-held barn cat like to be called?"

When she batted her eyelashes, he halted his reach for the second burger. "You mean I get to pick?"

She leaned forward placing her hands on her knees, and then blew into the fire. The coals glowed orange in response. "I suppose so—within reason."

He conducted the turnover maneuver in silence, causing the grill to spatter again. Once he'd dropped the spatula on the side shelf, he turned and decreased the distance separating them. "Okay, I'm picking out my own nickname. If you're ever trying to be sweet, you can call me Rancher." He inched closer as though to heighten the drama.

"Ooh, I think I'm going to like that name, yes indeed," Aley cooed. She pressed her lips together, forgetting she'd worn pink gloss. The slippery feel caused her a moment of dizziness. When Hake swooped in for a kiss, she grabbed his shoulders for stability. Though the grill hissed nearby, nothing could break the spell cast by the handsome cook. A few more paint flecks peeled off the barn before he got done, which suited her flirtatious mood.

He hovered cheek to cheek for an instant, gave a slow wink, and stepped away to resume his grilling duties. A moth fluttered over the grill, so he swatted at the air.

"I'm going to plug in the bean pot, and then I'll come back out to find the cat."

He pointed the burger flipper right at her. "That's Honey, Sugar."

She hastened a few steps, bristling at his nickname for her. After all, she wasn't *that* sweet. Once she had the pot in her hands, she climbed to the top step and turned, only to find him watching her every move. "Hey, I don't think the evidence supports your syrupy nickname selection. How about Miss Smart-and-Sassy instead?"

Hake got busy working some crusty buildup off the grate with the tool. "Oh, no. The lady adds only sugar to her coffee, so the Sugar nickname sticks. No swapping out. Go ahead and get those beans reheating. These burgers are almost done."

"Okay, I'll set the table then. Maybe I can cat-hunt later." She tipped her chin up to indicate victory. After stepping inside, she found condiments clustered on the bar near a plate of onion slices. Finding an outlet, she set the bean pot on high. A plastic bag abandoned on the bar soon contained the notorious onion slices. She rubbed her glossy lips together, conceding that condiment had to go into isolation for later consumption.

The dining area's buffet held an array of dishes. She chose a blue and white willow pattern and positioned them on the table by the window, with Hake at the head and her right beside him. That should be cozy enough.

"Here I am with the sizzling heifer patties," he teased, entering the back door with the platter balanced in his hands.

Her heart as light as a feather, she placed the silverware down and came right to him. "Oh, Rancher. I'm so glad you're home." Though her tone held a phony little tease, she made sure her gaze communicated something more genuine.

Hake slid the platter onto the cooktop range and hooked an arm around her waist. "Shoot me if I ever get tired of hearing that." He traced her jaw until his fingertip made her dangling earring wiggle. He pulled her close and seemed content to merely look from that proximity.

Caught between hunger and a warm sensation in her chest, Aley lost her focus right there in the kitchen. Out the screen door, she saw a tabby-colored flash run by. When Hake made a humming noise in his throat, she opted for short-term resolution. "Want some sugar on that order, Mr. Warren?"

"Most definitely."

Whatever message came next ended up muffled. Those gloss-waxed lips had to deliver the sweetener that this poor love-starved professional man needed. She'd break the news about the onion quarantine to him in a few minutes, but right now, she sensed his need for more immediate nourishment. A domestic mission of mercy, she happened to be in the right place to administer it, saints be praised.

~

Headed north to his rail connection, Hake pressed the gas pedal and took an old terrace like a whoop-de-doo. The Jeep responded with agile pep, catching a little air before it landed in a trackless pasture. The sun sank lower off his side-view mirror, so he tried to make a straight line north toward his destination.

"This could be addictive," Aley said, "riding with the wind in my hair."

"I'm stoked because the Jeep doesn't hide the land from me. Open air keeps me open to the elements. Hey, my old jean jacket looks good on you."

She folded the excess over her collarbone and giggled. "You might not get it back. This may become my official riding-the-range coat."

"In three weeks, it'll grow sweltering out here. I've

checked all the water tanks and everything looks good-to-go for grazing season."

"So is this some cow feature you're planning to show me?"

"Can't give away my secrets like that. Nope, you'll have to sit tight. I'll drive us right up to it. Give me forty-five more seconds." He jerked the steering wheel once they'd cleared the top of a ridge and veered east. A post from an old fence line went by, a lone sentinel.

"I love hearing the sounds of the closing day on the prairie. Once we get to wherever, let's stay until the last sunray filters through the trees along the creek." She turned and stared at the vast sweep of rolling prairie off her side of the vehicle.

Hake took in a different scene, one with Aley by his side coloring his world. A ranch this large could have been a lonesome place, but instead, God offered it to him in time to be part of their adventure together. He wouldn't squander that privilege, but he might ramp it with drama now and again. He spotted the elevated spur feature and angled for the right approach.

Aley tucked her fly-away hair back and gave him an inquisitive look. "What's this ramp thing doing right out in the middle of your pasture?"

"Hang on. You're about to find out." He wheeled the vehicle around, aligned the tires with the gravel ruts, and then added some speed for good measure. His third trip out this way, he knew right when to hit the brakes. The hood nosed higher as they rose above the prairie.

Aley scooted forward and folded her legs under, trying to see ahead. "What in the world?"

Just for heightened effect, Hake tapped the accelerator again before stomping the brakes. The vehicle slid to a halt at the edge of a sharp precipice. As he looked up, the sun began to touch the horizon. "Here's your incredible sunset, Sugar."

Aley stood up on the seat, peered down into the chasm off the front grill, and glanced over at him. "You're a madman, Hake. Where in the world did the road disappear to?"

"We're missing the old railroad bridge that used to span this spur line. They made an undercrossing for the cattle, back in the day. Looks like the bridge collapsed first, or maybe they removed it for safety reasons when they closed down the spur. The cattle pass-through down below looks really cool. They lined it with stacked stone to hold the train's weight."

"I'm so going down there." She jumped from the Jeep and backtracked until the ramp lost its steep sides and she could negotiate the sloped footing. In seconds, she became a shadow.

The decision to stay on top came with ease, as the rockwork would turn the low-lit setting into a picture postcard with Aley decorating the center. *Gotta see that.* When she came around the corner, he almost lost his breath, the scene turned so picturesque.

With the evening wind blowing her hair, she opened the jacket's edges like she was trying to take wing. Everything seemed to undulate like an ocean current swept through the cattle crossing. "This is totally amazing. Fly to me, Rancher."

Weak-kneed, he had to resist. "No—you're too…beautiful for me. I'd better stay up here." He extended his arms like a bird gliding by along some distant contrail. Only the Jeep's weight kept him tethered onto the ramp.

Aley walked deeper into the crossing until she stood directly below him. "One day, you will come to me, Hake." She held her arms up as if to beckon him like a mythical siren.

He wiped across his top lip as the sun melted into a saffron-banded sky. "Yes, one fine day—I'll fly to you. I promise." The last meadowlark called for its mate in the pasture and the prairie grew silent beyond the rhythmic thump of his heartbeat. As the sun dipped below the horizon, falling in love staked a claim, a high perch that left no room for turning around.

"We'd better get going while you have enough light to back down the spur's ramp—unless you want to try and jump the gap." She laughed and broke into a trot to circle around the far side.

Thinking that would equate to a Romeo-and-Juliet self-destructive move, Hake studied the narrow road back down and geared up for the challenge. "No jump attempts today," he muttered to himself, so used to playing it safe. When Aley appeared by the track ruts, he fired up the Jeep, let it emit its rowdy protest, and then reversed down the spur. Everything post-sundown had surrender written all over it, anyway.

Aley scrambled in and shut the door. Unwilling to be confined by her seat, she came across the console and soon held his chin in her hands. "This is for the gift of such a gorgeous sunset surprise, *Rancher*." Her kiss blurred the way she accentuated his nickname, and the two intermingled in a heated point of touch.

Gradually, Hake eased the taut pressure he held on the brake pedal and let the vehicle roll back to the face of the earth without over-steering the situation. With one hand on the wheel and the other in her hair, he had all he could handle at the moment. Level ground halted the Jeep mere feet from the north fence, as though he'd planned it that way. He took credit for nothing, except for having the right idea about coming here to end their dinner date.

Aley rubbed noses with him. A faint grin emerged on her expressive face. "Let's call this Sunset Spur so it can stay a special place for us."

"Glad you didn't say Lover's Leap." He gave her earring a teasing nibble and encircled her waist in a hug. "Sugar's Sunset Spur," he whispered. "I think we might have started something grand." Something airborne buzzed close by the Jeep in a whir of wings, barely missing the windshield as it banked away.

Aley flinched in reaction and buried her face in his neck. "Nighthawks are out already. Sure hope you've got headlights on this thing."

He laughed as he found first gear and set Old Betsy into forward motion. "There's no road anyway, so who needs headlights?" After navigating the first rocky ledge, he popped on the running lights just to illuminate the grass. Once she threw her arms around his neck, that equated to all the help he needed to find his way back home.

Chapter 9

Aley placed the storage boxes at the door to the garage. "Both offices agreed that I should start the new position at the beginning of the pay period, so that carves three days off of my two-week notice. She rolled her eyes at Reece, who stood barefoot at the bottom of the stairs. "Looks like I caught you off guard. Didn't we agree on eleven o'clock?"

He stomped into a pair of old sneakers. "Retract the claws, sis. Candice got up several times last night. She's growing more uncomfortable as each day passes. Less than two months to go, and then we can settle in for a bit more regularity in life."

"Hopefully. I do appreciate your offer to store my extra stuff—plus help unloading my trunk. Maybe you can work your way into a midafternoon nap." She wrinkled her nose with the tease and cracked open the door to inspect the promised space. From the cluttered accumulation of paint cans and yard tools, it appeared nothing ever got put away.

Reece led her into the garage and flicked on the light. "Give me a hand collapsing this workstation. I finally got the changing table done."

"Sure. I can fit four boxes in that space, maybe six." She lifted a plank off of two sawhorses and followed his lurching lead to the far side of the garage. "So, you think I'm doing the right thing, don't you? The relocation, I mean."

Reece slid the board in place beside another two-by-six. "Yeah, it's important to be happy in your work. However, Candice feels like you're moving away right when the baby's coming, so the distancing seems anti-family to her."

"Call me. I'll be right over. It's not that far, an adjoining county even." She followed him back and collapsed the nearest sawhorse. When Reece tucked his beneath the stairs into the house, she handed him the second one. "Let's retrieve the next round of boxes from my car."

He headed out, pressing his wrists together like a bound slave. He gave her a long look over his shoulder with one eyebrow raised. The overhead sun soon caused him to squint.

"What's with the penetrating stare?"

"Just wondering what your friend Hake thinks about the office switch. You went from his conservation field agent to his…well, remote consultant from the next county. That's a demotion of a different persuasion."

"Hake's not insecure enough to let a little distance between us shake him up."

"Oh, yeah? You're sounding pretty confident, like you have your cake and get to eat it, too. But if he's cool with the new arrangement, then that says something, doesn't it?" He stopped, stared into the trunk, and reached for the largest box. As soon as he lifted it, the packing tape popped off.

"I'll fix that later. Just get the box into the right corner for now. That one goes on the bottom. I'll bring another box to stack on top."

"That's my sister, the girl with the detailed plan." He grunted and hastened his pace when the box began to sag in the middle.

She struggled to keep pace. A tiny worry nagged at her, so she decided to disclose the situation to get her brother's trusted input. "Hake mentioned that housing availability might be an issue. Of course, I couldn't let something so trivial upend my plans for the office shift, which led me to ignore the entire issue—until now."

He crouched and dropped the mammoth box. "Well, it must be a pressing issue. I have to adopt your cast-offs until Council Grove opens its loving arms with a permanent address for its newest conservation officer."

She set her box atop his and flexed her shoulders, one at a time. "I'm staying at The Old Trail Inn, cabin two. They allow me to pay week-to-week. It will do in a pinch. The apartment options in town include a couple of complexes, neither of which has any vacancies. I'm on a waiting list for both. Short of looking for a house to rent or buy, that's all I can do."

His gaze cut away to a commotion down the block, but not before he regarded her for a split second. Wordless, he walked back to her car. The neighborhood kids broke up the rowdy pack and went their separate ways.

After tweaking her ponytail tighter, Aley wandered down the driveway and joined him. A quick assessment of the remaining boxes proved that any choice would mean the same amount of lifting—too much. She sighed. "I'm reduced to exist in a stash of liquor boxes. What a note."

Reece shook his head. "Take some advice from your brother. Don't go the house route. It's too permanent—and too much of a poke. I mean for Hake. He might concede you the job relocation, but the pursuit of a new house to nestle into, that's asking too much, from my humble perspective." A quick glimpse revealed he meant well.

"Is this some male territorial thing I might violate? I'm not really used to asking permission to live."

"He considers Bushong the halfway point, if I'm remembering right. That makes it neither here nor there regarding where you live—temporarily. If you two are building something together, you shouldn't make a move against that. A little cooperation on the surface goes a long way. In this case, shaky waters run deep. Save yourself trouble later on…if he matters to you." He hefted two boxes and returned to the garage.

Aley pressed her thighs against the rear bumper, letting his advice seep deeper into her contemplations. She envisioned Hake riding in his Jeep, happily acquainted with his section of land. Nothing about it seemed inconsequential. *Guess he does matter.* Duly warned, she released the house-buying option as improbable territory for further consideration.

∼

Only a couple of other ranchers had arrived at Bluestem earlier than Hake, which gave him a surge of pride in his purpose. After navigating an entire panel of paint chips, he'd settled on Old English Cottage for the ranch house, the barest color of yellow. A touch of tint might accent the house's symmetric features and give the gables some deserved attention. Trimmed in the sharpest white, he hoped the combination would prove eye-catching.

The attendant turned his back to the counter and a loud whirring noise soon began. Two bare wood stir sticks appeared next. The man held up a metal key used to pry open the cans.

Hake nodded and took possession. Funny how the right tool, no matter how simple, improved one's outcome. That thought jarred his contemplation toward the rented paint sprayer he had on reserve down the road. The manager assured him it would be easy to use, and the cleanup, a snap. Working with paint rarely had any ease to it, but he'd stick with the task and keep cleanup to a minimum. He figured to get the back and west side of the house done today, and then finish the front and east side on Sunday after church.

The constant hum of the shaking machine lulled him into such a deep trance, he almost missed the couple walking by. When the woman made a throaty noise, he glanced up to see a former client, the one with credit card woes. "Hey there. How's it going?"

Though the dark-haired guy's long stride didn't miss a hitch, she slowed and trailed her left hand behind. There, riding her ring finger, sat a glittery diamond band. She pressed her lips in a teasing circle as she left with a lingering told-you-so look over her shoulder.

Too early in the day for such conflicted input, Hake shook his head to help dismiss any further thought progression down that legal alley. He turned back to the paint station assistant only to realize the shaker machine had completed its cycle. Soon, the gallon can slid onto the counter beside the others.

The salesman popped the top and made a paint smear on the lid. "That's your light yellow. Here it is against the white trim color. There—that's a match made in heaven." The man grinned, seeming to enjoy his work.

The couple with trust issues flashed to mind. "Guess everybody can't claim that," Hake joked. "Thanks for your help today. I might have to make two trips to get all this to the register."

"Let me tote two cans for you." In a blink, he had them in his grip to make good on it.

"Thanks for the extra help—mighty neighborly. You don't live out by Bushong, by any chance, do you?"

"Nope. I live out by Olpe, south of town." He shrugged, but the paint seemed to weigh down the gesture.

"My next stop is for the rented sprayer. Hope I don't have to wear that yellow color to church tomorrow. Sometimes exterior paint can be a bear to get off."

The man nodded to the clerk as he sat the paint cans on the checkout counter. "Here's a tip—wear an old shirt with long sleeves. That's the fastest way to clean up."

Hake set two more cans on the counter. "Roger that. You really do have me covered this morning."

The man chuckled. "Hey, thanks for putting some fun back in my Saturday."

"You bet." Hake shook his hand before whipping out his wallet for the purchase. As the cash register rang up the items, he spotted the client again in the gardening section. In profile, the stocky guy looked familiar, but for the life of him, he couldn't make the connection. When the clerk announced the total, he slid his credit card through the scanner. Home improvement came with an incremental price tag. With the next stop, his tally would ratchet up another notch.

~

Grateful for the short drive over, Aley quelled her rumbling stomach and eased the car toward the house. A utility light shone on the western corner, where a bent figure seemed to be having a tussle with a gadget of some sort. She stifled a giggle and grabbed the takeout bag, achy from her day of packing and hauling boxes. From the looks of things here, Hake hadn't eased through his day either. "Intruder warning. Don't shoot me with that wand."

"Aley? Oh, thank goodness. Come over here and give me a hand, will you? I'm in rinse-out mode, but whoever typed 'easy cleanup' in the user manual could be found liable for false advertising. Yuck—I've got paint everywhere."

Once she'd closed the gap between them, she saw that his last statement rang true. His hands looked like a hazardous waste spill, coated and gleaming in the harsh light. Paint dominated the landscape, especially the rented sprayer.

"Got any suggestions? I can't get the paint to clear the lines. It's supposed to be pure water shooting out of the nozzle by now, but it still looks like paint."

"Warm water…maybe sudsy warm water. That's what you need. Let me take the food in and bring out a pitcher of water."

"Okay, use the dishpan though. Try to be quick about it, so the paint doesn't start to dry inside the line."

She broke away at a jog, resolved to bring him a ready

solution. An interior light shone across the back steps, helping guide her way. She slid the bag onto the counter and opened the cabinet under the sink to retrieve the dishpan. In one fell swoop, she plopped it into the sink, squirted dish soap in the bottom and jetted some hot water inside. Her gaze swept the room as the container filled. The table by the window held a lone book. Otherwise, the house seemed tidy, as usual. That lent some comfort, because the occupant couldn't say the same.

She shouldered into the back door and balanced the pan to avoid spilling. This would likely be the first of many loads in the cleaning process, so she tried to pace herself. Rounding the corner, she met the painter squatting to remove the sprayer tank's lid. "You bled the rest of the paint out, right? There's no buildup down there."

"I poured the leftover paint back into the can. Then I took a brush and swept out the rest. Take a look at my hands for the rest of the picture." He flexed his fingers to add drama.

"Sounds like you're ready for this then. You'll see…the warm water will help. Take this much. I'll go right back and make some more." Once the water had cascaded into the tub, she stood and gave him a prolonged assessment. "Yellow? You're yellow?"

He twisted the end of the wand and hit the power switch. "Not yellow. I'm Old English Cottage, thank you." The wand sputtered and then began to shoot a weak stream of tinted water.

Aley tried to work through her mild shock at the color selection. In seconds, the wand sprayed a stream of bubbles into the air. The happenstance almost annoyed her.

"Hey, hey—a little magic here," Hake quipped, aiming the wand over her head.

The utility light glimmered on the bubbles as they fell clumsily to the ground. The line spat water, coughed another line of bubbles, and resumed the watery spray. Aley tucked the dishpan under her arm. "I wish we could have discussed the color change beforehand, that's all."

"Sugar, I'm going to need more of that warm water. You might hold back on your dash of soap a wee bit next time. I'll work on clearing the gunk on the nozzle tip while you're gone. Who knows, by the full light of day, you just might like Old English Cottage."

She left without responding, not sure why it made such a difference to her. Since the first time she'd seen the house, she'd imagined it with a crisp coat of white paint. Yellow represented a departure from that dream, an infiltrating taint. She blew out a breath and hit the door latch, the day feeling too long at the moment.

A whiff of fried chicken made her wish the sprayer had already been tucked back in its box, clean and snug for the next use. Water soon filled the basin, and she lessened the soap by half. "Yellow," she muttered. "Didn't see that one coming."

~

Hake froze his expression like one of the faces on Mount Rushmore. Around him, the remains of dinner sat on the table. Now with his hunger satisfied, exhaustion overwhelmed him.

Aley took his chin in one hand and kept dabbing at his cheek. "You're beyond freckled. You're coated. Good thing this baby oil loosens the spatters, or I'd be using the scrub pad on you by now." She made an accentuated circular swipe and bent closer to inspect the results.

"Can you come out and help me tomorrow after church? I don't know if I can tackle the rest by myself." So tired, his words slurred. He hoisted an elbow onto the tabletop and propped his chin in his scraped-clean palm.

"I'm coming and bringing a crew along with me. This is a big job for two people. If you're going to be part of the community, you have to remember to let folks in the front gate." She ran a fingertip across his other cheekbone and inched closer. A new cotton ball soon found a non-scrubbed area.

"You're teaching me a lot of things, Aley—all of them are worth knowing. I thought you might be interested to hear the barn cat came and hung out with me for part of the afternoon. Maybe she's getting used to me." He shook his head which caused a brief disconnect with the cleanser. When her knuckle skimmed across his top lip, he could smell the soft scent of the baby oil. It brought a comforting response he couldn't name.

"Maybe she wants to be around more," she whispered.

He reached for the cotton ball and caught the hand that held it. The gravity of attraction held him suspended for a millisecond while Aley's oily fingers slid into his. The rest became a mix of withheld breath and targeted touch. When she brought warm receptivity into the kiss, he closed his eyes to savor the outcome, too tired to strategize beyond the truce. The day would end in powerless surrender. Tomorrow would be the Lord's Day of rest—until lunchtime anyway.

Chapter 10

From the harbor of her cubicle, Aley winced in discomfort, wondering why she thought her last few days might go smoothly at the Emporia office. Next week would be a mountaintop experience compared to this agonizing drag through the valley. An exit survey required her to overview the entire department, including leadership.

To further accentuate the departure process, Mr. Norman had scheduled a one o'clock appointment with her. The memo line on the e-mail had read "To Close Things Out." Mounting apprehension would make eating lunch improbable. She would ready her files for use by her forthcoming replacement instead. She deemed that task the professional thing to do.

She grabbed Hake's conservation folder and let it fall open. A lump tightened her throat when the aerial photograph showed the widespread boundaries within his care. Few men would dare attempt such a feat while working full-time at another occupation. She thumbed through the pages to make sure she had the enhancements all properly declared. Two stars indicated the location of the wildlife escape ladders, which she traced with her fingertip. Well on his way for the long-term management of the land, she knew he'd be successful—with or without her.

A commotion along the far hall distracted her for a brief moment. When she spotted Mr. Norman shaking hands with a stocky man standing back to her, she returned her attention to the plan and studied the implementation timeline. Nothing in this office concerned her—nothing until the one o'clock meeting. She sighed and closed the familiar folder, lining it up with twenty-five other active projects in her standing file slot. That would be her legacy—likely to a stocky heir with broad shoulders. He would fit in just fine, a real all-man squad. *Good riddance.*

~

Hake gave the agitated client a protracted look, not knowing what to make of his last insinuation. He had no intention of wallet gouging anyone. Maybe he had forgotten to disclose the entire setup. "Mr. Elliott, there is no direct cost to you—except your time in my office filing your claim. Dr. Atkins referred you to me, so you qualify. Today's visit represents a free consultation. As for my part, there's a set fee-claim evaluation provided for helping families like yours pursuing settlement. That comes after-the-fact, so there's nothing upfront to worry about."

"Oh." The man's bulging-eyed gaze drifted over the surface of his desk, skimmed him, and landed on his mounted diplomas on the wall. "I'm just being cautious. You lawyers have made a reputation for yourselves that isn't exactly flattering."

"Well, I'm new in the business." He flexed his palms up. "I'm held accountable to uphold justice, and this product liability case has victims here in Kansas that deserve compensation. Once I found out that exposure to this particular herbicide might be widespread, I set up the campaign to encourage settlement. Given that regard, I'm acting in the community's best interest." Out of breath, Hake caught the skeptic's gaze and held it like a set of vice grips.

Finally, the man gave a solitary nod, swept out his phone, and dialed with stubby fingers. "Yeah, I checked him out. It's legit, so come on in." He ended the call and passed a knuckle under his nose. "Got a few friends having me run scout for them, so we don't get tied up in something with shaky underpinnings." He tilted his head and shrugged.

The front door opened, and three stooped men filed up the hallway toward his desk. The lead man nodded at Mr. Elliott. They circled around behind him. A couple seemed unsteady.

Hake jumped to his feet. "Let's do this workshop-style. I'll take everyone through the claim form at the same time. First, I'll clear off my desk and pull up some chairs. Maybe I should put the coffee station table off the corner of my desk for more room to write."

"We'll help drain the dregs out of your coffee pot, Mr. Warren," the scout said. "Never any need to let good coffee go to waste."

Hake slapped his hands together and pointed at him. "Right you are, Mr. Elliott." He pulled up two more chairs, which were readily claimed.

"I'll take sugar in mine," the smallest man said, a crooked finger raised skyward.

Hake snapped his fingers to acknowledge the request. As he headed for the coffee pot, he thought to pocket the sugar pack for delivery. When he touched it, his mind flashed to Aley's first visit and how vulnerable she seemed. A smile soon spread on his face. He grabbed a stack of Styrofoam cups, hooked the coffee pot handle, and returned to get his victim compensation workshop going.

At this rate, he'd soon run out of forms. In problem-solving mode, he made a mental note to print more off at earliest availability—which certainly wouldn't be this afternoon. Excited beyond belief, he handed the carafe to Mr. Elliott for pouring and turned to retrieve the file forms. Translating the man's reactive grunt, he retook control of the coffee pot and did the pouring one steady cup at a time. Recovery always came like that—one step at a time, and today brought him a multiplier of four. *Taking off, for sure.* Viewing a rocket launch couldn't feel more exhilarating than this. He moved through the group, his feet light on the floor.

~

Aley froze while Mr. Norman centered her exit survey in front of him. His desk represented an expanse between them, one she had always honored by keeping her distance and not crossing. She glanced away to see if her squirrel friend might distract her today outside the window. That would help lower her blood pressure. One glimpse offered no such luck.

"To prevent our county resources from being understaffed for any period this spring, I hired your replacement today." Her boss stared at her as if to provoke a response. As the silence lengthened, he picked up the survey and tamped it on his desk. "This guy has been waiting for a prime chance to better his career, went back to college and finally earned his degree. I like a man who can pull himself up by the bootstraps like that. Plus, he'll be well-matched with this office, a sturdy outdoorsman ready to face the elements."

Every disclosure seemed to have an invisible barb meant to prick her thin skin. Aley inhaled through her lips and decided not to let him get her goat. *Two days and counting.* She could pull this off, remain productive until the end, and then life would improve by leaps and bounds. "I'm certain he will take off at a full run, sir."

He leaned forward. "I'm confident of that as well, which is why I've asked his boss to release him without notice, so he can report to us tomorrow for training. The county stays overstaffed in the noxious weed department, anyway. He'll be with us for your last two days, so I'm requesting that you to run him through the client list for familiarity, and then take him in the field for a couple of active site visits."

Aley's jaw dropped at the presumptive request. Her last hours of freedom evaporated. She'd have two days to bring an entry-level recruit up to speed, a grueling transition if ever one existed. The brief duration represented the only aspect that saved her from flat-out refusing. She could do the nerve-grating orientation—for two days. Her thoughts skittered across her client list to land on the perfect site visit to suggest. Hake popped to mind, but she dismissed the option, hoping to insulate him from the plagued tag-team excursion.

Mr. Norman leaned closer. "I'm thinking the larger the job site, the harder it will be for him to orient and navigate. Take that nine hundred-and-twenty-six acre parcel in Bushong. That would be a challenge for anyone, seasoned or not. I'd like you to work that one in—if the rains don't come Friday."

Her ability to shield Hake vaporized on the spot, in tandem with her freedom. She clenched her teeth, searching for a way to avert the collision. "That contract is brand new. There's barely been any action on it so far. With the cattle herd being delivered this weekend, the landowner is focused on fencing and other aspects of containment. Are you sure that would be a wise choice?"

"I figured the newer contracts would be the easiest, since they don't have any backlog of noncompliance. Sometimes, the less history is the best history, if you know what I mean." He exhaled while he fingered through the survey. "The new guy comes across firm as a regulator. I don't mind a touch of gruffness accompanying proper enforcement. That might keep a few borderline clients honest, who knows?"

Aley diverted her eye roll into a glance out of the window. The fox squirrel leapt from a landscape tree and ran across the parking lot. *Run for both of us, amigo.* An overwhelming urge to be out on the prairie struck her, causing her to rise to her feet. "Did you want to go over the survey with me, sir? If not, I'll go plan that orientation progression, as you've requested."

"Survey? Oh, no. I'll look over the whole works later.

These exit forms are worthless, if you ask me. Still, I'll sign off and send it on up the line to comply with procedure. Thank you, Ms. Halstead. I somehow knew I could count on you."

Her chuckle accompanied a single shake of her head. "I'll try to beat the rain on Friday and get that Bushong site visit accomplished."

"I'm not so sure the county's most neglected tract would be highly accommodating in a downpour," he quipped. As he tucked the survey into a drawer, he acted as if he wanted to add something more, but held his peace.

"We'll take boots and rain slickers, just in case." Proper field gear fell under standard operating procedure. The new recruit would get a healthy dose of that fed to him, as regulators always stood on policy. It had been their backbone for decades, so no reason existed to rebel at this juncture. *Frustrating yet fitting.* With a nod, she left the office and ended a pointless exit interview, which encapsulated her entire experience at the Emporia office.

~

Hake made the parmesan cheese shaker spin as Aley returned from washing her hands. Dinner together on a Wednesday represented a new treat, one he welcomed. Between his good humor and the cheese-laden pizza on order, they would abolish her downcast mood.

As she slid into the booth opposite him, Aley forced a brief smile that fractured her tight expression. "The scrumptious aroma from the kitchen almost makes me forget my woes."

"Good plan, right? I can be sinister like that. You have to watch me." He winked and gave her a furtive look that hinted at his capacity for being shifty. "Two more days. To my recollection, no one ever lost their sanity for exposure to the inane over a two-day period—unless water-boarding happened to be involved." He squinted for drama.

"Ha-ha. You're downright hilarious. Still, I operate

better when I get to pick my own company—not when it's forced on me." She picked up her straw and stripped off the paper.

A cozy feeling shot up his spine, realizing he'd landed in the insiders club. She'd even asked him to meet up for dinner before heading home. He reached across the table and found her hand. "I always want to stay a member of that uplifting brigade. Is there someplace I can sign on for an extended membership?" He raked his thumb over her satiny skin and rubbed her knuckles.

She exhaled, puffing her bangs up. Next, she gave her head a shake while glancing around the pizza joint. Finally, her gaze came to rest on him. "Hake, honestly. You make all the ugly go away when you're with me. It seems inconsequential on the surface, maybe because you make me feel like a part of something more consequential. Does that make any sense?"

"Well, you could say that what we have going on transcends any drudgery happening day-to-day. I hope you remember that after you move to Council Grove and start the new job, because I expect my regular Thursday night date, plus weekends with time spent together." He infused his expression with masculine interest, so she wouldn't decline. Nothing would change between them during the transition, not if he could help it.

A girlish grin crept through her stoicism. "You always seem to get what you want, don't you? Like when you offer consultations for free, and then end up with paying clients."

"That didn't exactly work with you, did it, Ms. Halstead? I suggested that you not sell your land, so there was no monetary entrapment on my part whatsoever." He leaned in and kissed the back of her hand, his gaze locked with hers in a magnetic standoff.

She tilted her head. "Entrapment might hint to captivation of another sort."

"Aha, but a much more voluntary kind, if I'm not

mistaken." He sent her a delving look.

"You shameless flirt," she replied under her breath. She wiped a napkin down her neck where a crimson blush had started.

"I dare you to come over here and talk like that." He tugged on her hand, wanting an immediate response. When she arrived on his side of the booth, he drew her in until their knees bumped under the table. He locked his hands around her neck and took an in-depth survey of her facial attributes, all of which pleased him without question.

"Hake Warren—do *not* kiss me in this restaurant," she whispered. One brow hitched and slowly retreated back to normal. The twinkle in her eyes spoke a different mandate.

He bowed his head, content to breathe through her thick brown hair. The smell reminded him of meadow hay, sweet and organic. "Oh, I thought you needed a little distracting…in a captivating sort of way. I'll hold off on the kissing…for now. Since we're going to sit this close, I'll think of something else you can do for me."

A scraping sound interrupted their intimate conversation. Hake glanced over to see that the pizza had been served. The footed pewter tray delivered dinner right about chin level. Under his grip, he felt Aley sigh. "How about this?" He nuzzled his cheekbone against hers which almost led to the prohibited action. Fighting the urge, he pulled back and looked deep into her eyes. "How about feeding me some pizza? In return, I'll feed you."

Aley snickered at the proposition. "Sounds like busy work to me."

"You know you want to."

Her gaze deflected to her lap, but drifted back to him. "Yes, you're right. I do."

He slid closer to her until their shoulders touched. With head bowed and eyes closed, he enjoyed the oneness of her proximity. "Thank you, God, for this captivity. And bless this food so we can last out the week, amen."

"Two more days—it's hardly any time really." She blinked once, her countenance light.

"Here comes my daily bread. I'll take the piece with the giant mushroom." When she freed it for his immediate consumption, he had the outcome he'd wanted from the start—dinner cooked for him and a dazzling date to deliver it. The kiss would come later. Definitely later.

Chapter 11

Already an outsider, Aley took the guest chair and sat away from the built-in desk of her former cubicle. The hulking mass of a man that sat in her place took up all the immediate space anyway, leaving her the passageway between sections of the natural resources office for a place to perch. The detachment felt appropriate, although the flirty wink her replacement had just sent her did not. Dane Burroughs could have her job, but not her feminine attention.

He gave the standing file of CSP participants a pat with his broad hand. "Maybe you could elaborate on that point, so I don't have to guess."

Aley shrugged her shoulders. "I'm saying that long before you switch to enforcement mode as a regulator, you owe it to the client to recommend the best land management for his particular acreage. Once you set the groundwork of cooperation, then you are in better position to enforce the stipulations of the contract. Since landowners receive monetary compensation from Uncle Sam, we have to make sure they remain in compliance throughout the contract."

"I landed this job because of my ability to ramp up enforcement. I merely mentioned my conceal-and-carry permit during the interview, and the match-up fell right into place."

Aley leaned forward, unsure he had received her full message. "Cooperation, Mr. Burroughs, will get you more respect from the ranchers than a show of force. This department wears its authority with a light touch, again, to foster cooperation. Plus, we need new enrollments to keep the local quota up each enrollment period, so we won't benefit from mumbled complaints among the ranchers. My last task here is to conduct your training, so you can advance in the position with procedural accuracy."

He flexed his stubby fingers before locking them together. "I'll stay within policies and procedures—but I still maintain the right to do the job my way."

She recoiled in her chair, wondering what kind of pig-headed replacement Mr. Norman had let into the building. The calendar somehow caught her attention. Maybe that represented safer ground. "We should concentrate on the time of year you're starting. The first of May is critical to the ranchers. The cattle arrive by semi-trucks, and the pastures get stocked, as set by contract, for the ninety-day short-season grazing period. As for exceptions, you only have one long-season grazer with cow-calf pairs, the McCaskey ranch."

"I have all the stocking rates recorded?" He reached for a file as if to find the answer.

"Yes, on the inside cover I've stapled our copy of the contract agreement that specifies the stocking rate. You'll find it pays to be orderly in the way you maintain your paperwork."

He thumbed across the notation, scanned the contract, and then slammed the file shut. "My plan is to make this job nine-tenths fieldwork, and one-tenth paperwork. I'm more of an outdoorsman, which is why I aimed toward a range management career in the first place."

The more she heard, the less settled she grew. Further correction would be antagonistic or disregarded at this point.

Maybe she should play off of his professed strength. "When we go into the field this afternoon, I'll narrate my management assessments out loud, so you can pick up on what to monitor based on the various enhancements in each CSP contract."

He stretched back in his chair, his arms over his head. "Finally, something I can look forward to beyond this gray jail cell of a cubicle."

"Welcome to NRCS. It's a good job, so take care of it. You can be influential, even from the plans you design from this little cubicle." She stood up, needing a break. "I'll give you some time to review the folders. We're going to the Douglas ranch this afternoon, so read that last."

He locked his hands behind his head, his chest puffed up like a tom turkey. "Will do."

Aley exited the front door, tempted to escape to her car. With Hake's office less than three minutes away, that destination sure tantalized her in the moment. They still had their regular Thursday night dinner plans together, so she'd hold off until then. Thinking about him seemed to make the day more tolerable. With birdsong in the air, late April soon teased her with its carefree persuasion. A gusty breeze sent her loose hair flying.

Remembering her identification badge in the console, she detoured to her car to retrieve it. When she flipped the console open, three wrapped caramels stared back at her beside the ID lanyard. "You're a sweet man, Hake Warren. I should have told you that by now." She took a piece of candy, grabbed the badge, and headed back to the building.

Before stepping inside, she unwrapped a caramel and let it sweeten her mood. The mail truck swerved into the parking lot, offering her the next work-related diversion. She'd teach her replacement how to check his mailbox. Perhaps he'd like that tight space even less than the standard-issue cubicle. *Not my problem.*

~

"Topeka?" Hake studied his host, trying to figure out the reference.

Dr. Atkins leaned over the cafeteria tray, his eyes twinkling. "I'm in a consortium of doctors that rotate specialized practices between three locations—Emporia, Topeka, and Pratt. An old medical school chum, John Hendry, remains based out of Topeka. When I told him about your settlement work, he promptly requested a visit. You can pick up the tail end of his weekly wellness lecture on Friday, add your summation, and then stay to complete the paperwork."

Something about working out of the area bristled against his mindset, but Hake couldn't put a finger on exactly what. It seemed unprofitable to incur needless expenses in hopes of gaining a handful of clients. "I don't know, sir. I'd have to close the office here not knowing how much business I might pick up there. Let me think about that."

"Well, if the sixteen Non-Hodgkins lymphoma patients John has on referral don't interest you, I'll try to understand."

His head jerked up, recognizing the bonanza. "Okay, now I have a quantified interest in Topeka. How would I make that Friday wellness seminar work?" He fiddled with his spoon, but couldn't feign any real appetite for the blob of yellow custard decorating his blue plate special.

The doctor scribbled a couple of lines onto his napkin, and then shoved it across the table. "Stay at my condo. I'll be up there Tuesday night for my Wednesday appointments. You can come up Thursday night. I gave you the four-digit entry code there. Remember to hit 'enter' after the number sequence."

Hake read through the address. It seemed the clinic and the condo shared a block with the main hospital. Talk about convenient. He could drive straight up the turnpike after the law office closed. He'd have to beg off of his regular

Thursday night date, but Aley would understand. "You're about to talk me into this Topeka outreach, Dr. Atkins. I can't see any downside from where I sit."

"Because there isn't one. Believe me. I had hesitations when they first suggested this three-city rotation thing to me, but now I admit that the patients receive better care, and we get to help more people. Seems to me, when you discovered that no other lawyers had addressed the Rid-A-Weed settlement close by, you had a similar motivation to help victims around the state."

Hake nodded, a smile emerging at the admission. "Rookie mistake—I thought those victims would travel to me."

Dr. Atkins gave a belly laugh and then tossed his napkin over the custard on Hake's plate. "Okay, one mistake per meal is my limit. Don't eat that gelatin. The glossy coat and strong nails promise reflects a nutritionist's over-exaggeration, I assure you."

Hake took a few seconds to enjoy the old sage's company. This professional association had added a few personal perks, like help deciding what boundaries could flex in a quest to reach more deserving victims. "Thank you for lunch, sir, and for setting up the Topeka session. After we give this a trial run, let's talk about doing something in Pratt, too."

The doctor stood with a grunt and slid his chair under the table. "Now you're talking with some forward-looking sense, young man. You need to allow your influence to radiate outside of your immediate sphere. That's the recipe for successful practice—be it law or medicine."

Hake rose from the table, awash in similarities between the two occupations. "I don't know, sir. Maybe you'd better tell me what the living arrangements are like in Pratt before I make another rookie mistake."

"Rick's Restaurant makes the food options better there, but for the rest, you'll have to take a baby-step of trust, young man." Dr. Atkins grabbed the register tickets and made for the check-out counter, an uneven hitch in his gait.

Lacking momentary direction, Hake let the hubbub of the room infiltrate his thoughts. Amid the din, two women dressed in comic book scrubs giggled at a nearby table. As he made a sweeping assessment of the dining hall, he realized he must have been the target of their feminine attention. Being oblivious had its perks. He probably strolled right through a few of those every day without notice. Today, he'd take baby steps past such meaningless scrutiny. Tonight, however, he would make a point to cash in on some better-targeted affection. His solitary afternoon began to shrink by increments. In the meantime, he had a trip to plan.

~

Not intending the hurt, Aley stepped closer to the man hugging the front door frame. Bent by a lifetime of ranch work, the host seemed on the verge of collapse. "I'm sorry, Mr. Douglas. I should have told you when I called. I'm relocating to the Morris County NRCS office. They have more clients than Lyon County and a diversity of personnel on staff. Dane Burroughs here will be your new CSP contact. I'm trying to show him some of the local projects, so he knows what to look for when I'm gone."

Dane stepped forward and offered his hand. "Thanks for having us out today, Mr. Douglas. You can reach me at the same number, as I'm taking Ms. Halstead's spot. My business cards won't be ready until mid-May, so they say. I'm not holding my breath on that one." He chuckled and pumped the man's hand.

"Okay then," the rancher replied. "Let me go get my hat. Meet you out the back door."

Aley stepped away with an exhale, relieved at the outcome. Dane's schmoozing ability had some meritorious benefit after all. With the enhancements fresh in mind, she tried to put a route into logical order.

Dane led back to the truck. "I'd like to see that new pond

first."

"Correction. First, we can check the location of his mineral feeders in these two front pastures. They are directly on the way out to the new pond."

"All right." He opened the door to the driver's side and gave her a hard stare. "I'd prefer to drive Mr. Douglas around. That emphasizes my authority to be out here in the first place."

Aley stood on the ebbing edge of this authority battle, and she knew it. "Fine. I'll ride along to keep the dialogue going."

"That sounds cozy with three of us in the cab," he replied, a thread of interest needling into his tone.

No stranger to his ladies-man tendencies, she'd managed to avoid Dane while living in the same town for years. Now, proximity in the truck's cab worked against her. Fortunately, she had a third party who could run some interference between them. "Hope you like rubbing shoulders with a bony old man. I plan to have Mr. Douglas sit in the middle."

She turned and retreated to the passenger door, in prayer mode that God would grant her the forbearance to withstand being tethered to Dane Burroughs for one more day. When the aging rancher ambled into sight, she tossed him a friendly wave. A cooperative gesture, she walked out to meet the aged rancher halfway.

~

Hake shifted the lifeless mass until sure he had it centered on the plank. "We'll never get to seesaw if you don't cooperate a bit." He clamped Aley's grip onto the handholds and trotted around the center fulcrum to man his end of the deal.

"But I don't feel like playing." She threw her head back and let her hair dangle in the late afternoon sun. "This has been the most trying workday *ever*."

"But it's over, so banish the thought. One training day

down, and only one left to go. That balances you right in the middle, which makes you the perfect teeter-totter partner." He jumped onto his seat and shifted to offset their weight differential. With a push, he soared from low to high while she did the reverse. "Look, Aley! We're flying."

By the second trip up and back, her groans had morphed through several gasps into a lighthearted giggle. "Okay, just take those pushes a little softer, will you?"

He cupped one hand around his lips. "Pilot to co-pilot, I think we're hitting some turbulence through here." His next push accentuated the jarring he'd warned her about.

She wrapped one arm around her midsection. "Good grief, Hake. At this rate, I won't need that sub sandwich you picked up for dinner. Whoa, Nelly." She rode the height of the crest and squeezed her eyes shut on the way down.

"Well, we're closing in on our destination called forget-the-day." He paused long enough to push off. "How am I doing so far?"

Her hair flounced as the momentum shifted again. She shot up with a laugh. "Getting there, believe me." Once at the pinnacle, she let her arm fly like a bronco buster.

"Are you glad I chose Peter Pan Park for tonight's date?" He had to know, as it was a key part of his setup.

She rode back down before replying. "Extremely glad. Thank you."

He pointed back at her, intent to keep the ride going.

His plan to end up at a destination called remember-the-day required certain careful navigation. A man need not push that distance too hard. He let the wonder of being together buoy his spirits, while his legs got a workout with the routine push-off. Overhead, a puffy cumulus cloud passed the canopy of two cypress trees before he felt the urge to stop. When his feet hit the ground, he cushioned the halt.

Aley tilted her head to one side. "Will you swing me next?"

He slid off the plank and lowered her to the ground.

"May the lady always get what she wants." He bowed with a flourish and crossed over to escort her to their next stop on the playground. The pavilion where they had first kissed lurked off in the distance.

Aley turned abruptly, just short of the swings. "How did you know this was exactly what I needed?" She gathered her hair and held it from the teasing wind.

"Hmmm. Fresh air, soothing repetitive motion, and an unbeatable companion at the park. Throw in something to eat later, and you have a winning combination. Right? Now, pick your swing, Wendy, and let's be off to Never Never Land."

She kissed her fingertips and tossed the sentiment toward him from afar. With a giggle, she turned and ran to a sturdy swing. "This one will launch me over the treetops. Push only to get me started, and then I'll take it from there."

He shook his head, squelching a grin as he bypassed her for pushing duty from behind. He drew her back in a sudden motion and held her against him in a halt. "I remember Wendy being a bossy character at first, but she eases that saucy attitude once she sees how much the Lost Boys need her." Intending his words to be intimate, he let his lips brush her ear with the delivery. The following second, he shoved her into the stratosphere without any mercy.

From her protesting scream, the launch succeeded in every respect. Her hair flew wild all around her, crowning her apex and then trailing her on the return. "I'm so free."

Not to be left flatfooted, Hake settled into the adjoining swing, gave the chains a testing yank, and then shoved off to match up with his dinner date. It took effort to gain equal altitude, but he soon managed. When she looked his way, he tossed her a wave as their arcs crossed.

Aley passed by flying forward, her expression euphoric. "Why are Thursdays the absolute best?"

He didn't have to over-think that response, though he did have to wait for her to return. "Because we get to be together, that's why."

On the next pass back, she reached out for him, wiggling her fingers in thin air.

Prompted to amend his premeditated plan for the pavilion, he shoved off to gain altitude and better match her trajectory. The added momentum proved to be just what he needed. He locked his fingers into hers and allowed the jubilation of the linkup to ramp up his courage. At the apex, the words seemed to rush right out. "Aley Halstead, I'm falling in love with you."

She squeezed his fingers and let out a cheer. "Hake, you make everything so unbelievable for me—in the best way possible."

The swing back to earth seemed to take forever. He needed to stop and close the gap between them. "Hey, put on the brakes, will you?" After dragging his heels, he managed to slow down first. When she came back again, he stood waiting for her. The chains felt warm where she'd been clinging to them. Breathless, he hovered over her, taking a long assessment of her wild state. "Tell me…what I need to hear."

She rose, locking her arms around his neck. "I love you, Hake. I love the way you make me feel when we're together."

"Welcome to Love Everlasting," he whispered as he bent closer. His kiss landed in an untamed hurry, capturing the wild woman in the swing next to his. For her part, she didn't fight love's entrapment. When he lifted her off her feet, she even displayed sweet cooperation, strong progress for a Wendy-type under necessary reform.

Chapter 12

Sick of having to share limited airspace, Dane glanced up to see the director in conversation with the departing conservation officer. Soon, the boss would rely on him instead of her. Monday couldn't come soon enough to usher in full possession. He already had one special date highlighted on his calendar. Yes, that first payday would be sweet, as the salary for this job topped his wages at the noxious weed office by a third. Funny that holding a college diploma could make that much difference.

He glanced back at the folder featuring the location of his afternoon site visit. The monstrous property covered almost a thousand acres. He'd probably be able to nail this guy with a number of negligent omissions to his new CSP contract. No question, one of them would come out looking ignorant in the exchange—and it wouldn't be him. He grabbed a notepad and sketched a shortlist of enhancements they should expect to find in the field.

Someone walked over from the copier room and waylaid the director. That bought him enough time to record the list of enhancements. The addition of wildlife ladders would be easy enough to monitor. The aerial photos showed locations for grazing cages, so he'd test that component, too. The mineral feeder rotation sat outside of his grasp—for today.

Once the cattle had been added to the mix over the weekend, his next trip out would be more productive. His gaze skimmed the aerial. The tract's perimeter seemed endless. With four individual ridges adding to the Flint Hills, his coverage of the vast territory might be tricky. A unique transportation option popped to mind and matched his maverick style. Radical enough to work, it gave him an unexpected edge. Dropping two wheels proved him capable of brilliance at quick study, nothing short of genius.

Aley Halstead stopped near his cubicle, rubbing her palms together. "Are you ready to head out for the Warren ranch, Mr. Burroughs? I signed us out of the office."

"Yep. Totally ready to execute compliance justice." He waved his notepad at her. "I wrote down a shortlist of the enhancements, in case having the whole file with us gets awkward."

"Oh, I'm fully anticipating awkward." With a curt turn, she headed for the parking lot.

Dane shoved out of the seat and grabbed his hat. Like a buck released into the wild, he felt his blood pressure surge. Restless, he needed a breakout. It matched Friday, too. As he flicked the back door open, late April hit him with a full case of wanderlust. A thousand acres would be plenty of room to roam…as long as she let him drive.

~

Aley's approach to Hake's ranch registered flat on her emotional Richter scale. The clod behind the wheel had everything to do with that failure. At least Hake wouldn't be home yet. Maybe they would have most of the training session accomplished prior to his arrival. She scratched an imaginary itch on her temple just to block the visual image of her companion.

Out of duty, she'd have to start the running narrative on the property in the next minute or two. The department truck navigated the slowdown for Bushong and almost halted at the turn-in. "Yes, this is the entrance. Turn left after the old loading pens."

"Gottcha," Dane replied. "I've never been out this way much. Lookin' forward to it."

"You'll know you've gone too far if you cross the old railroad tracks down the road. The Rails to Trails bike path traces the parcel's entire northern property line. The western property boundary is more natural, as a creek winds through the neighboring tract. Mr. Warren retains a minimal riparian woodland fringe along his fence line."

"Right, I'll be watching for that if we get that far over. I'm more interested in the central ponds and water tanks." He gave a slow nod as if he knew something she didn't.

She took a tranquilizing breath and studied the rise ahead. Once they made the curve, Hake's charming farmhouse would come into view. She spotted the pointed roof of the grain silo above the trees and let out an involuntary sigh. What she wouldn't give to see him standing on that front porch, ready to keep her company.

The truck maneuvered the curve with haste, sending the file folder skidding off the seat. In a flash, she stuck out her hand and trapped it against her leg. By the time she glanced up, the house sat straight ahead, basking in the full afternoon sun. For a golden moment, she enjoyed its gabled features, noting how the mottled roof shingles picked up the yellow tint of the new paint for a blended look. *Old English Cottage.* Today, she adored the paint selection.

"Left or right here?" the driver asked in a gruff tone. "I'm not sure where I'm going."

"Head to the right. That's north. The house sits dead center of the property." She pointed to the access road that would eventually take them all the way up to the burned-off pasture. They could backtrack from there, a great way to kill time.

He chuckled under his breath. "Thought I'd lost you to some daydream back there."

His ridicule jabbed her under the ribs. She'd better stow her sentimentality for now and begin her narration. With any lull, Hake would come streaming into her consciousness and sidetrack the training session. "I wanted to take you to the far pasture, which needed the most immediate improvement. I brought a crew in and burned a hundred acres bordering on the riparian woodland back on the second week of April."

"I always enjoy a good burn," he mused, his gaze trailing over to her.

Aley refused to look his way, allowing the memory of Hake's knockdown tackle at the spot-over fire to entertain her instead. She'd retrace that burn outline without revealing any of the personal interaction the fire ignited that day. Sensitive about revealing too much, she touched her forehead to make sure the scrapes had healed. So much had happened since that day. It almost left her off-balance to think about the progression.

"Oh, yeah. I see some hardwoods encroaching from the western boundary, for sure."

"I've advised the landowner to rotate the herd into this back acreage by mid-June, after the grass has recovered. The cattle have plenty of forage out in this adjoining portion. See the cross-fence coming up from the west there?" She pointed across the ridge, grateful they weren't headed down there today.

"A cross-fence means there should be two grazing cages, right?" He shoved up the brim of his hat as if to better inspect them.

Another stab pierced Aley's midsection. She chewed her bottom lip and looked down the slope as the truck navigated the winding road. "I'm not one hundred percent sure, but I don't think the landowner has those cages up yet. We'll keep a lookout for them, just in case."

"I believe the wording makes it clear that the enhancement has to be in place prior to grazing season. I counted the star symbols on the aerial. This guy has six cages to install. I'll be sure to express my expectations when we meet him later on."

"He'll have all weekend, if the cattle don't arrive early," Aley replied, sensing the need to defend Hake. In her single-minded devotion to landing the new job, she'd forgotten all about those grazing exclusion cages. Maybe she could sweet talk Reece into loaning out his trailer for the wire panels. She'd delay her Saturday moving plans to help Hake get the cages installed.

The conflict of interest now made walking both sides of the line agonizing. *Get out here, Hake.*

~

At three-thirty, Hake snatched the "Office Closed Early" sign out of the printer. If he taped it onto the front door now, he could beat the arrival time he promised Aley by almost an hour. Business had been slow since a solitary client left with advice for a traffic violation that couldn't be appealed. That eighty-two-dollar ticket would only escalate trouble from here on out, a point he made all too clear.

He reached back to retrieve the tape dispenser only to spot the red light of the coffee maker. Glad to catch that oversight, he didn't want to leave it simmering all weekend long. He stepped over to toggle off the power switch and relented to rinsing out the coffee pot, too. It held an acrid roasted smell and crinkled his nose after closer inspection. Swirling clean water in it a time or two, he tore off a paper towel and brought the pot back to the lobby for drying.

"Can you help me, sir?" a woman asked, her voice tempered by age.

Hake glanced up to find the tiniest old lady he'd ever seen, bent-backed and propped on a cane. "I'm sorry—yes. I can help you. I didn't hear you come in."

She inched forward. "I've come about the Rid-A-Weed settlement."

"Would that be for your husband, ma'am?"

She shook her head side to side. "Nope, I'd like to file

a claim for myself. I kept the arboretum over in Hesston for twenty-five years. I used Rid-A-Weed almost weekly to control poison ivy, as I'm deathly allergic."

A familiar wave of compassion swept over him as he gestured for her to take a seat. Moving behind his desk, he transferred the closing early sign and reached for the settlement claim form. "I'm Hake Warren, ma'am. I guess Dr. Atkins referred you to my office."

"After I saw your notice in the newspaper, I called over there to confirm. The nurse said Doc would give me the referral, so here I am—your Friday girl." She gave a weak smile and slid into the guest chair.

"I'm glad you came in then," he replied, trying hard to be sincere. "Are you getting along okay this afternoon?"

She opened her purse and placed her wallet on the desktop. "I'm beating the cancer, but I'm battle-weary. This settlement would be a nice reward for my perseverance, to tell you the honest truth."

Hake's gaze met her determined stare and every ounce of resentment for the late-hour drop-in vanished. "Let's get busy making that happen then." The smile he added had nothing to do with his ranching situation. Right now, justice resided in another realm, keeping company with the weak and the weary. "Let's start with your name—first, middle, and last."

She curled her fingers and rested her hands on the desk. "Janie Rose Steadman. I'm pleased to meet you, Mr. Warren." Her dark eyes twinkled at the admission.

Hake printed her first name and looked up, breaking his rhythm. Maybe the Holy Spirit had required the extra moment from him, so the process didn't seem so routine. "I hope you enjoyed your years at the arboretum, Ms. Steadman. It sounds like a lovely job."

Her chin tucked to her chest. "They named the path out to the sculpture island for me upon my retirement. I volunteered a bit afterwards, until the lymphoma got to be too much."

"Retirement has its blessings, too. Some may not be as familiar as your path, for sure."

She leaned toward him the slightest bit. "You may be right about that, as one such path led me right here to you."

Nailed in place by her purposeful stare, he read the next line from the form. "They want to know your date of diagnosis next, Ms. Steadman, Do you remember that?"

She pushed an insurance card toward him. "I wrote it on the back here. Doc told me to keep up my records, so consider this written in shorthand."

"Yes, ma'am, I will." Hake flipped the card and had to hold it closer to read the fine print. According to the date recorded, she'd been fighting lymphoma for over three years. That disintegrated his last ounce of hurry. Knowing she deserved his undivided attention, he silently vowed she would receive it. He recorded the date and turned the card over to learn the name of her insurance carrier. The Bushong address typed in below her name snagged his attention. "Hey, we might be neighbors. I bought the old Leet pasture this past winter."

Her gray-frosted eyebrows arched, while her hand covered her mouth. "Marcella Leet was a childhood friend of mine. I moved back to retire on some heritage family holdings. I live in the two-story white house north of the railroad tracks from your place."

He leaned on his elbows and gave her an animated look. "Well, how about that? I finally get to meet one of my neighbors. Talk about a blessing in disguise."

She nodded. "You'll have to come over when the peaches are ripe. I can always use an extra hand in the orchard."

Hake grabbed a business card and wrote his cell phone number on the back, then handed it to her. "I'm only a call away. Now, it feels like a real neighborhood, despite all the grass stretched between us." He found the smile she flashed him just darling, which fueled his determination to get the settlement form in the mail. His workweek would end on a high note, and then they would both take off in the same direction for Bushong, a destination not too many others could claim. That made it God's country, no zip code verification needed.

Chapter 13

Trying to pull some of the crumpled folds out of her over-shirt, Aley squinted into the morning sun and gave Hake a few extra moments to get acquainted with the fence post driver. With all her possessions now packed and poised for transport, she couldn't be picky about what to wear on a Saturday. This work session definitely fell into the cracks between greater works planned. On the flip side, at least they could be together.

"This thing's a real beast." Hake hefted the iron-clad post pounder onto his shoulder and joined her at the location they'd agreed upon, right in the middle of the grassland.

She hoisted a fence post vertical. "I'll hold the post in place while you pound, which is an all-out act of trust on my part."

"Watch your fingers, because I don't know what I'm doing." He grunted to lift the pounder's open end over the post. It slid down and made contact with a clank. "This is when an automatic power supply would come in handy."

"Yes, if you had a mile of fencing to do—which we don't. Consider it building character. You get an upper-body workout, and I get the peace of mind knowing these cages are in place."

"Before you abandon us for Morris County, you mean."

After shooting her a dubious look, he grabbed the pounder's shank and began setting the post. With the soil compliant from last week's rain, the post slid right into the ground until the stabilizing spade disappeared.

"Okay, that's down far enough." She released the post and wondered if she should respond to his Morris County comment or let it ride. She reported to work at the new office on Monday morning, the same day he had the cattle delivered to his ranch for the first time. Change seemed inevitable. "Who's this *us* I'm abandoning, by the way?"

He tested the post with a shove. "Honey and me, of course. She's becoming quite the fixture on my back stoop, like a furry consolation prize…lose a girlfriend, gain a cat."

"Let's throw the wire panel up instead of hoisting a pity party." She stepped toward the trailer and retrieved the first welded-wire panel. Though it slid from the trailer with ease, once it landed in the grass, her progress bogged down. "A little help over here, Hercules."

Hake chose the left side and manned the corner with a solid grip. "How do we get this flat panel circled up to form the cage?" He wiped his sweaty brow across his upper sleeve and led the way back to the post.

"You need a bend in the wire where there isn't one—so you have to force the panel to curl. Let a pro show you how it's done." She shot a smirk over her shoulder while doubling back to force her corner over the trailing edge. "Sometimes, you have to teach the wire a lesson to put the crimp in, so it stays bent. I'll use my body weight to add some leverage."

While positioning to conduct the crimping action, her boot caught against a clump of prairie grass and she launched over the wire out of balance. Though she managed to get one hand out, the momentum carried her down for a full-bodied impact. She set the crimp with an unceremonious bounce, like an overactive kid face-planting inside an inflatable.

A muffled laugh rang out from the far corner. Soon, a hand patted her back pocket hard enough the wire bounced.

"So that's how the pros set the curl in the wire—well, I'll be. And all this time I considered ranching nothing but hard work. Look at the fun we're having." Hake knelt beside her, his expression impish.

"I hadn't planned on that fall, for sure. At least I had a soft landing—which can't be said too often here in the Flint Hills," She lifted her shoulders to sit up, but her feet remained stuck. "Help untangle me here, will you?"

Hake knelt on the wire and plucked at her shoestring. "At least I got to see a few of your curves in a new light."

"Yeah, thanks for checking my back pocket, as you reminded me I don't have the baling wire cut yet for attaching this panel to its new best friend, the post." She held a hand up in his general direction, ready to separate from the springy wire.

Hake rose, braced, and tugged her up taut against his hip, so close the rivets in their jeans could have shined each other. "Something tells me I'm going to enjoy a few more of these lessons you have in store for me."

When he knocked the brim of his cowboy hat back, she knew what would be coming next. That answered the question of how long they could work together before it got more personal. At least the morning had crowned ten o'clock. Her work attitude shattered under his masculine influence, so she let the wind comb the grass for a few unproductive seconds. His whiskers felt like wheat stubble, lending the weekend a new reason to seem leisure.

Hake appeared content with the diversion until a horn sounded from far off on the road's edge. He pulled back, gave a strained look, and then waved high over his head. "That's Miss Janie Rose Steadman, my closest neighbor and a new client for the herbicide settlement. She lives in that neat two-story white house north of the tracks off my east corner."

"Well, how about that?" Aley gave the wire one final kick to free her left foot and then headed straight for the Jeep.

She found the loop of baling wire, located the fencing tool, proceeded to measure with her hand, and then cut three wire ties.

Hake stood the uncooperative wire panel on its edge and tried to fit it against the post. Dry grass tops flew away in the breeze. He kicked at the bottom to get it better aligned.

Aley hurried back to help him. "Here, it really takes two for best results. Pull the top closer, and I'll fasten the first wire." She stuffed the other two wires between her lips and laced the top wire through the panel grids and around the post. Once she found a nub on the post's spine to keep the wire from shifting, she twisted the two ends and held the panel at full attention.

Hake stepped beside her and clamped the wire to the post with his hands. "Go ahead with the middle tie." His shoulder bumped hers as they closed in on the work.

This time, Aley gave a little grunt as she put extra pressure to tighten the twist. A bit longer, she wrapped the baling wire a second time around the post for good measure. A slipping sensation distracted her next, as she lost the last wire from her mouth. A scrape of whiskers pinpointed the culprit. "Okay, you thieving rancher. You do the last anchor—and make it tight."

He knelt on one knee and spent a few seconds getting the panel into position. Next, he threaded the wire through and caught two grids just under the corner welds. With force, he made the wire bend into compliance, twisted the joint, and wrapped it the second time. For extra measure, he turned down the wire tips where they'd be harmless. "Don't want to scratch my cattle customers, now do I?" He glanced up with half a grin.

She tapped his knee with her knuckle. "That's right. God gave us lawyers to ensure our general wellbeing."

He grabbed the post and stood, drawing her up with him. His gaze seemed to dance across her face. "I'm not so sure that extends to Council Grove, but I'm ready to test it—

if you are." His statement came out more like a question, with a tiny poke at the end.

"Good thing we have five more cages, so I can work on getting that answer figured out." She'd no sooner made the admission than he hoisted her, tucked her over his shoulder, and headed for the Jeep. "Hold up, Hake—you're leaving the post pounder."

He pivoted and retraced his steps. Once back at the grazing cage, he tugged her waist, lowered her frame toward the grass, and let her dangle over the heavy iron tool. "Go ahead, you get it."

Upside down, she snickered and tried to secure the slender tool in her grip. She clamped the metal shaft to her ribcage and tightened her midsection. "Ready to go, Rancher."

Hake pulled her from the ground with a growl. He tromped back to the Jeep in giant steps. Soon, he squared with the rear swing-gate.

Using all of her strength, she deposited the pounder. It landed in the Jeep with a bang. Instead of being brought to her passenger seat, she soon found her bottom propped on the wheel well.

Hake leaned closer and cleared the hair from her face. "You know I love it when you call me that." A sparkle in his eyes accentuated the remark.

Pleased that he noticed her tossed-in term of endearment, she took the liberty of tipping up his hat brim. "This working weekend thing sure has a lot going for it, I must admit."

Hake placed his hands on the rollbar, trapping her in the middle. "Consider the invitation open any Saturday, Sugar." The cheek scrape came next, ending with a soft-lipped kiss that stole permission to linger.

Transported, Aley clung to him as all else fell to the wayside. The prairie had never felt like this before, a mix of method and masculine persuasion. She touched his stubble-strafed cheek and encouraged him to stay, another training session with a slight curve to it. Only the wind blew contrary, but the grass nodded in approval.

~

Hake stood in the parking lot at the outdated roadside inn. "This is where you're going to live?" He squelched the afterthought in a throaty rumble. A row of tiny duplicate shacks formed a half-circle with a larger office in the middle. Whatever accoutrements had existed in a grander day now shriveled to a solitary flagpole. Even Old Glory flew sun-bleached.

"Here's Cabin Two," Aley replied in a melodic chirp. She carried a suitcase to the front door and produced a key to get inside. "At least Highway 56 has been rerouted further south, so the traffic noise isn't so loud."

He assessed the hilltop location, shared by a ramshackle grain elevator and a brick building with an animal clinic sign out front. Except for grain trucks, it didn't look like any through traffic would come by this forgotten spot. For some reason, he couldn't gain any peace about it. "I hope this can be temporary as far as housing solutions go—like less than a month."

She shoved the door open and stepped inside with the suitcase. When she reappeared, she gestured to him. A truck hummed by in the distance.

Hake examined the contents of the rear hatch and picked up a box labeled "field references." Sizeable and weighty, she probably needed that at work, not in her cereal-box residence. Begrudging the transfer, he walked toward the hut. He'd seen outbuildings bigger.

"Keep that one right here by the door. I'll take that with me Monday when I settle into my new office." She stood stock still until he passed the threshold. "Guess that's another advantage, moving from a cubicle to a real office with four walls and a door that can close."

He sat the box down misaligned and then kicked it

straight. "I hope you like it—the new job, I mean. They're lucky to acquire your expertise, so they don't lose time having to train you."

She looked up and shook her bangs out of her eyes. "With growing season in full tilt and plenty of spring rains yet to come, I'd better be able to hit the ground running. Mr. Lightner mentioned how much older CRP ground they have—that's former cropland that's been put back to grass, so they call it throwback. I can hardly wait to see that stand of grass."

"There you go again, getting excited to take care of the land." He chucked her chin and headed back outside. "I hope nothing happens to quell that unbridled enthusiasm of yours."

She followed close behind. "Well, what could happen to squelch my excitement to do what I've been trained for all my adult life? Honestly, Hake, don't be a worry wort."

He slapped the sides of another box in partial protest. Caution never equated to worry. Attorneys were known for their caution. He lifted the box and turned toward her. "Call or text me at night, okay? Unless you want to check in daily with Reece instead."

"Okay, I'll text you. That box goes in the bathroom." She opened the rear car door to remove the hanging clothes and swept them out right behind him.

Hake entered the cabin, took two steps, and found the doorway to the bathroom. Though remodeled with modern fixtures, they couldn't improve on the old-fashioned lack of space. Exasperated, he stuck the box in the bathtub and backed out. When he spotted Aley, her armload had filled a tiny nook of closet space. A twin bed claimed the far corner under a crank-out window. He grated his teeth and headed for an awning of blue sky. A prayer leaked out from between his lips with a mention of protection somewhere in the middle.

"This day had a touch of payback to it, doesn't it?" Aley

shielded her eyes and stared at him. "I mean, I spent the morning helping you, so now you're helping me in return. Look at everything we're getting accomplished. What a way to end the month."

He heard the optimism in her voice and let it trickle down to sooth his irritation. Instead of picking up the next item, a broken-zippered tote crammed full of boots, he reached for her and skimmed his knuckles across her cheek. "I know. I just want better than this for you."

She moved closer and scanned his face as if trying to see deeper. "Trust me to find my way, Hake. This is the right move for me. Well, for the job anyway. The housing situation will get better, too. By this time next month, I'll be inviting you over to my posh apartment."

He had to smile at that prediction. Nothing about Council Grove appeared posh. Not that Bushong fared any grander, but he could fit her entire cabin inside his mud room. "You're shaming me with your positivity. Of course, I want you to be happy with the job shift. I'll try not to consider myself on the far side of that realignment."

She hugged his arm. "You know what I just remembered? The Rails to Trails line connects us. We could ride bikes to visit each other and meet in the middle. With the days getting longer in May, I bet there would be enough time after work."

He pressed his forehead to hers, hoping to trap some enthusiasm. "I don't have a bike. Would Old Betsy do?"

"You're being lazy. It's a designated bike trail, you know, for bicycles. The kind powered by humans."

"Guess I need to shop for a bike then, since I don't have one."

"We can borrow bikes from Reece this summer. I don't think Candice will be riding any time soon. Problem solved." She blew a puff of breath at him and backed away.

Hake hooked a hand through the tote's handle and lifted it out of the floorboard. "I bet Reece will be glad to get his garage space back when you move into something larger. Remember, I have the grain silo that stays pretty dry inside. Think about it, anyway."

"We moved the last of my furniture in yesterday, but thank you. Reece doesn't want hail damage on their vehicles, so I'm hoping to have my possessions out of his garage by June first. That gives me a month to find something, sign a lease, move in, and make both my brother and my boyfriend happy. Ta-da. Then I can go about having my illustrious career without all this worry hanging in the air."

He grabbed a small grocery sack of food items with his spare hand and headed for the cabin. Her plan sounded good, but small towns could be fairly unaccommodating when it came to life's basics, like adequate shelter and shopping. Her roadside inn made a perfect case for that caveat. With no place to put the load, he landed it on the bed and freed his hands.

Aley came in and swept by him with an armful of electronics. She plugged in her phone charger and laid it on the faded dresser. "Well, that's it. What should we do next?"

Claustrophobic, Hake back-pedaled toward the door. He threw his hands in the air trying to shrug off the place. "Can we find some dinner? I think that would help my mood."

A girlish grin embellished Aley's face as she reached for her purse. "Saturday night, fast food for dinner, and a handsome man at my side. Whew, boy. I must be living right."

He grabbed for her as she exited for the car, but she somehow eluded his grip. "Hey, thanks for the *handsome man* comment. That kind of talk might help lift my spirits."

She dropped into the passenger seat with a mysterious look on her face, as if she had a secret. Her door slammed and the vanity light soon illuminated on the overhead visor.

Hake glanced at the grain elevator across the street and noticed how it stood like a sentinel against the cloudless sky.

A verse about God being a watch tower flitted through his thoughts. Aley would need that kind of protection over her shoebox room. If God watched out for the sparrow, he could certainly keep watch over her. He dropped into the driver's seat, ready to explore the one stoplight town. *Don't blink.* As he backed away from the cabin, Aley's hand came to rest on his shoulder, a sensitive bridge over the gap threatening to divide them.

Chapter 14

For two days Dane had been a caged tiger, with rain streaks on the windows forming the bars on his cage. He took the procedure manual in hand and tried not to doze as he started reading section two. A creature of habit, he fought the urge to head for the back room to mix up some chemicals for the sprayers. This new office had no back room. Plus, he no longer had any obligation for the spreading noxious weeds that always seemed to assault the county.

A loud-talking field agent two cubicles down finally finished up a protracted conversation over the phone, and the office area fell silent. Wheels slid across the tile and the agent soon walked by. "Putting on another pot of coffee," the man mumbled as he passed.

Fighting heavy eyelids, Dane leaned back in his chair. "Hey, make mine a double." He'd have to remember to bring a caffeinated refreshment to jolt him out of the regulatory doldrums when the weather turned inclement. Maybe he should review his files, make a list of head counts for each client's pastures, and reserve the end of the week for field verification.

The thought of outdoor freedom birthed a restless itch. He'd spent the weekend tuning up his Honda CRF 230 motorcycle for getting around each ranch. With a portable ramp, it would fit right in the bed of the NRCS truck. He had no intention of asking in-house permission, though he hadn't read any prohibition of such use in his field techniques manual. Call it imaginative, but he intended on using the motorcycle starting with the first site visit. He'd cover more territory that way, a real ace-in-the-hole strategy.

The loud talker returned and paused beside him. "Say, you might want to check the gear locker for a decent pair of boots. I don't think Al's old ones are going to fit you. I'm Brody, by the way."

Dane tipped the procedure manual toward him. "Who's Al and where's the gear locker?"

The man chuckled. "We called Aley Halstead *Al* just to give her a hard time. Norman said that's partly why she left. Go figure. It was just innocent jesting. We never thought twice about the ribbing. It kept things lively around here."

Dane rose to his feet, aching for something productive to do. "Guess we'll have to find a new game, as Norman's got an all-buck herd now. Would you mind showing me that gear closet? Something tells me I might need those boots, if it ever stops raining."

"Sure thing. You'll find some division uniform shirts back there, too. If you're out in the field, Norman prefers you wear the uniform for identification by the general public. Then, if you have to shift into enforcement mode, your sign of authority is already riding your chest." He tapped the badge on his faded green polo shirt.

Dane squared with the man and flexed his biceps. "I definitely plan to transition into enforcement mode, so I'll grab however many I can find in the XL size range."

Brody nodded over his shoulder. "Right this way. Word up—the boss is particular about us not leaving behind any messes. I'm in charge of the coffee station. Aley used to maintain the gear closet, so I guess that falls as your territory now."

He gave a little growl as he followed the man down the

back hall past the restrooms. Just past the break room, they stopped in front of two louvered doors. "Aha, the gear closet, I presume." He jerked open both doors and beheld a jumbled mess.

The agent backed up a step. "Hmmm, looks like Aley ran out of time her final week in the office. She didn't get to this task, for sure."

The irony of inheriting the mess hit him full force. "No, she had to give up her last two days to get my training done, so I'm indirectly to blame."

"Well, it's a rainy day, so what can you expect?" Brody shrugged and disappeared into the men's room nearby.

Feeling like a demotion, Dane stepped closer to take a bunched wad of unfolded uniform shirts in hand. He threw them on the floor until he had the whole shelf cleared out. Once he located the extra-large shirts, he'd fold and put them back in some semblance of order.

A pair of good-looking boots caught his eye. Maybe he would claim his loot first and then restock the closet. Under a buzz from acquiring new gear without forking out any compensation, he soon found the silver lining for the gear closet duty. He could become an expert at taking without giving back. He definitely had the credentials for that job.

Mr. Norman walked up, his arms folded. "Hey. What kind of whirling dervish is this?"

Dane gestured to the pile-up on the hall floor. "Halstead left you an A-1 mess back here, sir. Brody said the gear closet's upkeep likely fell to me, so I decided to tackle some organization now while it's raining. I won't have a spare moment later this spring, so why not today?"

The man's expression froze for a few critical seconds. "I hope you have that much gumption in every aspect of your work, Mr. Burroughs. Some of the things Aley took on, she did because she wanted to. Don't feel like you have to wipe up the kitchen at the close of day, or anything like that. We employ a janitorial service for building upkeep."

"Good to know, sir. You won't find me being too domestic, I can assure you." He flexed a muscle like the Incredible Hulk and gave a laugh.

The boss chuckled in return. "Is that fresh coffee I smell in the break room?"

"Yeah, Brody just put on a new pot to fend off a lunchtime nap. I'm making some checklists from the CSP contracts, so I can hit the ground running once the rain quits."

"Smart move. Just remember to use the sign-out board, so I know where you are. We keep things kind of loose around here, as long as the fieldwork gets done."

"I'm a big respecter of loose. And I'm chomping at the bit to get outside, believe me." When the man backed toward the break room entrance, he dismissed his boss with a mock salute.

Glancing up, Dane spotted a stack of neatly folded smaller shirts in the corner of the shelf. Just for meanness, he grabbed them and tossed them into the messy heap. Since he had every intention of undoing her kingdom and making it his own, that might as well start in a by-passed nook of little regard. Something told him he had all afternoon to address the task. He'd snarf up the new boots while they were free for the taking, too. That made it all the better to walk up the back of his predecessor, perfect though she might have appeared. The fieldwork would be another matter, enforcement-heavy and attitude-strong. He only needed a little sunshine.

~

With the office devoid of life, Hake let his mind wander to the muddy mess his ranch had turned into over the last two days. Were it not for the limestone outcrops anchoring the slopes, he wondered if his grass might have floated away. Schedule-driven semi-truck drivers from Texas had delivered countless loads of cattle to the ranch. He tried to check scale reports and document the number of head per load, but at best, it came off a water-soaked estimate.

The unloading chutes created an instant mud bog, a problem he hadn't seen coming. If he could borrow or rent a front-end loader, he would scoop some river rock up from the creek along the western gully. With a redistribution of his natural assets, he could avoid further wear-and-tear on the land. That after-the-fact wisdom put him in stop-gap management mode. Yes, this would be a learning year. Next grazing season, however, he pledged be more on top of such matters.

He reached for his ranching journal and thought to add a note about the chip-rock to fortify the loading entrance to each pasture. Remembering how a single gate had constrained the unloading process compared to several sets of double gates, he added a note to widen the east pasture entrance. Sensing some traction with the proposed improvements, he let a ripple of confidence straighten his spine a bit. A dual-career man, he had successfully pulled off the tandem occupation, after gaining a bit of help along the way.

His thoughts detoured to Aley when she had fallen on the wire panel helping him Saturday. A smile pulled across his face as he recalled using her compromised position to his immediate advantage. Having a beautiful helper bore its own fanciful distractions. He couldn't get enough of having her around lately. Come Wednesday night, she promised to meet him in Emporia to move up their regular dinner date, doubling as Candice's birthday dinner.

A moisture-laden suction on the front door threshold snapped him out of his reverie. He doubted any of his elderly clientele would be out and about on such a drenching day. When a curvy figure stepped in using a soggy newspaper for an umbrella, his alertness ramped a level or two. Once the paper lowered, he recognized the woman with the credit card woes. Given her wet-rat look, her diamond ring didn't seem to shine as bright today.

She gave her colored tresses a limp shake. "Well, I hope this stop's gonna be worth it."

Hake reached for his free consultation file and laid it out. Fingering through his collection of scrawled notes, he found the one bearing details of her situation. "Oh, Ms. Tillison, isn't it?"

She came closer, giving the hallway a suspicious glance. "Can everything I say from here on out be held in total confidence?"

"Certainly. Please take a seat and tell me what compels you out on such a dismal day." He gestured to the guest chair with the ink pen still in his hand. As a matter of procedure, he recorded the time.

She eased into the chair, but only sat on the edge. "Trouble brings me out. Brewing trouble's headed for an outright eruption. I need more legal advice, but I want to know if it will cost me. Everything seems to have a hidden price tag lately…and I do mean everything."

At some point, Hake knew he had to stop giving his services away. If they went much further down this path, she was sure to hit that tripwire. Still, he wanted to render some aid, if he could. "Tell me, does this involve the original problem of the unauthorized credit card use?"

She tilted her chin up, as if trying to save face. "Yes, that's right. The fraudulent claims department gave me a call this morning. They are asking for names and phone numbers for anyone with access to my credit card. I hope asking you one more question won't start the meter for legal assistance I can't afford." She arched both plucked brows and stared him down.

Hake leaned back in his chair. *Time is money.* "How's this, Ms. Tillison? If I can help you in a minute and a half, I'll not charge you for any assistance. However, if you return for another follow-up consultation, the billing clock starts the moment you walk in."

She nodded and seemed to collect herself a bit. "Like a

provocative idiot, DJ signed his name on the receipts for the unauthorized charges, so it's not like *I* have to turn *him* in."

"The credit card company will expect to see his name on your shortlist of suspects then. There's no avoiding that option, or you'll appear to be in collusion with him. Such an act might actually turn the suspicion back on you as the defrauding party, I'm afraid. I warn you to be cautious about that outcome as it will leave you having to pay for the charges."

She made a clicking sound inside her cheek that was followed by a heavy sigh. In a weak gesture, she held up her left hand and brought the promissory ring to his attention. "Guess I am in collusion with him…now. I still don't want to pay for those unauthorized charges, though."

A redeeming angle came to him in an enlightened moment. "Well, there's this. You could let them conduct an investigation as the due course of action. Like you said, he's already turned his own name in, so the blame can't be pinned on you. These transaction follow-ups are notoriously slow, but when he's finally confronted, that could be the corrective fulcrum DJ needs to better respect your assets. He's toeing the line of propriety here, but he wouldn't have put that ring on your finger if he didn't have honorable intentions in the long run."

She looked away, her gaze skimming the far wall where his diplomas hung. She flexed her fingers and curled them around the zippered top of her purse. "The follow-up won't look like I caused it then. It's what you called *due course of action*. He had to figure there would be some kind of kickback when he used my credit card, right? He likely still has the gift cards he bought riding around in his wallet."

"That's a strong thought. If he's asked to make restitution, he can just return the gift cards and recoup the money. He's playing the risk of a kickback against the thrill of holding this over you, Ms. Tillison. You're an agreeable partner in this either way it plays out. You call his bluff as a silent opposing witness, or you omit his name and continue to let him run roughshod over you. The more you allow him to get away with, the more confident he'll be to try it again."

She rose with deliberate effort, seeming a million miles away. "So, I'll turn in several names, and one of them will be DJ's. If and when he comes complaining to me about the credit card company hounding him, I'll play the part of the powerless fiancée."

Hake threw up his palms to absolve her of further guilt. "You are the victim, after all. I hope the two of you can reconcile this temporary glitch and get on with planning your wedding. In the meantime, try to stay dry out there, Ms. Tillison."

She took a couple of steps toward the door and bent to retrieve the soggy newspaper. "Thank you for hearing me out, Mr. Warren. I just needed the voice of logic to tell me I'm doing the right thing. Maybe I'll see you around town. If not, have a nice…life." She hoisted the paper and disappeared out the door into a blur of rain.

Hake made a notation of the follow-up visit to record her decision to move ahead. Afterward, he drew a long, cleansing breath. "Have a nice—if not somewhat conflicted—life yourself, Ms. Tillison. You may want to keep your purse hidden, all the same." He shoved away from the desk to go reheat his lunch, an unglamorous reflection on the day.

~

Aley stared down her brother across the booth, intent to make him lose the I-don't-care look. "Phone call logs have to document every communication, e-mails must be blind-copied to the director, and all outgoing mail has to pass across his desk. I tell you, it's micromanagement in its finest form. Mr. Lightner wants to know e*verything*. Compare that to Mr. Norman, who didn't care to know anything. Surely there's a happy medium between the two extremes."

Hake bumped her shoulder, accompanied by an

amicable wink. "Try the Bushong office. I hear the manager there is one cooperative dude."

A girlish giggle followed. Candice fanned her puffy face with a napkin. "Not to change the downer subject, but how about showering some attention on the charming birthday girl?"

Aley looked at the once lovely woman who now bore a red-blotched complexion. Her swollen abdomen made the booth an incredibly tight fit, even though she had insisted on it. Wondering what to say, the waitress saved the day by popping the deep-fried appetizer platter onto the center of the table. When Hake tried to abscond with a sizeable fried zucchini, she stabbed it back onto the platter. "Let me say grace first, so I can thank God for the birthday girl."

Hake entwined his arm around hers and eased the fork out of her grip.

Maybe going to God empty-handed was more appropriate. "Gracious Lord, today we thank you for Candice as we celebrate her birthday. May this year bring her blessings beyond what she can imagine as she becomes a mother. Thank you that she can continue the Halstead family name for another generation. Bless her generously and bless the baby she's bearing during its growth and development. May they both walk close to you. We thank you for this better-than-ordinary food, dear God, as I no longer take eating out for granted. In Jesus' holy name we pray, amen."

She caught Reece's vulnerable look seconds before the platter gained assault on two flanks. To keep the mess contained, she passed out the small plates stacked on the table's edge. "What's the hesitant pause all about, dear brother of mine?" She slid his plate toward him in extra-slow motion.

"If it's a girl, she won't get to keep the Halstead name when she gets married." He shrugged his shoulders and reached for a fried mushroom.

Hake leaned over and placed a fried cheese curd on her plate. "Your baby will still be a Halstead, always and forever."

She leaned forward, her mood improving by increments. "That's why I keep this man around—for his sound reasoning."

Hake waved his zucchini in rebuttal. "Aha. I thought it was for my handsome face." He gestured to Candice, as if bringing her into collusion. "I can't figure out this woman. She does get grumpy if it rains several days straight."

"Also if you make her record her phone conversations," Reece added, "she starts raving." He popped the entire mushroom into his mouth.

"Don't mention being steamed at having dinner run late," Candice said with an animated expression. "I find myself totally respecting that particular point."

Aley dropped her arm across her abdomen. She only had normal hunger driving her need to eat, while her sister-in-law had the urgent demand of prenatal development. For the first time, she wondered what that dependency might feel like to a woman's body. When Hake focused on her a split second later, a heated blush birthed from under her peasant blouse.

Hake leaned over to whisper in her ear. "Take two cheese curds and call me in the morning." As he retracted, he winked and then held her gaze.

In one fell swoop, a cheese curd landed in her mouth. Rubbery and cheddar-packed, it melted in total satisfaction. She had to have another one in short order.

Hake must have sensed her reach, as he leaned in to block the platter.

"You're a lawyer by the way," she quipped, reaching past him. "Not a doctor prescribing treatment."

"Oh, I have a cure, Sugar" he whispered through her hair.

The skin on her forearm prickled at the innuendo. She

might need treatment…and she might not. Either way, she wouldn't let him know. "I want to try your Santa Fe chicken, and I'll let you have some of my blackened tilapia."

Hake shook his head, his gaze riveted on her. "No deal…unless you sweeten the pot."

Aley dragged a fried zucchini stick off the platter. Goodness, where would she steer the conversation from here? She picked at the droopy coating and ate the whole spear.

Candice paused between bites and giggled again. "He can help me eat my birthday caramel sundae. They'll serve it with or without singing. All we have to do is make the request."

Aley chewed and snuggled ever closer to her date. Once her mouth cleared, she wiped her lips with her napkin. "Is that what you want, Hake? Do you crave a caramel sundae?"

He stabbed a mushroom and hoisted it. "What's your favorite flavor, outdoor girl? I'll share a bit of whatever you order for dessert."

Pleased the choice had come back to her, Aley nestled a cheek onto his shoulder. "I would enjoy a strawberry sundae, without any hot fudge sauce on top."

Hake's nose did an exploratory run through her hair. "Add sprinkles and it's a deal."

"Okay, okay. What a merciless negotiator." A blackened fish soon stared her in the face. She made quick work of moving the appetizer platter, since the main course had arrived. "Thank you. Could you bring two dessert sundaes to us in about twenty minutes?"

The waitress produced a pad. "Sure thing. What kind would you like?"

"One birthday girl special," she replied, gesturing to Candice. "With the singing option. And one strawberry sundae for this side of the table, with non-singing sprinkles, please." After the server disappeared, she ventured a glimpse at Hake. His grin bordered on silly, but she found it endearing. *Let me cut you a deal.* She sliced into the blackened fillet and offered him the first taste. Back in Emporia for the festive evening, she felt jubilant seated at his side.

Chapter 15

Hake watched the slender doctor handle the audience in the room with folksy ease. He guessed the attendance to border on sixty, mostly geriatric individuals, but not all. Several tables in back had been claimed by staff members on lunch break. It appeared the hospital fully endorsed these wellness lectures. That made total sense to him. He'd even learned a thing or two about managing cholesterol levels. The fried sampler platter had to be a vestige of the past.

While the doctor fielded the last question about the use of olive oil, he readied the stack of claim forms from his briefcase. In an attempt not to appear unapproachable, he'd skipped the business suit for khakis and an ironed shirt. Make that a somewhat wrinkled ironed shirt, as his packing job left a lot to be desired. Next time, he would leave it on a hanger in the car.

Dr. Hendry moved back to the center of the room. "Remember, you are the best advocate for your own good health. By the time you've asked me to join the partnership, we've likely shifted into fix-and-repair mode. My dear mother used to say, 'at the beginning of the semester, everyone starts out with A's.' Think of wellness like having straight A's. What you do with your good health will determine your GPA in those senior years. Live well until next week, when we'll tackle a few current topics in the autoimmune arena."

A case of the last-second jitters started working on Hake's chest. Bound to be thrown into the spotlight within seconds, he had little time to recover. He took a sip from his water bottle and defaulted to silent prayer. Somehow, the peaceful scenery of Psalms twenty-three inched into his consciousness and tamped down the flurry of sudden apprehension. He made eye contact with an elderly woman and her slight nod registered as reassuring.

Dr. Hendry approached. "At any rate, it's not like me to expose my flock to a predatory lawyer, but my partner, Carl Atkins, has been telling me about the good works of this particular young man. So I now present to you Attorney Hake Warren, who has committed to representing the victims of Rid-A-Weed herbicide on a statewide basis. For those of you on lunch break, I bid you adieu at this point. For anyone interested in hearing Mr. Warren and possibly filing a settlement claim, the lunchroom remains yours."

Hake stood and shook the doctor's hand as the room began to bustle with activity. "Thank you so much, sir."

"You're quite welcome," He patted the back of his hand. "Make a transition from all this medical talk by telling them a personal story about yourself."

Hake nodded and stepped to the front as several retirement-aged lecture participants moved closer. Thinking maybe a law school story might fit the bill, he tried to reflect while making eye contact with several attendees. Somehow, none of his stock stories seemed to work. He'd have to come up with something else. After one more group of listeners settled in, he decided to go ahead with his introduction.

"Doctor Hendry was partly right about me. By day, I'm a lawyer with a new practice in downtown Emporia. At daybreak and dusk though, I'm learning to be a rancher north of town in a tiny crossroads called Bushong. First of the week, I learned that rain and unloading trucked-in cattle don't mix. Well, they mix if you aim to produce mud—for which I proved highly talented." He paused to shake his head and received a few audible chuckles. "I guess in that line of work, a strong fence could be considered your wellness plan."

"Amen to that," a man with leathery skin replied with a nod.

Encouraged, Hake continued. "In life, a whole series of caveats and cautions exist to protect our wellness. Unfortunately, bouts of negligence occur in the most innocuous spots, like unforeseen breaks in the perimeter fence. That's when the judicial system steps in to protect the unsuspecting victims in these instances. When multiple victims result from such a breach, the legal addressing of the widespread slight is referred to as a class action lawsuit.

"I'm here to guide anyone who thinks they might have been affected by a particular case of negligence by the manufacturers of Rid-A-Weed, a commonly used herbicide. A settlement has already been determined in the courts, which makes financial compensation available for individuals diagnosed with Non-Hodgkins and a host of similar lymphomas. If you have that confirmed diagnosis, I can lead you through the process of applying for the settlement."

"There's a bunch of us here recommended by Dr. Hendry," the weathered man said. We're liable to have lots of questions as we go, but for starters, did the manufacturer admit guilt in order to reach the settlement?"

Hake tipped his head to acknowledge the man. "No. From what I've read, the company's researchers still contend that their product does not cause cancer. The glyphosate in Rid-A-Weed had been examined for hazard identification, which they held as moderate and only a slight risk. Yet, the manufacturer of this popular weedkiller failed to warn of *any* cancer risk, which the courts deemed negligent in providing the user adequate warnings and safety instructions."

"Toxic like cigarettes…only we inhaled it through our skin," the man replied.

For the first time, Hake sensed the blatant suffering caused by negligence. "I'm as sorry about that as I can be. I take my call to uphold justice as part of my Christian stewardship. If you can trust me as your advocate, I'll continue with this free consultation in a general workshop style to get your claim forms prepared for submitting."

"Free consultation?" a woman asked. "Do you mean we don't pay you?"

"No, ma'am, you don't need to pay me. As part of the settlement's provision, the court allotted for a set fee-claim evaluation. So I get paid when you get the settlement. It's a tandem payout. I've printed a summary of the terms on page one of my handout, and then the claim form is page two. Are we ready to move forward?"

He glanced across the group of about two dozen people and received scattered nods. Some regarded him with a hollow stare, while a few held angry glimmers. Pain and suffering represented deep personal anguish. Maybe he was still too young to relate fully.

"I'll not be shy about taking a handout," the wrinkled man said. "If the court has already decided it, and the doctor has already diagnosed my cancer, then nothing's gonna keep me back from getting my rightful share."

Hake reached for the handouts. Once in hand, the stack felt weighty. Justice could be like that, a tangible reward. "Let's get the compensation train rolling then. I'll give you a few minutes to digest the settlement summary on page one. After that, I'll lead you through the form, line by line, as all the blanks have to be completed for your claim to qualify."

As he handed out the forms, he decided to look at each individual eye to eye and affirm their participation. By the second person, it began to bless his socks off to serve as an agent of fairness. His day job possessed such significant moments, though they seemed slow to arrive and too far between.

"Am I too late?" a woman inquired.

Hake straightened and saw a young woman with her head wrapped in a kerchief. "No, please come join us. We are just getting started with the claim paperwork."

She nodded to a matronly figure at her side, and they moved to the second row of tables.

He softened his expression when he delivered her form, which left him only one blank set to use for his presentation. At some point, he would need a headcount to make sure the form count matched once he returned to the office. Maybe he could do that while they read page one, if he could still enumerate to twenty-five.

He glanced across their bowed heads and caught sight of Dr. Hendry standing solitary in a far doorway. The moment of professional accountability dissolved with the doctor's immediate disappearance down the hall. In a blink of an eye, the truth hit home. He'd been trusted by the local health guardian, a notable commendation that made him glad he'd ironed the shirt.

~

In the chronicles of humankind, there had been better first weeks at a new endeavor. Aley rode silently as the department club cab maneuvered some paved road north of Council Grove. Several staff members had joined the show-and-tell outing to break up their Friday afternoon workloads. Others had disappeared into the field earlier in the day.

For the fifth of May, the day had been extremely mild. Besides temperatures in the low seventies, there was virtually no wind, a rare happenstance in Kansas. She tapped her jeans pocket to make sure she had her phone. Not that anyone needed to contact her, but she might want to snap a photo or two if this sixty-three-year-old throwback proved scenic in nature. A large body of water opened to the right and she gawked at the city's reservoir.

"Here's the turn-off for the city lake," Mr. Lightner said, pointing left. "There's a social riff between lake dwellers and city citizens, but most of it's fabricated by the county tax office, I think. Both their addresses still read Council Grove, so let's consider it one big happy family."

She nodded and took in the expanse of tallgrass prairie opening up on both sides of the road. Unprepared, her stomach flipped when the truck dropped off of the pavement where the road turned to gravel. A dilapidated windmill stood frozen in time, its rusty hull testifying to an unknown duration of hard work. The sight made her wonder how long she might last at this job, given next week improved on this one.

A distant ridge struck her as similar to one on Hake's ranch, though the alignment held a different angle. Most hills in this section bore the familiar notch on the southeast corner, like a nose carved onto a green horizon that seemed to roll on forever. An occasional brome hayfield would cut into the mixed grasses of the prairie, but little cropland existed here. She took that as a good sign, as wider tracts meant better survivability for the prairie and its residents.

"That's the Neosho River under the bridge up ahead," Lightner said. "It looks small like a creek north of the reservoir. They dammed it up after the flood of fifty-one, so the outfall you see running through town is controlled by gates on the dam. I enjoy boating and fishing out on the reservoir, so I guess there are perks for water management."

Aley tried to get a look down at the river as they passed over the bridge, but the concrete railing prevented any close-up study. The watercourse seemed narrow for a river. When she glanced back up, a two-story white structure loomed on the side of the road. "Is that a church way out here?"

"An old one-room schoolhouse, converted to a Methodist church," her boss replied.

A staff member who occupied the opposite corner office leaned between them. "Welcome to Kelso, Kansas, the little town that isn't one anymore," Jo-Belle teased.

They slowed for an intersection where she spotted several residences tucked under a canopy of elm trees. A mongrel dog raced out and announced their passage. Down the road, limestone rocks signified a loose fence for a playground that didn't appear heavily used. From there, the world opened up to tallgrass prairie, countless miles of it rolling to the far horizon.

Before they could traverse the next crossroad, the truck eased to a halt. "Okay staff," Lightner said. "Pick out the sixty-three-year-old throwback section. Find it if you can."

On high alert, Aley threw open the door and stepped out onto the roadside. She scanned the horizon to the north where one of the Flint Hills eased down to the lower elevations of Kelso proper. A herd of Angus dotted the far pasture where a second hill arose. From where she stood, she could spot three different fence lines bisecting the square-mile acreage. Nothing stood out as different or recovering in her estimation. She turned a complete three hundred sixty degrees to make sure the answer didn't lurk right behind her.

"Let's walk in a ways." Lightner held the barbed wire strands apart so they could traipse across. The closest gate stood a quarter-mile up the road.

"I'm game," Jo-Belle replied. With a slap on her thigh, she crossed the roadside swale and leveraged between the wire strands.

Aley approached and met her boss's imploring gaze with an inquisitive look of her own. "Okay, I'm hooked on your cliffhanger, Mr. Lightner. Take me to your secretive throwback."

"I'm just Ron out here—as long as there are no clients with us. Watch for prairie indigo blooming, which always reminds me that Mother's Day is coming up. Heaven forbid if I ever forget that particular holiday." He rolled his eyes to dramatize the potential ruination.

Aley focused on the bottom wire as she cleared the

fence in a squat. The grass here looked tall, so the cattle must be rotated into the back pasture for now. That made walking easier, as she didn't have to perpetually watch for fresh cow pies along the way. The creamy stalked blooms of a nearby prairie indigo beckoned to her, so she reached out and caressed its velvety cluster as she followed the others.

Within seconds, she fell into a tranquil state of mind that walking off the beaten trail lent. Transfixed on what she might discover next, she walked through a patch of gramma grass and back into the thick cover of the dominant big bluestem. By autumn, the grass would measure up to her cheekbones, a glorious encounter. For early May, at least the late-season grasses had awakened to put on their most vibrant shade of green. Rain had softened the ground, making their hike all the more pleasurable.

The boss stopped thirty yards short of the nearest fence and turned north to study the massive hill. He took his chin in his hand and seemed lost in thought. Jo-Belle joined him, one hand full of some early-flowering sedge she'd stopped to pick. Colorless as a bloom, the green-on-green was almost comical for a bouquet.

Aley stepped closer and examined the rise. "Surely not the hill itself." Uncertainty marked her questioning tone.

"There, beyond the road over the far hill," Ron added, "you can still see the tin roof of the old Henning homestead."

Aley squinted, as the late afternoon sun competed for the western horizon. "They would have been the agents converting the sod to tilled farmland in the first place, I suppose."

"Probably the same farmer who let the grass come back in, too," Jo-Belle said.

Aley shrugged to dismiss the hunt. "I honestly don't see any former cropland."

"That's because you're standing on it." Ron fought off a teasing smile, but failed. "Forty acres right under our boots were broken by plow, cleared of grass, and farmed for a handful of miserable years. The moisture regime just wasn't right. So fed up, the farmer surrendered his agricultural dreams, and left the ground fallow to recover."

Aley found that hard to believe. "So, the grass just happened?"

The teasing look returned to Ron's expression. "They call it throwback or go-back, when the land reverts to grassland, but here's the clincher. The old-timers say that the grass walks back in from the edge. They never planted the first seed or sprigged the first plug. Nature took over and reclaimed what belonged to her. You have to admit, the end result is stunningly similar to the virgin prairie right over the fence. The hill, Ms. Halstead, remains true unbroken prairie, and what you're standing on is the throwback. Would you have figured that out on your own?"

Aley spread her arms parallel to the ground and turned her back to the road. Everything looked natural and carpeted with green as far as the eye could see. The beauty of it filled her senses. "No, sir. Guess I still have a lot to learn. Maybe give me sixty years to let the grass walk back in and cover my blind spots. I sure appreciate you bringing us out here this afternoon."

He nodded and checked his watch. "Let's head down that gully and track the water's flow. After three solid days of rain, every drainage crack in the county should be functioning. Plus, the bank below the old pond always holds a badger hole or two. We could see if they're still keeping house there—or not."

"I'm so in for that," Jo-Belle replied. "It would be a good day to spot a mudpuppy, too."

Lightner gave his hat brim a tiny tweak to lower it as they headed off.

Aley took a grass-covered path to the south, determined to learn this re-grown grassland and pick up hints as to its success. The land needed cover, and grass seemed the logical choice. Leave it to their department to try and complicate matters.

They had ventured for less than a hundred yards when Jo-Belle squealed in delight. When she squatted to take a closer look, Aley responded at a trot. "It's a baby ornate box turtle just getting moving for the season. Isn't he outright adorable?"

Aley glimpsed the whirled markings on what appeared to be half a baseball propped on four stubby legs. She wondered what odds the little fellow had of surviving in such a tall-growing environment. It took a few clumsy steps and thumped over the yielding grass.

"Ladies, I found an active badger hole over here," Ron called from the pond dam.

Aley drew a quick breath and bumped shoulders with Jo-Belle as they jogged to see the next quiet wonder of the prairie. The surrounding habitat struck her as pretty mesmerizing, even for throwback. Somewhere on the vast landscape, her contentment returned, another unsuspecting walk-in occurrence straight from the plowed-up edge.

~

Hake knocked on the weathered surface of the door, determined not to cross the threshold. He had everything he needed right outside here. Well, everything but the occupant. He raised his hand to knock again when the door opened.

Aley peered through the crack and then pull it wide open. Dressed in a cropped pink T-shirt and form-fitting jogging shorts, she seemed incredulous. "Hake? Wow, what a nice surprise." Her gaze darted to the bag in his hand and then back at him.

"Happy Cinco de Mayo, Aley. I come bearing Mexican food for your dinner, and tales of Topeka for your entertainment pleasure. How does that sound?"

A hand crept up to smooth her hair. "Oh my gosh, too good to be true. It hadn't registered to me that today's a Mexican holiday. Want to come inside?"

"I definitely do not. I want you to check out what I

bought from a secondhand store." He jutted a thumb in the direction of his car. With the trunk propped open, his clue would be hard to miss. "I think we can have a self-contained little dinner party right out here."

She hurriedly scuffed her feet into a pair of slip-on sneakers and ran past him toward the car. "Double wow. You bought a patio table?"

Enjoying her enthusiasm, he stood right behind her, intent on the show. "Plus two chairs. I thought it would help me extend my living space to the farmyard. Now I can catch nature's show at dusk and eat dinner at the same time."

"That sounds so perfect. Let's give it a trial run right here, shall we?"

He stepped around her and tucked the bag into her midsection. "That's exactly what I had in mind." He loosened the bungee cord, grabbed the table's wrought iron rim, and guided it clear of the trunk. You pick the right spot."

She soon pointed to the north corner of the cabin where a late-in-the-day shadow had formed. "This location shouldn't bother any of the other residents."

He followed her direction, impressed with her consideration of others sharing the limited space. "I'll get the chairs. Maybe you could give the table a wipe-off."

"Roger that." She popped the bag onto the table and retreated into the cabin.

Buoyed at seeing her so happy, Hake slid one chair off the backseat upholstery. He mated it up to the table and returned for the second chair. The whole set had been less than half a settlement claim evaluation fee, so he counted that as gain. If it gave them a place to be together more often, the value would double—in his heart. He pulled out the chair and shut the door.

Aley gave the table one last swipe as he approached to get the patio threesome reunited. "This strikes me as an impromptu date. How about you?"

He stroked a wisp of her hair back, his finger brushing

her cheek. "Anytime you're with me, it automatically escalates to date status." When she tiptoed closer for a kiss, he took that as confirmation. *Roger dodger.* Everything for a Cinco de Mayo Friday night now fell into place.

Chapter 16

From the smallest spread to the largest, Dane had been busting clients for violations over the past two weeks. He checked his master calendar to assure his week would progress intact. Three large ranches loomed dead ahead. He'd have to alternate in and out of the office, but he could manage the get-acquainted visits and put his heavy-handed stamp on his new job.

Bearing authority and not afraid to use it, his tour of duty outmaneuvered the previous regime. Those soft-treatment days had ended, a point he'd made clear to a bevy of landowners. In this business of regulatory compliance, a bit of fear lent the enforcer a slight advantage. As he studied the file for a spread of three hundred twenty acres, a shadow appeared off his shoulder.

Mr. Norman stood towering over him. "Hey, Dane. I wanted to make sure you saw the staff memo regarding the joint-county training session on Thursday. It's a plant identification workshop at the Morris County office, focused on Old World bluestem. We're trying to get on top of spotting it in the field for our clients, so landowners can treat it before further spread. Mark yourself out for the whole day. They're providing our lunch, so that's a little something extra to look forward to." He smiled and walked away.

Dane pulled out his notepad and bracketed in the day-long training. That addition would put a crimp on his field schedule. He'd ditch the day planned in the office instead. On Friday, he needed to ride the open range, because that strategy shrank the workweek. While in the field, no one could make any further claims on him.

He pulled the file on the McCaskey ranch and studied the cow-calf pair allotment. Too bad he didn't know more about the agricultural practices in the region. He'd have to research that before going out. Even if he couldn't find any violations to the contract, he could have a general grumble regarding the condition of the grass. Those full-grown cows likely ate more than their share anyway, so he'd be right on target to protect the resource.

Gratified that nature fit into his authoritative plan, he regained some confidence. The training session would be a distraction, but he would cooperate like a good new employee. He was all about compliance, most of the time anyway.

~

Aley straightened her desktop for the second time that morning. With two other sets of area staff meeting here at nine for the joint training session, she felt the pressure of pending scrutiny in her immediate future. She'd brought in a few more of her books from storage after church back in Emporia on Sunday.

Reece had been on a reactive short fuse that day, once she confessed to no prospects for a more permanent living arrangement. She'd wasted her Saturday placing her name on the waiting list of every apartment complex in Council Grove, which wasn't many. Always the first thing on her prayer list, she tried not to let the transience of her roadside hotel stint cast pallor on her promising new job. Making friends and getting a feel for her place in the office hierarchy held more priority than where she slept at night. At least she tried to believe that.

A good-natured rumble of men's voices echoed from the entrance corridor. Jo-Belle joined the conversation with directions to the meeting room. A quick glance at her cell phone told Aley that prep time had run out. She silenced its ring and snagged her notebook to enter the realm of Old World bluestem and other nefarious encroachers in the botanical realm.

With a goal to remain invisible, she entered the room and slid into a chair at the back table. From there, she could watch the camaraderie from behind. It seemed a harmless ploy.

Jo-Belle walked up holding a cup from the convenience store down the block. "What? You want to mope here in the back row? That's antisocial for playing host."

Aley looked up, her thoughts racing for defense. Their lunch flashed to mind. Since she had to coordinate the carryout, it seemed like a fair excuse. "You know, I might have to dart out when the catering order gets delivered. It's best not to be a midsession distraction."

"Oh, right," she replied in a flat tone. "Guess I can visit around with the guys at break." She popped her writing pad down in front of the adjoining seat. "Maybe I should warm up my coffee one last time."

"Most definitely," Aley replied, her tone more animated than she felt. She wrote "Old World Bluestem Training" across the top of her page and looked up to locate the presenter. Maybe they could actually start on time. When Brody from her old office tossed a wave back to her, she flexed her pen at him and pushed a weak smile in place. Ron Lightner took the front, and she knew the session would get underway at last.

By ten o'clock, Aley had a good grip on identification of Old World bluestem, as long as the stalk bore a seed head. She noted in the margin that fall months would be critical. The plant scientist from Kansas State University took his seat after fielding the last question.

Ron Lightner assumed the podium. "Ladies and gentlemen, how about a fifteen-minute break? You'll find some granola bars and water bottles stashed on the hall counter. Bathrooms are to the right halfway down the hall. We'll start back promptly at ten-fifteen with an update on tantalizing new candidates for the noxious weed list. Enjoy the break."

Determined to lay low in her office, Aley shot out of the meeting room doorway and made haste down the hall. When she got abreast of the ladies room door, an instinctive urge caused her to divert inside. She caught a glimpse of her uptight expression in the mirror as she passed and blew out a pent-up breath. *Relax.* She shook off her defensive attitude and vowed to find something redemptive about the gathering.

Once back in the hall, she had to dodge a few broad shoulders to make the trip to her office. She'd barely stepped around the corner of her desk when a knuckle-knock sounded from her door. The hiding gig she'd hoped for wouldn't happen.

Brody teetered through her doorway, a grin on his face. "So, these are your new digs, huh? A private office? That's super nice. Good move."

She tossed him a smile. "Well, that particular aspect wasn't planned, but I am happy for it. Lots of contracts run through this office, so the privacy helps me stay focused."

A second figure shoved in behind Brody. "Ooh, first class upgrade," Dane Burroughs said, eying the office features. "This sure beats the messy gear closet you left me." His mouth popped open in feigned surprise.

The guilt needled Aley's ribs. "Uh, sorry about that. I can't say that I gave one thought to that closet's upkeep last month. Having the files in order struck me as much more important."

Brody nodded. "So, are you all moved to Council Grove and everything?"

She folded her arms over her midriff. "Not exactly. I've been a little frustrated in the apartment hunting arena. Options here are limited. I'm at a primitive roadside inn right now."

Dane swiped a knuckle under his nose. "You should take my old place and let me get shed of it. I kept an apartment here so I could shuttle up to K-State for classes three days a week to finish my degree."

"I thought you were living in Emporia now," Brody replied.

Dane gave him a loaded look. "Yeah, my girlfriend made that switch convenient."

Aley questioned the validity of the offer, given the source. "Well, I'm on the waiting list of every complex in town. Where did you live?"

Dane lifted one brow. "The Wayfarer Apartments up north on Union Street. That's less than a mile from here. Unfortunately, I still have three months left on my contract, but would welcome any way to get out of that burden."

She had admired that apartment complex at first inspection. Still, something told her to be cautious. "I wouldn't want to rush your personal plans. I can wait for a legit opening."

Brody threw up his hands. "Aley, are you crazy? Take Dane's apartment on a sublease, for pity's sake. It happens all the time."

"Oh, I don't know," she replied. "I can wait and go through the normal channels of leasing. It won't kill me to live in my cabin a few more weeks."

Dane fished into his pocket and soon dangled a key ring over the desk separating them. He pinched a gold key between his thumb and middle finger. "Listen, if I can haul a load of my stuff back with us today, the apartment will be empty by nightfall. Please, consider taking this financial burden off my back. I can pay off my student loan quicker and get on my feet with the new job. What do you say?"

Brody clamped an arm around Dane's shoulders in a show of solidarity. They fist-bumped and both stared at her as if to leverage a positive response.

A glimmer of spacious resolution made her reconsider. Within a day, her top hindrance to settling into Council Grove could be overcome. The remedied offer came so fast it almost left her dizzy. She needed more time to think things through. "Hey, I appreciate the housing offer. I really do. Let me have until lunchtime to think it over. I'll let you know something then."

Brody nodded at his accomplice. "Perfect. We'll ask Mr. Norman if we can detour by the apartment and haul Dane's stuff back when we're ready to go. I'm sure once he realizes it will help you, Aley, he'll say yes." The two men bumped knuckles again, this time with a vocal explosion added at the end.

Sensing the momentum had somehow bypassed her permission, Aley rolled her eyes. It would be perfect to get this hassle over with, even though a sublease rated less than ideal. Reece would be thrilled, no doubt. Hake detested her current accommodations, so he'd likely welcome the switch, too. Given that added reasoning, the pros began to outweigh the cons. She gestured at the door to usher the men out. A granola bar would fuel her next contemplation, which would hold her until noon.

"Save us a place at lunch," Brody insisted in a hushed voice.

Aley squirmed at the sudden show of camaraderie. "I'll ask Jo-Belle to join us then."

"Sounds like a double date," Dane said with a waggle of his thick brow.

"What about that girlfriend you mentioned?" Brody posed.

Dane waved him off with a laugh and stepped up to the snack table. He took one of each treat and stuffed his pockets full.

Aley inhaled. She needed to regain balance. After checking the selection, she took a granola bar with almonds, not chocolate chips. She refused to cheapen the morning with a sugar rush, even if it helped keep her alert. She was plenty wary already. Good thing plants comprised the subject matter for the training, as she'd meet enough carnivores at lunch.

She would make a final decision on the apartment then, if it hadn't already been made for her. The lesser of two evils had never interested her before. The new job came with unforeseen compromises, like requisite call reports and blind-copied e-mails that lurked just below the surface of everyday awareness. Subleasing would be an adjustment, but one she could handle.

~

Hake waited his turn until the patron in front of him relinquished an amateur-wrapped box to the care of the U.S. Postal Service. He hoisted the stack of envelopes holding claim forms onto the counter. The pace in the room seemed molasses-slow.

A middle-aged female clerk soon returned empty-handed from the back of the room. "Yes, how may I help you?"

"I need postage on these today. They're all the same. Last week, the postage ran a dollar twenty for each one." He released his grip and the stack slumped toward the worker.

"I'll have to weigh each one solo, just the same," she replied. The first envelope found the scale. "That's a dollar twenty, just like you predicted." She pulled it off, entered an amount on her register, and passed the envelope through a narrow slot. In rapid succession, she repeated the process until all the envelopes bore the metered imprint.

"Wow, that was a time saver," he quipped, gratitude making his tone light.

"We've both got better things to do," she replied. "I see you're a lawyer. I might need your services. We've had a death in the extended family and need some help with the will."

"Sure, I do all types of estate law. My office is on Merchant Street a block south of campus. Drop by anytime. Walk-ins are welcome."

She gestured to the room's perimeter. "Here's my prison ball-and-chain. I'm here nine to five. Maybe I could just drop it off and have you review the papers."

"Nonsense. I can stay open late for you, if that would help. I'd be glad to, in fact." He gave her a sideways look, hoping to get a favorable reaction. When she further scrutinized him, he added a slight grin.

She chuckled under her breath. "I do have it out in the car. If you could stay late today, I'd be much obliged." She fiddled through several sheets of stamps and finally held one up. "If you buy these, you can pre-stamp the manila envelopes and put them with your outgoing mail."

"Great. I'm all about efficiency. Thanks for the suggestion. By the way, I always give new clients a free initial consultation. When we meet at five, I'll take a complimentary look at the will for you and render my advice. We'll take matters from there."

A bit of color flushed through her cheeks. "Thank you for that. I don't know what I'm getting into, but we can't leave the will unresolved. That's fifty-seven dollars and sixty cents for the metered postage plus the stamps."

Hake retrieved his credit card, taking time to memorize the woman's features. He'd get her name later. After sliding the card through the scanner, he held it up for her inspection. In seconds, a solution to his chronic trips to the post office had been rendered. He'd cherish that outcome every time he took a peel-and-stick stamp off the sheet.

"See you after five then."

He nodded and exited with his stamps in hand. A quick assessment of his afternoon brought Aley to mind. He'd have to cancel their regular Thursday night date, not knowing how long the will review would take. Content in the sunshine, he stopped at the curb and brought out his phone to send the text. *Working late. Can't make it over tonight. Catch you this weekend?*

He had barely slid behind the wheel when a reply dinged for his attention.

Perfect plan for a girl on the move.

He winced at her cryptic message as he started the ignition. He'd call her later in the evening to get the full scoop. Right now, he needed to bone up on his estate inheritance law, a prerequisite for the five o'clock consult he hoped would lead to a paying customer. Such matters tended to be complex, the reason why folks hired a lawyer in the first place. *Job security.*

~

Aley stood in the middle of a spacious living area, enjoying the late afternoon sun that poured through a series of west-facing windows. The NRCS men had left with Dane's furnishings over twenty minutes ago, allotting her enough time to dispose of the meager contents in the refrigerator. With so much natural light, she could arrange all her houseplants in here with room to spare. Excited to make the step up into a fully-accommodating rental, momentum began to lift her mood.

She walked back to the bedroom to mentally arrange her furniture along the walls. Two closets interrupted one interior wall, while the two exterior walls framed out a pair of glorious windows that had mini-blinds for coverings. She'd select some curtains after she got the place cleaned up and her furnishings in place. Reece would shout hallelujah at regaining his garage space so readily. *What a relief.*

After pacing off the space for her double bed between the windows, she clapped her hands. More than enough room existed for her to fit the bed and matching dressers. She returned up front, catching an acrid smell from the bathroom as she passed. "Note to self—pick up bleach-based cleaner at the store."

She snagged her purse from the kitchen bar, determined to move from the cabin that evening. Such a shift might take her two trips to accomplish, but the focused effort would be worth it. Tomorrow, she'd make her new commute to work for the first time.

She could hardly wait to tell Hake when he called to catch up later. Maybe she'd string him along and make him guess. *Let's hear it for affection migration.* After spilling the news, she'd offer the address to see if he could discover her new improved location. So lighthearted, she practically skipped to her car.

Chapter 17

May had fallen into a pattern of oppressive heat with an occasional rain shower. Hake noted the effect of a humid environment on the grazed pastures closest to the house. The stench of active ranching permeated the air, making it seem less like a weekend hobby. He smoothed the metallic silver paint over the rails of a pipe gate he'd targeted for the east pasture. Pressure on his left ankle made him realize he'd gained company in the farmyard.

"Hey there, Honey. How are you getting along today?" When he stooped to attempt contact, the barn cat froze and glared at him. "Okay, we'll keep things on your terms…until you can trust me." He dipped the brush and made another stroke across the top rail. The cat rubbed against his right ankle. Soon, he heard a soft purring noise. "I think you've filled out some since I've been feeding you. That's a good sign we're making progress, isn't it?" He dabbed at some brush marks and worked the thick paint into an even coating.

For the second time that morning, his thoughts flitted to Aley. She seemed genuinely happy the last time they'd been together. He'd asked to see her this afternoon, but she'd begged off, opting to get her apartment arranged like she wanted instead. He contemplated her readiness to settle into Council Grove for the long-term, something that rubbed against his inclinations for the future. Still, he could retrieve her in fifteen minutes. Council Grove wasn't an eternity away.

Unhurried, he made several long strokes along the upper surface of the top railing. The coating seemed too thin, so he dipped his brush and reapplied a heavier layer. After dabbing several spots where rusty red peeked through, he finished the job. Intent to leave it on the makeshift rack to dry, he tamped the lid back on the paint can and headed for the barn.

Once he'd stored the paint, he exited and took a long look at the horizon. Everything in sight he could claim as his own. Not too many men could say that. Instead of weighing him down with concern, it lifted his spirits. His phone pinged, so he retrieved it from his shirt pocket.

Perfect bike riding day. Leave at one to meet halfway on Rails to Trails. You game?

Aley's prompt birthed a smile. Maybe he wouldn't have picked the heat of the day to exercise like that, but he wouldn't ask for a delay from a woman who evidently couldn't wait to see him. He doubled back into the barn and returned with Reece's borrowed bike. Honey came trotting behind him, seemingly interested in the bike's wheels. "I don't think this trip is for the likes of you, little kitty. Stay here and do some mouse killing for me, okay?"

He dashed into the house to clean the paint off his hands. Maybe he'd toss on a clean T-shirt, too. He only had twenty minutes to improve his status, if he wanted to synchronize his trip with hers. He considered shaving as he turned on the kitchen faucet. Saturday warranted a break from such stringent upkeep, so she'd have to embrace the casual version of her boyfriend instead. That would become another part of this biking rendezvous experience—accepting each other under as-is conditions, come what may.

In fifteen minutes, he started up the access road toward the north gate. That would leave him a bumpy ride across the length of one pasture, but the cattle had been rotated out a week ago, so they wouldn't interfere with his planned route. He soon stopped for the gate, pushed the bike through, and latched the chain back for security. Plowing through the grass clumps gave his thighs a good workout.

He spied the railroad tracks up ahead and aimed for the tall posts marking the north gate, studying his kingdom as he went. Even with the grazing pressure, the grass's growth proved sheer wonderment to him. Nature's cycle possessed more traction than his bike tires. He stopped for the north gate, entered the combination for the lock, and let it swing wide open. After pushing the bike onto the gravel trail, he doubled back and closed the gate.

With a quick glance at his phone to document the time, he mounted the bike and started west on the refurbished rail line headed for Council Grove. Realizing a woman represented his actual destination, he gained motivation and pumped the pedals with extra force. The bike gained momentum under his determination to meet her more than halfway.

~

The thrill of exploration drove Aley beyond a lengthy pasture that looked double-stocked for the short season. Uncountable Angus steers dotted the sloping landscape like an agrarian connect-a-dot game. Wildflowers passed in and out of focus, dominated here by the white petals of daisy fleabane. She began to prefer this linear course, because it offered extended time to investigate the surroundings without the constant threat of navigational adjustments.

Up ahead, the tree canopy closed over the top of the trail. Such shady spots had been few and far between on her segment of the trail. Maybe she'd stop for a quick drink from her water bottle before pressing on. Unclear how much more territory she'd have to cover in her portion of the meet-up, she could pause and rest a brief moment before heading east again. The trail seemed underutilized, as she hadn't met a single soul since starting at Council Grove.

Headed into the shade, she soon became aware of a small creek that flowed in the valley between two sloping hillsides. The overhanging trees hid the short length of railing for a bridge crossing the intermittent waterway. Generous spring rains had fed a healthy flow of water into the drainage. So slow, Candice's bike began to teeter until Aley put her foot out to stop.

She grabbed the water bottle below the seat and opened the spout with her teeth. A soft gurgle emanated from the creek's flow over several rocks exposed in the gully, lending a tranquil atmosphere to her place of respite. With shade overhead, she'd found the perfect spot for a break.

A streak of orange in the sky revealed a Baltimore oriole. She looked around for a nest but didn't find one among the dense foliage. As the sun peeked through the leaves, she squeezed her eyes closed and listened to the sounds of nature filling the wild. The creek's melodic trickle almost made her sleepy. She took a long drink of tepid water and tried to memorize the spot, in case she needed a break on her return trip.

A far-off movement caught her attention as she stared up the trail. A biker approached, bent over his handlebars in a hard ride. Self-conscious about having stopped in the middle of the trail, she propelled the bike against the right railing and debated whether to get underway again or not. If their two paths crossed with equal-but-opposite momentum, there would be less time for any awkward greetings. As she stepped onto the pedal with her right foot, her thigh muscles launched a heavy protest.

"Okay, guess I'll wait. No one could fault my monopoly of the shade on a hot day anyway." She forced her rear tire closer to the bridge rail and waited for the casual passing.

The rider seemed to glide without effort into the shade. His head tipped up as he regarded her position. The brake pads squeaked and gravel skid beneath the tires.

Aley recognized Reece's bike before she identified the rider. A flicker of joy leapt in her heart. She'd already made the halfway point, or close enough for the planned meet-up.

His neck ringed with sweat, Hake swung his leg over the bike seat and took a couple of stiff steps toward her. "Water, please."

When Aley held up the water bottle, he dipped under and opened his mouth. She gave the plastic cylinder a squeeze and delivered the liquid refreshment he'd requested. The oriole flew back by overhead, lending some magic to the reunion.

Hake drew the bike closer and leaned in toward her. "Here I am, as requested." He tipped the brim of his ball cap up and made a quick study of her face.

"Welcome to the bridge over Halfway Creek," she whispered, enchanted at his proximity. When his arm slid behind her back, she relented and came to him, stealing the last droplet of water off his lips.

Labored breathing chopped at the kiss, but he inhaled and returned for more affection. He pulled away and gave her a satisfied look, placing his hot hand over hers on the seat. "I think I'm going to like this halfway bridge. Call me anytime you want to meet in the middle."

The oriole began to sing from the top of a towering hackberry tree. Aley traced a finger along the ribbed neckline of his T-shirt, feeling the rise of his next breath. "It's our little paradise, isn't it? I didn't think I could wait until Sunday morning to see you. Plus, I really needed this exercise."

He wiped his face on his sleeve, mopping up sweat off his temple. "I almost had to bring the cat. She ran with me all the way to the first gate. If I had a basket—"

"Honey wouldn't stay put inside. You know that. Don't even try." She raised one brow as if to test him.

"Flighty women," he replied, his tone a bit on edge. "One wants to go yet has to stay, and the other just wants to flat-out go." He shook his head with the admission.

Aley knocked her kickstand in place and released the bike. She had something else that needed propping up, a boyfriend with a faltering attitude. She started to slide the water bottle back into place and thought better of it. Instead, she handed it to him. "Why don't you tell me about your week?"

"Well, my trip to Pratt is planned for this coming Wednesday. Over thirty people signed up for the settlement workshop." He shook his head and then took a long drink.

Proud of his success, she gave his chest a pat. "I admire your dedication, Hake. You're doing a vital service for these poor victims. How's the ranch work coming along?"

"I have the east pasture gate ready for installation. Reece promised me a quick trip out after church tomorrow to help set it onto the post. It's nice to check that off my list. The cattle lend an element of life out there I didn't realize was missing. I like it, the smell notwithstanding."

With a laugh, she popped his cap off. In a flick of her wrist, she fanned him with it a time or two. Just to get a reaction, she feigned tossing it over the railing.

Hake caught her wrist and drew her closer. "Oh, no you don't. You might want to borrow that hat, since you're riding straight west into the sun—unless you'd rather ride east beside me so we can talk along the way."

"Are you asking me over, Mr. Warren?" She let a tiny smile chase the question.

"I most certainly am. After we eat dinner, I can fit your bike in the trunk of my car and drive you home."

She pressed her forehead against his. "My legs are going to be killing me tomorrow."

He held up a finger. "It's the same distance either way, and with Plan B, we get more time together." He squinted and held his scrutiny.

"Okay, east it is then. Are you ready?" She handed over his hat and headed for her bike.

Hake made a broad turn that put him right up against her beside the rail. He slid his cap in place and glanced below the railing to the gully below. "I'm fond of this halfway bridge, especially if I find you here waiting for me every time."

Aley got on the bike and pushed off the railing, leaving him without an answer. Her destination now comprised the full distance between them, twice the effort she'd intended. His invitation for more time together sounded too good to pass up. Maybe her legs would forgive her tender heart after a long soak in a hot bathtub tonight.

Hake zoomed by, rocks skittering in the gravel from his hasty passage. "I plan to kiss you again before the north gate," he called over his shoulder.

Drawn by his momentum, she began to pedal faster. Her knees gave a slight objection, but she soon closed the gap between them. The landscape eased into a sizable crop field, green with soybean plants all lined in rows. Now she saw the wisdom in moving forward, as it held an unexplored satisfaction over backtracking. Plus, she had Hake with her, a double pleasure.

He looked back over his shoulder as she approached. "I bet the cat will tolerate you holding her tonight. I'll let you put her food out."

Excited at the chance, she thought about minimizing her risks. Cat scratches proved notoriously germ-filled. "Do you think she would mind if I wore gloves?"

He laughed and reached for her across the trail.

Aley navigated closer and put her hand in his. When he kissed her knuckles, it felt like a blessing ahead of the potential cat damage. Too bad kisses didn't really protect anything—or maybe they did.

~

No matter how many times he tried to divert his attention on the return trip from Manhattan, Dane couldn't shake the mischievous idea. Access would be easy enough, as he'd commandeered the extra key to the old apartment from his fiancée earlier in the week. A brief stopover couldn't hurt, whether the occupant was at home or not. *Not* struck him as the better scenario. With no one home, he could take a look around at what she'd done to the place.

The more he thought about the option, the more he felt compelled to follow through. *Naughty and then nice, the spice of a crooked life.* For devious pleasure, he'd throw in one case of the old switcheroo trick, too. He liked to keep the women in his life guessing, because possessing the upper hand represented a real man's territory.

When the speed limit lowered at the edge of Council Grove, he spied the old apartment complex and headed for his target of his fond fetish—toying with the minds of the weaker sex. Too bad he couldn't lurk to witness her confused expression. *Maybe some other time.*

Ripe to start the mischief, he hit the turn signal and indicated his intention to trespass without invitation. He could scarcely quell his excitement as his truck coasted to a stop in a remote parking spot. Subleasing now presented him with a brand-new playground. The prickle of excitement enticed him all the way to the entrance steps, a perversion that he fed with titillating enjoyment.

Chapter 18

Hake peered past the bifocal glasses of his guest to read the earnestness in her eyes. "I don't recall ever eating rhubarb before. Looks like today's the day."

Janie Rose extended the margarine tub to him. "I kept this in the freezer, but thought I would free up some space. The strawberries will be ripe by next week. I want you to come over one afternoon and pick as many as you want."

He took the dessert and thought it felt a touch on the heavy side, given the container's size. "Thank you for the rhubarb and the invitation to pick. Would you be open to my bringing a friend? I'd like you to meet my girlfriend Aley. She just moved to Council Grove, but I try to have her come out once or twice a week to enjoy the fresh air in Bushong."

She turned sideways as if giving the matter further consideration. "That sounds fine. We'd get more berries picked, wouldn't we? Sometimes, the heat gets to them faster than the birds do. I have three varieties, so one should be ready for picking. What day works best?"

After checking his desk calendar, Hake needed to go with an afternoon he could count on. "Let's say Thursday for now. I'll have to check with Aley, but we typically reserve that for our regular date night, so I don't think she'll have a conflict. She works for the conservation service, so she's pretty outdoorsy."

Janie Rose sat her purse on the desk and made sure it snapped closed. "I might show her my favorite flowerbed then. Most of the plantings came with the house, but I've been trying to spruce up the side yard some. I even mulched a trail out to the peach orchard, to give the plot better definition." She bent closer and put the back of her hand close to her lips. "It looked like a side car add-on when I first moved in. Slowly but surely, I'm working my landscaping magic."

"I bet you are." Before he could forget, he took a pen and sketched in the visit for Thursday afternoon. "Janie Rose, I'm so glad you happened by today. I'm closing the office tomorrow, so I can be in Pratt for a settlement claim workshop there."

"Well, I'm on my way to the Federated Women's Club meeting. I thought it might be time for my fruity invitation, so here I am. But I need to scoot. Come as soon as you can after work next Thursday." She pulled her purse off the desk and took a step for the door. With a click of her fingers, she turned around. "Knock on the back door—if you don't see me outside in the yard. I think next-door neighbors should use the back door, don't you?"

"Sure sounds like the neighborly thing to do. I'm looking forward to seeing your orchard. I regret not having any fruit trees of my own." He rose to walk her out.

Her crooked finger pointed to the ceiling. "Nothing says you can't start one. Plant some of the pits from my peaches and see if you might finagle a sprout."

He pulled open the office door and let a heated breath of late May pull the oxygen from the room. "I might do that. It sounds easy enough."

"Don't wait until August, as the rains will stop and woeful drought typically besets the state of Kansas." She gave him a knowing look and stepped out onto the sidewalk.

"You stay safe over Memorial holiday weekend." He

hooked his smile to one side to drive the tease home.

"I don't need the calendar to tell me when to recreate—I'm retired and set free of all that. See you Thursday, Hake. I'll look forward to meeting your gal." She wiggled a few fingers in a farewell gesture and stepped down the curb to her car.

A skateboarder pushed along the sidewalk, drawing his attention to the letter carrier working his way closer. One day soon, that public servant would be delivering the first of the class action lawsuit settlements. Hake anticipated that income, as trips to the bank to make a deposit had been few and far between. He waved goodbye to his neighbor and returned to his office to plan out the Pratt workshop. His immediate destiny involved heavy use of the office copier, as he needed thirty more sets of the settlement claim form.

The "Closed Early" sign caught his eye as he walked past the coffee station. In four hours he would post that message and be on the road to Pratt. Dr. Atkins had recommended the steak dinner at Rick's Restaurant, but he hated the idea of dining alone. Aley flickered to mind and set off a longing for companionship he couldn't seem to quell. That steak dinner would have to be a takeout order. Afterwards, he'd call her and get caught up on her week. Besides, he had a strawberry-delight offer to entice her to Bushong. He smiled, knowing she wouldn't pass that up.

~

Aley ducked the kitchen cabinet door and slid the sugar sack onto the lower shelf. Rethinking the arrangement, she switched the flour and sugar around. That left enough space for her spice rack on the same shelf. Cereal boxes stood on their sides on the shelf above, beside her collection of boxed herbal teas. The pantry stock had started falling into place.

Her phone ring tone sounded, and she glanced over, recognizing her brother's sly mug shot on the cover. She grabbed the phone and took the call. "Hey, Reece. What's up?"

"I wanted to call you early enough to claim a day out of your holiday weekend."

Somehow, the mention made her protective. Three-day weekends didn't come around too often. "Depends on what you have in mind."

"Not me—Candice. She says we should get out more before the baby comes. I could stand a day away myself. She wants to see some water. How does a picnic at Wilson Lake State Park sound for Saturday?"

"Ooh, I like the idea. Could we make it a double date and invite Hake? I think he's caught up enough with his ranch work to miss a Saturday."

"Yeah, that was my next suggestion. He seemed pretty happy about getting that new gate installed last weekend. Sometimes, he looks more like a rancher than a lawyer to me."

She ambled into the living room to check the houseplants for moisture. "He'd take that as a high compliment, Reece. Tell Candice I'm game. Let me call you back about Hake. He's in Pratt tonight getting ready for another one of those settlement claim workshops."

"Ha—a traveling attorney. He's like a truck driver delivering a load of justice."

"Pat the baby for me."

"He kicked my hand tonight after dinner, the little scoundrel," he replied, his tone softening at the admission.

"Count your blessings, brother. I'll be in touch." She ended the call and stuck a finger in the rabbit's foot fern. The soil felt dry as a bone. She reached for the mini-blind rod and gave it a slight twist to reduce the amount of sunlight.

When her gaze swept the array of miniature animal figurines she'd scattered around the row of plants, she hesitated. *That's odd.* The tiny fox led the tortoise and the rabbit. She'd never arranged the painted clay pieces like that before. A prickle of unease lifted the hair on the back of her neck. Unsure what to make of it, she reached for the mischievous fox and placed him behind the rabbit, well out of the proverbial race. The turtle had to stay in first place.

Before she could give it a second thought, the phone rang again. A casual shot of Hake from their last visit to Peter Pan Park indicated the caller. She headed down the hall to her room. "Hey there. I hope you arrived in Pratt without any trouble."

He chuckled. "My only trouble is that you aren't with me. I took my dinner back to the condo because I couldn't stand the thought of eating out by myself. Guess I've gotten spoiled by having such first-rate company to dine with lately."

She stretched out on her stomach across the quilted bedspread. "Well, if that's the case, how does a picnic by Wilson Lake sound to you for Saturday? Reece called and said Candice wants to get out and see some water. I think she's getting antsy for the baby to come."

"You're probably right. That sounds fun. If they have boat rentals, I wouldn't mind getting in some rowing and trace the shoreline."

"Okay, I'll check for boat rentals during my break tomorrow. I don't feel like bringing up my laptop tonight. Tell me about your day."

A soft snicker trickled down the phone line. "At lunch, I discovered that I don't care much for rhubarb. My neighbor Janie Rose stopped in and brought me some cobbler. I rated the taste as marginal, but I couldn't get past the slimy texture. I only ate a spoonful."

"Poor guy. Rhubarb might be an acquired taste."

"Anyway, Janie Rose said her strawberries were almost ripe, so she invited me over to pick next week. I chose Thursday after work and asked if I could bring you along. Would you like to meet my neighbor and pick some strawberries?"

"My, my." She swung her feet off the end of the bed. "You really know how to tempt a girl, Mr. Warren. That is our regular date night, so I just might have to accept."

He hummed into the phone. "I thought so. She wants to show you her planting beds. She's been making improvements. Wish I could say the same."

"Hey, you have an improvement—a new gate on the east pasture."

"True. That felt great to cross the last pasture improvement task off my list. Summer is just kicking off, so there'll likely be a whole lot more chores."

"You have strong fences. That's half the battle. Maybe we could start a raised bed garden together behind the house. That way your barn cat could guard it."

He laughed at the notion. "I don't think cats are known for protecting against rabbit nibbles. You're the wildlife expert."

His mention of rabbits reminded her of the figurine misalignment in the living room. Aley propped her chin in her palm, wondering whether to tell him or not. If she kept it casual, that would still count as full disclosure. "I had a little surprise today in my indoor garden. When I checked my houseplants to see if they needed watering, I found my little clay forest critters out of alignment. To tell you the truth, the discovery startled me for a second."

"Women and their incessant need for rearrangement," he teased. "You've probably relocated everything at least twice since you moved in."

"Not true, as my bed is still where you and Reece put it. But you're right, I likely slid them around out of order in an unfocused moment. Goodness, and I was so ready to blame a poltergeist. It's funny how the little things can mess with your head when the day goes quiet."

Hake grunted, sounding far away from the phone.

"Hey, do you need to go? I fully understand if you need to prepare for tomorrow's presentation." She crossed her ankles, hopeful for a negative reply.

"Nope, I was only throwing away my carry-out

container. The next time I have the privilege of ordering a steak at Rick's Restaurant, I want you right across the table from me so I can stare into your beautiful hazel eyes."

"Ah, finally we get to the sweet talk. A girl like me with a hard regulatory job might need to hear more of that kind of exchange." She softened her voice until she practically cooed, hopeful to keep him on the line. "What else?"

"Well, the tiny mole by your left earlobe sometimes distracts me when I'm trying to be a serious rancher."

"Like when you were pounding those cage posts in, right? You can't stay focused when we're working side-by-side. Now, I see the truth of the matter. It's not work when we're together, is it?" During the pause, she could hear him exhale. She captured the faint sigh in her heart to treasure later.

"I thank God for you every night, Aley Halstead," he whispered. "If not for you, I'd only be half as motivated here on the ranch. What a blessing you've been to me, a real angel-on-the-prairie."

His velvety tone caused a heated blush. She rubbed her neck, but couldn't stop the reaction. "You're my Rancher…so I need to spend some time with you."

"Thursday night, let's plan to grill out at my place. You can step off that raised garden bed, and we'll set the planks for the edges. I might even let you drive my Jeep when we go searching for dirt to fill the bed."

"You truly need a tractor—or a mower with a bucket on front."

"I think I know what I need. How about an answer to my Thursday night offer?"

"Yes. Let's do chicken, since you just had beef. I'll take care of it. You're out of town."

"Too far away," he replied, his voice drifting.

Aley pressed her wrist against the lump in her throat. "You're the best part of my week, Hake. I can't wait for tomorrow night. See you then." She ended the call and fell face-first on the bed, letting the dreamy effect of Hake's voice take her to an imaginary place where they could be together morning, noon, and night. That progression seemed so natural, she drew great comfort from it. Eyes closed, she planned the layout for her garden with every hope that it would grow. Along the way, plant nurture melded with attraction to a handsome lawyer, a seamless fit.

~

Thirsty, Dane headed for the fridge to check what they had to drink. After he'd received his first paycheck, he earned bonus points by giving his fiancée extra grocery money. He needed to offer her a few pointers on better snack selection, but he couldn't complain about her cooking. A phone hummed on the bar where it sat recharging. Once he checked the caller, he snapped his fingers to get her attention. "Hey, Dannie. Do you know anybody in Sacramento?"

She lowered her latest People magazine and knit her brow. "No, I don't think so."

"That's the third time this number had come up this week. I can't take calls at work, so I wish this pesky salesman would buzz off." When she disappeared behind her magazine again, he continued to the kitchen to get that drink. "Loser," he muttered under his breath as he snatched open the refrigerator door. As king of his domain, he didn't appreciate any meddlesome jerk trying to chip away at his throne.

He opted for a pricey-looking bottle of organic protein blend, hoping it tasted better than it looked. Directionless, his mind skipped to work. Tomorrow he had a site visit planned. That should keep him sane, if the fair weather held. He twisted off the cap and headed for the back to watch TV. The protein would lend him a good head of steam for his regulatory work, a testosterone-driven objection to the shortcomings of others. Oh, yes. He loved the new job.

Chapter 19

Hake stood under a small arbor, letting the late afternoon sun spackle light onto the empty cartons he carried. Compared to his stark yard, Janie Rose's landscaping represented a modern-day version of the hanging gardens of Babylon. What incredible options the shade lent, with waves of colorful flowers everywhere he looked. He definitely wanted more trees.

Aley straightened from the nearest row. "Hey, I need a carton." Her hands brimmed with bright red berries.

Aluminum pie pans shifted in the breeze as he stepped down her row to deliver a crate or two. "I think someone's in hog heaven." He handed over two containers.

She deposited her harvest in one and then gestured in a long sweep. "This is all so inspirational. I want more time to roam the yard once we get done picking this last row. I honestly don't know how she keeps up with all of this."

"Perseverance, my dear," Janie Rose interjected with a wink. She took half the cartons from Hake. "First you dabble here, and then you check over there. There's always something to plant or prune. When I get a new idea, I set right out to make it happen. I inherited a wild tangle for a yard, so it's taken me two full growing seasons to tame the mess."

He followed her halfway down the row. "I need more shade," He straightened his back and enjoyed the breeze riffling through the large round leaves of cigar trees along the back lane. It would take him forty years to gain that effect.

"If you're picking, then I'm talking," Janie Rose said, an ounce of correction in her tone.

Hake stooped and pushed the jagged-edged leaves back to search for more berries. Five or six perfect-shaped strawberries dangled from arching stems. The plant was worthy of a still-life painting. As a second thought, he pulled out his phone and shot a photo of it with the empty crate waiting nearby. That should remind him of Christ's vine-and-branch promise of the ability to bear much fruit. He had every intention of staying connected.

Aley giggled and made a move to leap-frog past him along the row. "You're as slow as strawberry jam in a squeeze bottle. You won't ever earn the nickname *gardener* at this rate." Her expression animated, though her sunglasses played down the silly look.

The idea hit him from out of the blue. "Can we make jam from these berries? Really?"

"Yep, I make some every year," Janie Rose replied. "It's a good way to use up the ripest berries. I can give Aley my recipe, if you want." The straw brim of her hat lowered as she continued picking.

"Yes, we'll borrow your foolproof recipe. Thank you. I think it will help broaden her domestic skills." When Aley looked up with a sharp cackle, he pretended to throw a berry at her.

"True, I haven't done much home canning." With a broad step, she straddled the row and knelt to pick.

"It takes a fair amount of equipment to do the water bath right," Janie Rose replied. "Let me invite you over to use mine."

"I'll be back on Saturday. Would that work for you?"

She placed a medium-sized berry on top and set the carton aside to start filling the next one.

Their hostess stood, a hand propped on the small of her back. "Saturday around ten-thirty is best. That lets me get my yard work done while the day's still mild. You'll need to buy a dozen jelly jars. I prefer the diamond-cut ones."

Hake worked until he could top off his current collection. The way the women were bonding added extra enjoyment to the task. Plus, he'd gain some strawberry jelly out of the deal. After adding a handful of berries, he set the carton down next to Aley's and shifted to the end of the row.

"Almost time for the yard tour," Janie Rose said. "I'm 'bout ready for the shade. It's roasting today, but those peaches need it hot to fill and ripen."

Appreciation flooded his heart. "Thank you for including us in all of this,"

"You're welcome, Hake. I should have invited you over before now. The strawberries are a good excuse for neighborliness, and you won't believe how good they make rhubarb taste."

Aley couldn't contain her snicker as she shifted closer to him.

Hake gave her a hidden gesture to keep quiet, as he didn't want to offend the gardener. When she looked at him over her sunglasses, he took her wink as a conspirator's sign of muted compliance.

He'd wait to tease her until he tasted that first batch of jelly, a noteworthy sign of capable kitchen skills. After all, if he learned to garden, she'd have to do her part. The idea gave him a surge of connectedness for their future together. He patted her hip as she passed by, transfixed by the berry she held between her lips. Janie Rose wouldn't appreciate any sort of amorous conduct in her strawberry patch, or that fruit would belong to him in two shakes of a bunny's tail. He glanced at the empty container in his hands and moaned.

~

Dane twisted the throttle on his motorcycle, trying to make up time. The day had gotten away from him because the humongous tract bordered around a thousand acres. He didn't have time to waste coming back out, but he definitely owed this landowner's new CSP contract some scrutiny. Riding low along the western fence line, his tires bogged down in a hillside seep that he failed to notice in time.

Soft from the late rain on Memorial Monday, the ground tracked in places where the water collected. Those ruts weren't his fault. He would defend his right to access the pasture as the conservation officer in charge. Besides, the department truck would have left ruts on the land ten times worse. In that light, he was doing the landowner a favor.

He headed north to check the last solar-pumped tank for its wildlife escape ladder. Compliance played out in black-and-white. Either you had one or you didn't. An expanse of nothingness greeted him at this northern pasture. He made quick work of the distance and jammed the brake, letting his back tire drift on the gravel surrounding the tank. Instantly peeved, he spotted the required ladder in perfect operating position. This landowner had been a veritable choir boy of compliance.

Before he could shift his mindset to the next plan of action, the cell phone rang from his back pocket. Late for returning to the office, maybe he had some fessing up to do. With the setting sun glaring off the screen, he hurried to accept the call. "Burroughs here."

"Yes, Mr. Burroughs. This call is regarding a claims investigation on the Central Bank credit card of Danielle Tillison. We have your name associated with two unauthorized purchases that Ms. Tillison has declined payment on dating back to February. I'd like to discuss those unapproved transactions with you, if I may."

The investigator's accusation blinded him for an instant, so he clenched his eyelids shut. Rocked to the core, he steadied the motorcycle by shifting his feet and cut the engine. Incredulous guilt slithered through his veins as a risk he'd played against months ago now boomeranged. "Well, I had no idea she would decline payment on those charges." He groped for solid ground to strengthen his stand. "Danielle's my fiancée now. We share household expenses. That should help authorize my use of her credit card."

Steady blood pressure mounted and began to block his hearing while the man elaborated on several options to correct the situation. Every time his heart took a beat, it exploded in his ears. *Caught in a trap here.* His neck overheated under his uniform shirt, the late afternoon sun baking him out in the wide open. He glanced at the water tank to assess any relief it could offer.

His teeth gnashed as the representative enumerated on how he could pay back the initial purchases, along with the accrued interest, to avoid further legal action. With no way out, he'd have to pay the two hundred-plus dollars. He squeezed his eyes closed, trying to moderate his ramping rage. Dannie popped to mind, an obvious traitor, which infuriated him further. The man's last question sliced through his semi-conscious rampage and made him sober up.

"Yes, I'll certainly commit to making good on those expenditures. Expect it to come by online payment this evening, for sure. I'll get Ms. Tillison's approval to pay through her account, so all will be back to normal. Sorry about the mix-up."

Stomach clenched, he feigned through a few more conciliatory comments and ended the call while the steep payout reverberated through his mind. Seething, the tranquil tank seemed to call to him as it reflected the sky. He ratcheted the kickstand down and dismounted, approaching the water hole. Four steers stepped back, apprehensive about his lingering presence. In his brooding contemplations, his elbow brushed against his conceal-and-carry handgun.

With cold premeditation, he scanned the steers, selecting his target. His palm skimmed the NRCS logo on his uniform which quickly sobered him up to the possible ramifications of killing livestock. His vengeful knee-jerk deliberation faltered. He glared at the tank, saw the ladder, and jerked it out of the water with a huff. After straddling it across the handlebars, he started the motorcycle and headed back south, his brain a seared battlefield of indignation.

At some nebulous location along the back fence where it bordered the wooded creek, he braked and formulated a hasty plan. He dismounted and propped the ladder on the soggy ground. He took a moment to fit the handgun into his grip and stomped to the woodland's edge. Giving a guttural grunt, he slung the wire ramp toward the tree canopy and opened fire as though trying to down an oversized clay pigeon. Twice the metal pinged with a direct hit.

The entire shooting action gave him immense satisfaction. Not only had he vented a little steam, but now the landowner could be found in noncompliance. Realizing the leverage arrow pointed in his direction at long last, he drew a deep breath to calm his temper a notch.

Returning to the motorcycle, he determined to end the site visit before he wore out his welcome. The drive back to town would lend him plenty of time to figure out how to approach Dannie. She would have to own some of this payout. Yes, without question, she would.

~

Aley knelt below a cluster of ancient ash trees, admiring the lilies that Janie Rose had just pointed out. Cream-colored, a light brush of crimson streaked patterns down their delicate throats. She leaned in to sniff one bloom, but detected no scent.

A series of three or four explosions shattered the afternoon's tranquility. Hollow fear filled the old woman's eyes as she stood erect. She waited for Hake's return from depositing the strawberries onto her back porch. "If I'm not mistaken, that's shooting action from your place." Janie Rose nodded at him in a knowing way. "You might have a poacher trespassing."

A tendon flexed in his jaw. "I have three truckloads of cattle out there. Guns and livestock don't mix."

Aley placed a hand on his forearm as he flinched. "I'll go with you to check it out. We'll look for potential damage and document it, if we find any. I've got my phone."

"Take the rail line for faster arrival," Janie Rose said. "You've got access at the north gate, right? The poacher would never suspect you coming to track him from the north." Her gray eyes widened with the insinuation.

"Let's go," Hake replied, his voice taut. He headed for the car with no-nonsense strides.

Aley patted Janie Rose's arm. "We'll call later and let you know what we found. For now, maybe you could take a break from yard work and rest inside."

The old woman's lips pulled flat. "Don't be concerned about me. I'll lock the doors and pour a glass of lemonade." She nodded and walked toward the back porch. When several crows flushed from the redbud tree as she passed, she shooed them off with a dismissive gesture.

Aley exhaled, her throat desert dry. Their blissful afternoon had just oozed through a crack in the sidewalk in a hammer strike that sounded like a rifle firing. *What good can come of that?* She prayed the whole trip over, though it didn't seem to help.

"Get the gate, will you?" Hake stared ahead without further acknowledgement.

She slid from the vehicle and began to fumble with a heavy chain. Soon, a lock rested in her palm. "Hey, what's the combination?"

Hake's chin tipped up as he scouted the near horizon. Finally, his gaze came to rest on her. "Enter Christmas Eve—month and day."

She dialed in the date and the lock gave way, freeing the chain. She pulled on the gate until the gap could accommodate the width of his car. Once the back bumper had cleared, she locked the gate again. Without a doubt, they wouldn't return through this access.

Only the first week of June, the grass had already grown tall enough to whack the front bumper as they drove through the uneven pasture. Hake cut a diagonal as he headed for the gate leading to the road off the south end of the pasture.

Aley scanned the grass tops, looking for signs of disturbance. They passed a water tank where a foursome of cattle stood drinking. The right front tire hit a hole and the car lurched.

"Never thought I'd be out here driving down my own grass," Hake muttered, his grip tight on the wheel.

"I'll try to help you watch for holes. Maybe we should go retrieve Old Betsy and gain more clearance over the terrain."

"We'll head that way, but keep your eyes open."

They hadn't advanced twenty more feet when she first spotted the ruts in a low spot. "There, see those tracks in the mud? Someone's been in here all right."

Hake threw the car into neutral and killed the engine. He slid out and met her off the front fender. After toeing the track, he started following it back toward the water tank.

An ominous chokehold began to squeeze the air out of Aley's lungs. Her ability to read the land had never sunk to detective work before. She didn't care for the digression, though it fit the bill today. With a couple of hasty strides, she caught up with Hake. "Two tires, not four."

"Yeah, I noticed."

The hoarseness in his voice heightened her apprehension. Tightness in her midsection made it hard to breathe. The cattle stirred at their approach and gave way to the tank.

Hake knelt to study the tracks. He shook his head and fingered something in the chip rock. When he withdrew, the hand clamped around the back of his neck.

Aley squeezed her eyes closed, wishing it would all go

away. She should be eating strawberries right now and feeding them to Hake at his request. When she opened her eyes, she only saw the sky being mirrored in the round by the water tank. Then she noticed what the sky-circle lacked, which made her instantly queasy. "Hake, the wildlife ladder is missing."

With his jaw dropped, Hake grabbed the side of the tank and peered over the edge. "Maybe the cattle—"

"And maybe not," she replied. In her days, she'd seen many "No Trespassing" signs spattered with buckshot, but this had to be a new level of low. "Let's check your other tank."

He shot to his feet and began to search the immediate area. After circumnavigating the tank, he strode back to the car. "No. We're following these tracks." He gestured for her.

"Lord, please keep us safe," she prayed as she broke into a run. She didn't want to go check out any more clues. In the back of her mind, she didn't want to know. As she slid into the car, safety became paramount. "Remember, the poacher is armed."

Hake started the car and moved out straddling the single set of tracks. His features seemed to freeze for the longest time. Once they drove onto the access road, he ventured a glance her way. "I'm going to need a gun."

"Talk to Reece." It was a knee-jerk response, but not a total dodge. She knew her brother had a cabinet full of family rifles. That reflection split off a new worry. "I hope he locks the gun cabinet before the baby learns to walk." Their gazes met, a tangle of apprehension and crossed messages. As the tracks veered off toward the burned field, she closed her eyes and fended off the urge to get sick right there and then.

~

More perturbed than mad, Hake didn't cherish the idea of someone knocking around taking casual target practice on his land. Still new to the responsibilities of stewardship, this unwarranted trespass came across like a thorn in his boot.

With few options, he would have to add locks on all the perimeter gates and loan the cattlemen a key for access.

He parked the car atop a rocky outcrop not far from where the spot-over fire had caused him to tackle Aley. The tracks descended toward the riparian woodland where it hugged the fence. Giving Aley the option of hanging back, he slid from the car without a word and went down to investigate the clues. The more he could find out, the more details he could provide the authorities. He most certainly would report the incident.

The tire tracks stopped just short of the rock line. Hake stooped to examine the rocky hillside. A seep ran from under the rock outcropping, making the hill appear to be weeping. He could relate, as this proved to be a sad footnote to a promising evening. A regular pattern pressed into the mud made him kneel to examine it up close. The diamond grid of the wildlife ladder stared back at him like a clue cast in plaster. "Aley?"

"Right here," she replied, stooping beside him.

"Get a photograph of this imprint. I'm going into the woods to look for the ladder." Since the tiny sound she made in her throat wasn't much of a protest, he proceeded down the slope and slid between several red shoots of a shrub he remembered as rough-leafed dogwood. Once in the shade, the lateness of the day began to work against him. He slogged through the underbrush, searching for an area recently disturbed.

Five minutes turned into fifteen. Several times he heard Aley step in from the edge only to pop back out again. He mentally ran through his Friday morning agenda, thinking he'd have to continue the search by the morning's light. On gut instinct, he stepped further into the woods and circled back.

Within steps, something hard whacked against his shin. He bent and grabbed for the culprit. As soon as he touched it, the metal seemed all too familiar. He hoisted the ladder from the brush and made his way to the clearing. "Aley—I've got it."

She came at a trot, her eyes wide at his discovery. She pointed with the camera's corner at two distinct bullet holes that had penetrated the wire mesh. The third time she made an indication, her expression changed. "Poison ivy, Hake. You're probably covered with it."

"Take a picture right here," he insisted. Covered with sweat, he likely had the essence of the evil vine in every pore. "We'll also get one inside under better lighting. Tomorrow morning, I'll ride out and put the ladder back into the tank."

"Then what?" Aley took one picture and looked up at him for an answer.

"Then I find the straightest path to justice, which is what I do for my day job. Pretty convenient, right?" He waggled his brow while hoisting the ladder toward the car. "You drive to the house, okay?" He unlatched the trunk and heaved the ladder inside.

Aley stood off the driver's door, her hands on her hips. "Where are you going to be?"

"Riding in the trunk, stripped to my shorts. Unless you'd rather have me ride up front?" He pulled off his contaminated T-shirt as a point of emphasis.

Sporting a look of mild shock, she ducked into the car's interior without further comment. Soon, the engine revved. The car lurched forward a foot and halted.

"Thanks for waiting for me," Hake quipped, rolling into the trunk half-dressed. Right away, his back itched against the trunk's wooly lining. He knew not to scratch, but every time the car lurched, he received a little rub on the sly. He gave the wildlife ladder a pat as if greeting a long lost friend. *Some holy reunion.* A meadowlark called full-voiced from atop a post as they passed by, a sure sign the prairie would regain its reverie with the setting sun.

Chapter 20

After last week's holiday followed by Hake's trespasser, Aley found it difficult to settle into a regular workweek. Monday morning's staff meeting grinded to an end. She could hardly wait to get her letter-writing underway to remind several clients of their contract obligations.

Ron Lightner looked around the table, his expression complex. "Before we adjourn, this just came down from headquarters. Human Resources will have a speaker at the Emporia office Wednesday morning for a mandatory workshop on ADA compliance and sexual harassment prevention in the workplace. Sorry to ask on such short notice, but could you all clear your agendas for this workshop? They're expecting one hundred percent participation."

Someone across the table groaned. Another notebook slammed closed. Jo-Belle stood and left the room.

The irony of it rippled through her mind in slow motion. She now had to return to the scene of the chronic violation to learn how to avoid harassment. Hesitant to have some fabricated textbook examples tossed at her in training, Aley sat limp in the chair at a loss as to what to do. When she looked up, she found her boss sitting beside her. Everyone else had left the room.

He stared at her for a few seconds. "Want to talk about it, Ms. Halstead? I'm going to guess it's the sexual harassment issue that has generated the crestfallen look on your face, not the disabilities access issue. Is my hunch close to being right?"

Aley exhaled and leaned back. Maybe she should ask to opt out or somehow feign pending sickness. Her momentary nausea couldn't be attributed to an invasive germ, though. A little internal prompt nudged her to get the truth out on the table. "Going back to the Emporia office for sexual harassment prevention training will be a tough pill to swallow. The walls of that building scream something else to me. For that reason, I can't let down my guard there."

"I see." He shifted in his seat until he directly faced her. "Did you ever think to report the incidents? Maybe your superiors could have intervened on your behalf."

Aley tossed her pen on her notebook and shoved her hands into her pockets. "No, sir. Mr. Norman remains unaware of situations in the workplace. His management style is quite loose, compared to yours. As long as the work gets done, he looks right past what many might see as petty grievances. At first, I shrugged it off, but their harassment got so chronic, it leaked into the public arena. That's when I realized I couldn't do my job to my full capability. I searched for other NRCS offices that had a gender-balanced staff, which led me to apply here."

He nodded. Seconds ticked by. "I'm going to ask you to attend the workshop with the caveat that I'll sit right beside you for the training. That will make us both equally accountable to each other for the content. Before you protest, let me add this. I'm aware that if you don't face the demons that constrain you, it inadvertently gives them the upper hand. It takes strength to rectify a wrong, just as it requires light to expose a dark act. I think you have these attributes inside you, but I'm willing to give you a day to agree with me. Come by Tuesday afternoon and let me know what you've decided." With a flicker of a smile, he rose and exited the room.

Pinched into a corner, Aley sat heavy-hearted, not wanting to move forward or reflect back. Sometimes the middle ground of denial held the uncomplicated neutrality one's soul needed. Thinking her schedule might bail her out, she flipped open the day planner portion of the notebook and read "office" printed across Wednesday's ledger. *Too generic.* She had plenty of time to attend the workshop. Now, she had to figure out if she possessed the courage.

~

Hake winced at the pressure being applied to his left forearm. Aware that he shouldn't have let this outbreak go so long, he now paid the penalty. He flinched as another medicinal blob made contact with the outbreak.

"Sit still young man," Janie Rose said, her tone stern. "You've managed to get a first-class case of poison ivy here. It looks like you've been chaffing at it with your towel. That only spreads the rash, you know."

"So glad I caught you before leaving for town this morning, if that's your regular Tuesday routine. I thought about calling you for the remedy last night, but I thought the pink stuff I put on it would suffice."

She shook her head. "You need ointment and the oatmeal poultice. Once I get this patch smothered, I'll wrap a cotton bandage around it. Have you taken anything for the itching?"

"Yes, an antihistamine about an hour ago. Boy, I sure can tell when that stuff wears off." He laid his head on his right forearm and took the rest of the misery blind. Within seconds, soft cotton pressed against the inflamed skin and brought instant relief.

After a small tug to secure the wrap, Janie Rose's hand patted his shoulder. "This too shall pass, but I wouldn't go rampaging through the creek's shade again, if I were you."

"Another truism that I've learned a smidgen too late,"

he replied, sitting up to face her. "Feel free to wash your hands in the restroom prior to your women's club meeting."

"Thank you, Hake. They'll think my bursitis is acting up if I go in smelling all herbal like this. Don't get the wrong impression, as these are mighty fine women, but club is our excuse to eat out for lunch, most of the time."

"Ah, well my public appearances will have to hold off until my pustulated skin is no longer an affront to the average citizen." He rolled his eyes in exasperation.

"Now you see why your claims settlement victims used so much Rid-A-Weed in the first place. It's a jungle of harm out there." She patted the ointment jar lid and headed for the hallway.

With his itch now soothed, he let her comment about the herbicide sink in deeper. Prevention seemed so much better than a poultice remedy after the harm was done. Too bad widespread physical damage had followed from the preventative use of the herbicide. He let the skin irritation build a sympathetic bridge to these individuals who had suffered so much more. When he heard the restroom door unlatch, he rose to walk his summoned guest to the door.

Janie Rose gave the bandage a lingering assessment as she headed for the exit. "Repeat the application tonight before bedtime and tie a pillowcase around your forearm to keep it off your bedding."

"Yes, ma'am. Thank you so much for coming by. Maybe now I can think clear enough to get some work done."

She offered him a faint smile. "Wear long sleeves if you're worried about what your arm looks like. Tomorrow will be a better day, and so on until the rash dries up."

"Enjoy your lunch bunch. Feel free to tell them about the rookie lawyer you've been doctoring. Who knows? It might serve as good advertising for me."

"I plan to tell them about Aley, too." She peeked over her bifocals with impish zeal. "They all love to hear a good romance story." She walked out and headed for her car parked in the closest space.

Hake leaned out with his unaffected side and evaluated the Merchant Street traffic. To his delight, the letter carrier popped out from next door. "Hey, how's it going today?"

The man reached into his leather pouch. "Oh, fair to middling. How 'bout you?" He thrust a handful of mixed mail toward him.

Hake took the delivery and thought about his reply. "Mostly fair and somewhat rare," he replied, lifting his bandaged arm.

"Better stay out of the sun," the carrier quipped. With a tap on his hat brim, he moved on down the block.

As his vision adjusted to indoor lighting, Hake shuffled the envelopes and headed for the desk. Once seated, he spied the return address of the firm handling the class action lawsuit. Apprehension stabbed his midsection. The rectification on behalf of his clients sat on the threshold of being a two-way endeavor. That realization made him stop and weigh the matter.

"Dear Lord, you know more than I how much these hapless victims have suffered. Though the compensation doesn't make up for that personal loss, it can help offset their current financial woes. If it falls within your divine will, may this be a payout, not a decline of consent. I ask in the powerful name of Jesus, amen."

He reached for the letter opener and tore into the corner of the envelope. As he slid the letter out, he could see lines of typing from the back of the paper. It appeared to be a list. He unfolded the letter and a check slid out. His focus dropped to the names listed in the middle of the communication. Eldon Wilms led the listing. Each name possessed a settlement amount to the maximum extent allowable under the class action lawsuit settlement.

Adrenalin shot through his veins. The compensation process had begun to run full cycle. With exacting care, he read every word of the letter. In closing, he learned that the enclosed check represented his set fee for handling each claim. Using a multiplier factor of six, it generated a significant total.

He picked up the bank check to verify the amount. It matched to the last penny. A new detail caught his eye on the memo line. *How about that?* He'd been assigned a processor number. For once, he didn't mind being represented by mere integers. In fact, he approved.

Thinking to make a bank visit over lunch break, he skimmed through the rest of the mail, most of it advertising junk or nebulous services. A business-sized envelope with NRCS in the return address caught his attention. Buoyed by receiving his compensation payment, he dove into what appeared to be a form letter without any hesitation.

"Dear Mr. Warren, regarding your CSP contract number 600830-NJ, you are found to remain out of compliance with the following contracted enhancements."

Hake's eyes began to burn as he read the hand-printed block letters that spelled out his insufficiency across the allotted blank.

Wildlife escape ladder.

Sharp-focused, he reached for the envelope. The postmark read Monday's date, which meant the noncompliance letter had to be sent out during the workday Friday. He mentally retraced the progression. The ladder had only been missing late Thursday after the shooting incident, since he had replaced it Friday morning before coming to town.

A sinking realization hit him like a kick in the gut. *Lord help me.* He had a problem—a big problem. He picked up his phone and texted Aley to call during her lunch break. Before he could hit "send," his mouth went dry. Numb from the non-compliance letter and its insider ramifications, he stood, tucked the check into his wallet, and headed out to make the deposit, wondering all the while how to put a renegade conservation agent back into the bounds of his regulatory cage.

~

Wednesday morning bore so many levels of discomfort, Aley could barely breathe. Hake would arrive anytime now for the closed-door session with Mr. Norman over his lunch break. She tried not to look at her watch again. It wouldn't forestall the complexities about to unfurl from Hake's well-founded accusations, to which she served as eyewitness. She recorded a concluding comment from the workshop presenter who made a matter-of-fact declaration about modern-day professionalism. No proper arena existed for sexual harassment, including the workplace.

When she looked up, Mr. Lightner gave her a slight smile as if rewarding her for having gone the distance. She tried to let his gesture evoke a positive response, though tension knotted her stomach. She rested her pen atop the notebook and flexed her fingers. Having used profuse note-taking as a dodge from making eye contact with other staff members, she now paid the penalty for her scribbling zeal.

The lights came up, fading the last slide of the Power Point presentation. The speaker sat down, and Mr. Norman took the podium. "Thank you, Mr. Roberts. Now for lunch, we have hot pizza in the break room for everyone. Grab what you want and overflow into the conference room to sit and eat. We'll reconvene in here at one o'clock for closing comments before the visiting offices depart. There's a post-workshop survey that is—you may have guessed—mandatory for all personnel, so we'll tackle that after lunch. You're dismissed until one."

Aley took advantage of the restless transition to get a necessary message relayed. She leaned over to her boss to keep it private. "Mr. Lightner, you'll have to excuse me for fifteen minutes. I have a former client coming in for a closed-door session with Mr. Norman."

He studied her face for a few seconds. "Anything I should know about?"

She tipped her head, squinting. "Possibly. Let me see what course the outcome takes, and then I can relay the summary to you in a nutshell."

His expression warmed. "I do appreciate nutshells. Let me get going to the break room, before there's no supreme pizza left. I don't handle the meat lover's option as well as I used to. See you at the wrap-up." He knocked his knuckles on the back of her chair and rose to exit.

Aley stuffed her notebook into her bag, unsure of where to head. An attempt to hit the ladies room down the back hall would put her shoulder-to-shoulder with the Emporia staffers she'd avoided all morning. Too nervous not to make the trip, she ducked out the classroom door and headed in that direction. She glanced at her watch and figured she had ten minutes before expecting Hake at the front door. He'd likely text her upon arrival, so first things first.

In a series of dodges and hasty steps, she maneuvered past the gear closet where she noticed a new inspection listing had been posted. Only one entry had been inked in, but at least it represented a start. A tangle of concerns accompanied her into the ladies room, which stood empty. Maybe things had improved since she left.

That the office switch might have been mutually beneficial lightened her mood. As soon as she dried her hands, she grabbed her bag and headed for the front alcove to meet Hake. She made it to the conference room's double doors where she thought she heard her name called.

Brody approached the hallway. "Hey, Aley. Got a minute? Members of the old gang have something they want to say." He nodded sideways with a pleading look on his face.

Aley regarded him for a split second. A quick glance at the front told her Hake hadn't arrived yet. "Okay, I guess. Just one minute though." Determined not to over-explain her lunchtime plans, she followed him into the lengthy room. A corner of the dark walnut table separated her from four of the men she had worked beside for the past three years.

Brody swayed back and forth behind the seated men until he placed a hand on two sets of broad shoulders. Steadied, he looked right at her. "Guess I've been elected our speaker. Anyway, we all found it hard to sit through the harassment workshop, knowing the chiding we'd put you through. It might have started out as good-natured ribbing, but we let things progress out of hand. I regret my part in it and want to say that I'm sorry those incidents ever happened."

One by one, the others spoke up, some only choking out the *sorry* part. Since she hadn't expected any remorse from them, the impromptu contrition struck her as genuine. A heavy weight shifted off her shoulders. She looked at Brody who seemed to anticipate her response, so she dug deep. "Look, no one is casting any stones here. I think this is where Jesus would say, 'Go and sin no more.' Seriously though, awareness is the benchmark for realignment if you've been off-base, so I hope today offers us all a new starting point."

"We'll sure take that," Brody replied. His gaze shifted over her shoulder and clouded.

Aley turned to find Hake standing in the hallway. How much of the apologetic exchange he'd witnessed would be deciphered later. For now, they had acute pending business. "Right this way, Mr. Warren." She noted his long sleeve oxford shirt and creased black khakis, which gave the impression he was about to deliver a somber eulogy. As she approached Mr. Norman's closed door, the swelling lump in her throat seconded the grim emotion of death pending.

~

Hake allowed his rapid breathing to level off. He'd laid out the succinct timeline of action, the outcome of the trespass, and pictures of the damage from the photos Aley had e-mailed him. The evidence spoke to one obvious outcome, that the replacement conservation officer had been the trespasser. Finding nothing redeeming about the conflict of such a connection, his mind had galvanized to one favored outcome. Still—for Aley—he would defer to the office director for a decision.

After a few lengthy seconds, Mr. Norman placed the pictures on the desktop and looked up at him. "Well, this leaves us at an awkward juncture, doesn't it?"

Aley glanced between the two of them, her face looking pale. As they had previously agreed, she held her silence. Her straight posture spoke of unleashed strength as though she'd be ready for backup, if called upon.

Hake leaned forward, his fingers locked together. "From my perspective, there are two clearly defined ways we can proceed, so I'll pose them for your consideration. Option One, you decide to do nothing in-house and I take legal action against Mr. Burroughs for trespassing on his motorcycle without prior notification and for subsequent damages to my property."

The director waved a hand through the air. "Our agency isn't required to give advance notification, due to the regulatory compliance aspect of our work. We can visit whenever."

Hake leaned closer. "On a motorcycle that left damaging ruts all over my pastures?"

The man worked his jaw. "Well, no. He's out of line with the motorcycle. I can handle that in-house without getting some court involved."

"You mean that's outside of policies and procedures for the NRCS, don't you?"

"Yes, I can reprimand Mr. Burroughs for his use of the motorcycle…and include a directive to back off on some of his aggressive tendencies with our clients." He looked a touch vulnerable as he scratched the back of his head. "I got a call-in complaint from Mr. Douglas last week, Aley. He sure misses your visits out there."

"Poor Mr. Douglas," she replied in almost a whisper.

Unwilling to allow any softening of his stance, Hake straightened in his seat. "That brings us to Option Two, where I allow you to handle the reprimand in house. Since I would be abdicating justice to you as his immediate superior, I can settle for nothing less than my complaint representing strike one on Mr. Burroughs' permanent record. Please consider these options for a few moments, Mr. Norman. I can either press charges in my venue of familiarity, or relinquish the matter for your procedural handling. I relegate that final decision to you."

Silence held for seconds. Hake knew that suing his conservation officer may be construed as giving himself a black eye in the community, but Aley had warned him that the lax director would sweep the allegations under the rug if he didn't come in with a hard-line approach.

Mr. Norman fingered the photo and glanced up at Aley. "You realize that he only gets two strikes under the new statewide protocol. This puts Mr. Burroughs halfway to mandatory termination within his first two months of employment."

Hake stared at the man behind the desk. "He's the crazy man running around like a renegade on my property, shooting up the place like it's the Wild West or something. What if he had shot a steer instead? That would have represented a monetary loss for my cattlemen. We wouldn't even be having this conversation, as my first call would have been to the sheriff."

"Regulators don't like to play the *what if* game, Mr. Warren. We have a job to do which is normally quite predictable in outcome. I'll admit that this case falls outside of ordinary, but I personally don't think it constitutes legal action. For that reason, I am deciding to handle this in-house. Mr. Burroughs will receive a first strike for his erratic visit to your property last Thursday. I'll take care of that paperwork before close of work today and meet with him as required to file the action. That's my final decision on the matter." He handed the photos back.

"I'll watch for my copy of your reprimand within two days." Hake stood to leave. "In light of this early trouble, I would like to insist that my CSP contract be overseen by another conservation agent on staff, as Mr. Burroughs is no longer welcome on my property." *Good riddance.* He tucked the photos inside the file folder and walked out, abandoning Aley in the no man's land of her chosen profession.

Chapter 21

Aley sat in her apartment Thursday night, fussing with the arrangement of various trinket boxes on her dresser. She opened the ceramic clam shell and slid the garnet cocktail ring her mother had given her onto her finger. It looked out of place on her work-hardened hand.

Her thought progression skittered to Hake. Under normal conditions, she'd be at his ranch tonight sharing dinner and doing something productive by his side. The week had turned out anything but normal, fracturing their date night routine. He hadn't even called since the NRCS office visit. Maybe he wondered if his girlfriend happened to be more of a Benedict Arnold than trustworthy companion, or perhaps his skin rash lent him reason to hide.

She sighed and slid off the ring, clueless as to what to do about the distancing. If they saw each other in church on Sunday, that could mark a peaceable end to the stalemate. When Ron Lightner invited her to attend his church, she'd made some excuse about needing to stay connected with Reece and Candice in Emporia until the baby was born. Lame as excuses went, it still held relevance.

Headed for the bathroom to take a lengthy soak, she gave that excuse further evaluation. Council Grove seemed too far away to maintain closeness with her coming niece or nephew. Outside of work, she didn't know anyone in her new location except a few clients that lived on the rural outskirts of Morris County. For once, Emporia didn't seem lackluster by comparison.

She placed a jar of scented bath salts on the vanity top and stepped back into the hall to confirm she'd slipped the security chain in place. The sound of a key fitting a lock clicked from close by. Her heart skipped a beat as the sound of a door squeaking open echoed her way. The muffled sounds of a female neighbor welcoming her husband home filtered across the concrete hall. She blinked, bankrupted by a moment stolen from someone who enjoyed a shared life. Hollowed out, she excused away the sensation as borne of exhaustion and headed for the tub, bluer than blue.

~

Hake wrestled with his pillow, awake and listless. The coyotes' howling had forced him to shut the window over an hour ago. Still, sleep wouldn't come.

Details of the workday circled endlessly in his mind. The verification of disciplinary action for the errant conservation officer arrived by courier right before the close of day. That seemed to overshadow a partial payout for the Topeka clients, as the settlement company could only process the claims in groups of ten or less. That should have felt like two steps forward, but fell short by a disappointing mile.

"Dear Heavenly Father, if I didn't pursue justice in a way that honored you, could that be why I'm losing sleep? Don't the innocent have a right to be protected? Examine my heart. Is it as festering as my left arm? Don't allow me to linger far away from your will, even if it means correction for my unyielding part in this. Like King David once begged, create in me a clean heart, oh God. In the name of Jesus, I pray, amen."

A glance at the alarm clock revealed he could take another dose of anti-itch medicine. He swung his feet to the warm planking of the floor and wandered unbalanced into the kitchen. Once he'd drawn the glass of water, he flipped the lid off the antihistamine bottle and got a pill in his palm. Tossing it into the back of his throat, he took a long drink. As he lowered the glass, he saw the face of his cell phone light up even before it rang.

Startled, he grabbed its slender hull, punched the accept call symbol, and hoisted it to his ear. "Hake Warren here."

"Mr. Warren, this is Chief Mike Anders of the Emporia Fire Department. We've had some arson on Merchant Street and thought you might like to come down and check your law office for damage or loss. As far as we can tell, only the awning over the front window burned up, but I wanted to alert you to the breaking incident."

Hake pulled his fingers through his hair, thinking in slow motion. "Who'd do something like that, sir?"

"I'd have to guess at this point. Young punks come to mind, maybe looking for a late-night thrill. Listen, I don't seem to have a key on file to your law office yet. That's standard operating procedure for our department. The reason will be evident when you get here, so try to get me a copy made and forward the key to the station in the near future, okay?"

"Yes, sir. I'll do that tomorrow afternoon. I'll get dressed and come on into town." He ended the call and hastened back to the bedroom to retrieve his jeans and T-shirt. Thoughts of restless urban teens darted about in his groggy mind. He jammed his feet into old sneakers and headed out for an unsanctioned middle-of-the-night trip into Emporia. Bushong lost its peace in the process. Even the coyotes stopped howling, too wary for the disruption as his headlights split the canopy of darkness, ever pointing the way back to town.

~

His options narrowed after the knock-down fight he'd had with Dannie last night. The credit card dispute erupted again, and he had no patience for it. So help him, after she confessed the new town lawyer had advised her to decline payment, his blood boiled so quick, he could have busted a vein. That same lawyer had dared to taint his permanent work record with a strike. Livid at the link, he'd struck her without thinking. When blood spouted everywhere, he stormed out of the apartment to give her something more to wonder about. He'd call in a favor for a place to dive over the weekend. That should give her time to cool off. Then he'd turn on the charm again and win her back. She had a weak spot, one he knew by heart.

He entered the office like an upright public servant and decided to spend some time in the field. Brody passed the sign-out board, tossing a wave while he balanced the coffee pot filled with water in his other hand. It looked like Friday could transpire without further wrinkle. Dane signed out his favorite truck and didn't bother to duck by his cubicle. Nothing but a gray three-sided trap, he had better places to spend his valuable time.

~

Aley drove east on Highway 56, headed for her morning site visit west of the Lyon county line. With an empty weekend looming, she wanted to call Hake and get this impasse behind them. Each mile that passed put her closer to him. When the turnoff to Bushong came up, she realized she must have missed her intended destination. After nosing the truck into a culvert crossing, she turned around. Redirecting her heart proved to be a different matter.

Easing back toward Council Grove, she became a woman pulled in two opposite directions. The indecision worked on her resolve. If she arrived at the site visit early, she would give Hake a quick call and needle him into making some weekend plans. They had to push past this rough spot and gain ground. *Love endures all things...right?*

Seeing the Native American metal cutouts propped on a hill south of the highway, she remembered the note in her file to watch for that telltale sign on the landscape. The Pickett pasture should be directly across the road to the north. She slowed to find the heavy-set landowner standing in his pasture, waving her into the open gate. She sighed, knowing the call to Hake would now take low priority in her non-stop day. For the first time in her career, the pending fieldwork held no appeal.

~

Hake braced his chin in his hands. The second portion of the Topeka client payout lay on his desk in a lifeless check. He'd have to put a portion of it toward replacing the awning. Axe cuts in the exterior door would have to remain for now as forceful reminders to give the firemen a better way to gain access. *What a debacle.* At least his office's interior remained unmarred.

The clock on the opposite wall pushed ten-thirty. No one had needed his services since Tuesday when Janie Rose had visited. In truth, he had needed her, not the other way around. The lull offered him incentive to research yet another way to attract business. Somehow, the combative week had drained him of any ambition.

He had scarcely brought up the computer screen when his office phone rang. He grabbed it with low expectations. "Hake Warren, attorney at law. How may I help you today?"

"Carl Atkins here. Can you drop what you're doing and come to the ER? There's a young blond damsel asking for your help. She's being scheduled for rhinoscopy, but she'll be available once she comes out. How about by eleven o'clock?"

"I'll be there. Is there a name you can give me? I might have a file on her case."

"Sorry, I can't release a name, knowing you're not family or her spouse. I'll tell her you'll be on your way."

The phone went silent, adding further mystery to the beckon. Noteworthy, this represented his first hospital call. In seconds, his heart sank at the implication. Today, he became a full-fledged ambulance chaser. *Welcome to the stereotype.* He collected several files from his standup organizer and stuffed them into his briefcase, wondering how much help he could lend. As an afterthought, he grabbed the check, deciding to loop by the bank's drive-through lane on the way.

Twenty minutes later, his footfall echoed up the entry of the emergency room. Half a dozen people sat in the waiting area. A short line formed in front of the admittance clerk. Hake defaulted to the line until he could come up with a better plan. When two women wearing scrubs walked past, he saw his chance. "Excuse me. I've had a client summon me to the ER. I'm her lawyer, Hake Warren."

The older woman faced him. "Can you give me the patient's name to help me find her?"

"No, I can't. Carl Atkins called me on her behalf. All I know is that she was being scheduled for rhinoscopy at the time of the call."

The two women exchanged a knowing look. "Just one moment, please," the woman replied. She shifted to a side desk and selected a clipboard hanging on a hook. She returned and eyed him with scrutiny. "Can you show me some identification, Mr. Warren?"

He dug into a side pocket and produced his business card.

Though she declined possession, she nodded for him to follow.

Hake passed a grid of curtained-off enclosures. Sounds of the ill being attended to filled the area. Countless staff members came and went, some pushing equipment carts with IV lines. He kept pace with his guide while the distractions clawed at him from every angle.

The woman stopped abruptly at the end of a second enclosure. "You can only stay about five minutes. She has a date with the anesthesiology staff next." She lifted a hand and drew back the curtain.

On edge to face the client, Hake took two steps inside. When the patient turned toward him, there lay his credit card client—with her face rearranged. Black-eyed and in obvious pain, she seemed helpless. "Miss Tillison?"

"You came? Great. I wanted to show you what your good advice bought me—a trip to an unwanted nose job. It seems DJ didn't appreciate me turning him in. To add to his ire, something went wrong at work yesterday, so he came home to take it out on me. Does that news bring you any shame?"

He bent closer, struggling to maintain his decorum. "Domestic violence is never warranted, Ms. Tillison. You are a victim who may need some protection. I want you to think about your own well-being from here on out. We can arrange for a restraining order from DJ."

"What about this?" She shoved her hand into the air. Once her thumb pressed on the diamond ring, her meaning grew clear. "What should I do about my engagement?" Her voice cracked with emotion that eased into a simpering whine.

"Consider the cost of going through with that promise. Right now, there's nothing legally binding you to DJ. That's a personal decision you're going to have to make in the not-so-distant future. Do you want me to obtain a restraining order? If so, I'll need his full name."

The simpering turned to sobs about the time the curtain parted again. An orderly came in with a breathing apparatus, so she gave him a look of desperation. "Let me call you tomorrow after I've had some time to think. This is worse than him messing with my mind, much worse."

With the orderly gesturing for his prompt exit, Hake slid his business card between her fingers. "Call me if you decide to get protection underway. I'll wait to hear from you." He stepped from the enclosure, wishing he'd said something more uplifting in parting, like he'd pray for her. Out of sorts, he headed for the exit. The prayer happened without further hesitation, a real plea for relief from further human suffering.

The sunlight brought healing as he walked outside, though the brutal vision of the woman's damaged face replayed in his mind as he found his car. On a lark, he thought of Bluestem and decided to spend his lunch break in friendly territory. He could get some paint cards for the barn color and have the office key copied, too. When Aley popped to mind, he knew what else he'd be picking up. They were due for a reunion. Overdue, in fact.

Chapter 22

After returning the department truck, Aley decided to flex out an hour early since she'd worked through lunch. Once she'd stopped by her apartment to freshen up, she would drive to Bushong and surprise Hake when he came home. His earlier text about sharing Bluestem treats broke the stalemate and welcomed her company. Her heart longed to be with him.

Jo-Belle appeared in the hallway. "Are you back in the office for a while? I need someone to proofread a report for me."

"Sorry, I'm not staying. It's been a long day for me. I really need my weekend to start." Aley animated her expression a bit. "Hake and I have some catching up to do. Hope you have a great weekend." She signed out and headed for the parking lot.

The sky seemed endless through the tempered windshield as she navigated toward the apartment. Two minutes later, she skipped up the stairs to her entryway. She unlocked the door and headed straight for the kitchen bar to unload her bag. As the door clicked closed behind her, she made a mental list of items to pack for a weekend adventure. She'd stay overnight with Reece and Candice if her plans worked out.

Aley started down the hall when she spotted something littering the carpet. She stooped and snagged it on her way. Once under better lighting in the bedroom, she took a closer look. The tip of a fern frond had broken off. *How on earth did it get in the hall?* Maybe she had rats.

With instinctive assessment, she glanced back out to the hall. Another green fragment lay just inside the bedroom door. *Uncanny happenstance.* The hair rose on the back of her neck. Her heart pounded as she opened the closet door to grab her overnight bag. Only her shoes and clothes stared back from the closet's recesses. Relieved to find normalcy, she yanked a couple of outfits off their hangers and turned to dump all the selections onto the bed.

The bag landed with a whoosh, making something small fly off the far side of the bedspread. Unable to ignore it, she stepped around and knelt to lift the bed skirt. Another snippet of rabbit's foot fern nestled by the edge of her nightstand, green yet lifeless.

"I need to see that plant," she muttered. Resolve propelled her back into the front room where she headed for the west windows. At first glance, everything appeared to be in order with the plants. When she stepped closer to peer out the window, she caught a glimpse of something out of the corner of her eye. Looking down, she saw three shattered piles of clay fragments where the turtle, the rabbit, and the fox had been. They'd been smashed to bits.

A sob rattled her chest as her hand covered her mouth. No rat had the power to do that kind of destruction. The truth tumbled in from nowhere. Someone had infiltrated her apartment.

Fear drove her to the phone. In a second, she had the call placed. It rang for an eternity, her chest quivering all the while.

Finally, the call went through. "Hey, how's my favorite lady this afternoon?"

"Hake," she replied, her voice nothing but a squeak.

"I'm at the apartment. Someone's been in here again. This time I'm spooked because they pulverized the little clay animal figures I told you about."

"Look for a logical explanation, Aley. Maybe the curtain rod fell down."

She turned to look at her plant corner again. The curtains hung intact. "First, I found little pieces of my fern all over the floor leading to my bedroom. Then, one floated off the bed when I started packing." She paused for a breath, but hiccupped instead. "That's when I checked the plants and found the figurines demolished. This really has me shaken up, Hake."

"Go ahead. Pack your bag to leave. If you get to my place first, you know where I hide my spare key. Help yourself. Sorry, I have to go. Another call is coming in. See you in an hour or so. Goodbye, Aley."

Willing to face her fears, she took a few steps to re-examine the plant corner. *Am I missing something?* A particularly large fragment caught and held her attention—the fox's head. The wily character been placed at the lead of the line again. No fallen curtain rod would have done that kind of rearranging prior to smashing it to bits. The whole thing struck her as vengeful. A chill crept over the top of her shoulders. *Lord, please get me out of here.*

~

Hake tried to compose his thoughts before taking the next call. He lifted the office phone and held it to his ear. "Hake Warren, attorney at law. How may I help you today?"

"It's Danielle Tillison. I only wanted you to know I represented myself and had the court place a temporary restraining order on DJ. You won't have to get involved unless things get complicated before the follow-up hearing. Sorry if I was a little accusatory earlier. Nose pain hurts like crazy. Guess I was a bit edgy."

"No, that's quite all right. It sounds like you're thinking clearly now. You seem to be on the right track. I'm sure you've thought of this, but you need to change out your door lock."

"Yep, the police gave me some pointers. Believe me, my eyes are wide open."

"I wish you a speedy recovery, then. Stop by if you ever need help with another legal matter, hopefully something more innocuous like a traffic ticket." When she gave a chuckle, he felt the positive payback of investing in a non-paying customer.

"Guess I better go. Thanks again for everything."

The call fell silent, leaving Hake in a span of meditative thought. The need for keys and locks swirled in a representation of an imperfect world. Remembering Aley's panic, his mood turned abysmal. *Why isn't her lock holding trouble at bay?*

Danielle Tillison had to change out her lock, because DJ would pose a constant threat until she did. Now Aley seemed to need the same adjustment. The parallelism didn't escape him. He opened the walk-in client folder to make a new notation to maintain the record's progression. On the scrap of paper from her initial visit, he'd underlined four little words. *Messed with my mind.* His next breath caught in his throat as he realized Aley had used the exact same words.

Unease overtook him. Had he missed something along the way? The thought that he might know this DJ character persisted. But Aley had gotten her apartment from the new troublemaking agent at NRCS, Dane Burroughs. At the immediate contrast, a sense of foreboding hit him full force.

Breathing in dread, he pulled out the CSP file and threw it open to examine the final document. Aley had switched offices before the contract received its official number. He flipped to the signature page to find out who had signed it. In type under the scrawled signature was the name Dane J. Burroughs. His worst case scenario, the renegade conservation agent and the domestic abuser were one and the same. Hake had managed to antagonize the man on two fronts.

In rigid pursuit of full disclosure, he picked up the office phone and redialed the most recent call. When he heard the line click open, he spoke first. "Hake Warren again, Ms. Tillison. I have another lock and key question for you. This issue dates back to early May before DJ moved into your apartment. By any chance, did you have a second key to his old apartment?"

"Sure, I did. It was a thick brass thing. Guess I could take that off my key ring now."

When Hake heard the jingle of keys close to the receiver, he withheld his follow-up question. He had a slight inkling it would be unnecessary. His throat went dry at the prospect.

"Huh, that's odd. That key isn't on my ring anymore. Maybe DJ had to turn it in when he moved. He never mentioned taking it back. Sorry if that doesn't help you, Mr. Warren."

"No, you've been plenty of help. I'm sure there are lots of other unwanted reminders you need to clean out of your apartment. I'll let you go then."

"Well, the police took care of most of it. I've trashed a few small items. DJ is getting a big box of his belongings along with the temporary restraining order this afternoon. It won't be his best day, I'm sure of that. Still, I have to worry about myself at this point."

"That's the spirit, Ms. Tillison." Hake paused, acutely aware he had another opportunity to say something meaningful with his farewell. "As you rebuild your life, let me pass along this helpful advice. Give church a try. I think you'll find that these are the individuals you want making your life more positive."

She exhaled into the phone. "Why is it that I never like your advice at first crack, but you somehow prove to be wiser in the end?"

Hake chuckled at her hesitant relinquishment. "On this

particular wisdom, I just know what's worked for me. Thank you for answering my question regarding the key. I'll wrap up this file for now. You've done the right thing. Speedy recovery to you, Ms. Tillison. Goodbye now."

He dropped the receiver and picked up his cell phone. Without delay, he typed a text to Aley. *Leave your apartment ASAP. Lock door at my place and wait for me inside.* He would owe her an explanation later. Since he wasn't constrained to protect client privilege in this case, he certainly would offer her a pain-filled one.

~

Dane turned around when someone standing by the director's door cleared his throat. Two uniformed police officers kept company with Mr. Norman, one holding a white envelope. He closed out his file and powered down the computer.

"Here is Dane Burroughs, officers," Norman said. His expression remained stoic.

The man with the envelope strode forward and held it out. "I'm here to deliver this temporary restraining order which protects claimant Danielle A. Tillison from your company for three hundred and sixty-five days. That requires a separation distance of one hundred yards at any given time. At the second court hearing, you'll have an opportunity to present your case, but until then, this restraint prohibits you from being anywhere in her immediate proximity."

Stunned it had come down to this, the mention of future court action prompted an irate reaction Dane had to control. The whole thing stunk like the pesky lawyer had stirred things up again. Though the officer still spoke, his escalating blood pressure kept him from hearing.

The cop hunched to make eye contact. "Do I make the department's stance clear, Mr. Burroughs? There's zero tolerance for any violation of this order. No communication of any type shall be allowed. The court date is printed on the order, so please be sure to read it carefully."

The second officer stepped forward. "We have a box of your personal effects that the claimant released to us. If you could step outside, we'll make that transfer of possession happen."

Dane rose in response. His knees quaked, but he wouldn't show weakness in front of these drones. *Don't shoot the messenger.* Right, he'd hold his rage until the proper target availed itself. He knew just how and where to make that happen. He stepped between the policemen and allowed them to escort him out, the model of a peace-loving citizen.

"I believe you're done for the week," Mr. Norman added in passing.

Dane nodded, fingering his car keys in his pocket. He didn't have time to stay put anyway. He had to return balance to his life before sunset, a ride on an angry horse.

~

All this commuting hit her right in the gas tank. Aley glimpsed at the clock on the dash to gauge how much of a time penalty the fill-up had caused. Hake would be home in twenty minutes. She slowed for the Bushong turnoff, happy to be within a mile of her destination. The country quiet worked its spell on her, a respite she truly needed after such a hectic week.

As the big two-story house loomed on the horizon, she slowed the car. If she saw Janie Rose out in her yard, she might stop to exchange a few pleasantries. Though she scanned the recently-mowed yard, she didn't see the seasoned horticulturalist outside. Maybe she could drop by tomorrow. The car eased over the old railroad tracks that divided Bushong in half.

A broken-down truck hugged the ditch beside the entrance drive to Hake's house. She navigated around it, letting her car roll to a stop. A stocky man darted out from beneath the open hood and came right for her. The pointed handgun made his intention clear. It took Aley several seconds to recognize Dane Burroughs because of the crazed look on his face.

"Keep heading up the driveway, and I'll follow you. We're going to pay your boyfriend a little surprise visit. Now, hand me your phone so we can get going." He jammed an empty palm through the window.

For a millisecond, Aley wanted to stomp on the gas and crimp his plan from the outset. A saving grace, at least he let her stay in the car. Forced to comply, she surrendered the phone.

"Good. Now park your car in the same place you always do. I don't want him to notice anything amiss when he comes up the drive. I'm right behind you, so don't try anything."

Aley eased off the brake and let the car pick up speed gradually. In the rearview mirror, she soon spotted Dane on his motorcycle, riding the left-most rut. She felt the threat, as he could ride up and strike her right through her open window with little provocation. At the last second, something silver glinted on the northeast horizon. She glanced over and saw Janie Rose up a ladder in the orchard. *Please send help.*

The countryside seemed fragile during the awkward processional. Aley needed to concentrate on helping Hake as much as possible. With minimal motion, she reached behind the seat and snagged her overnight bag. She tucked it behind the console and worked the zipper open. By the handful, she removed clothes and scattered them around the backseat. Typically a neat-nick, he'd see that clue and know something was wrong.

She fingered a tube of lip gloss and brought it to her lap. Now she had a writing utensil, but needed a place to write a message. Her heel butted up against the present she'd made for Hake laying in the floorboard. She angled the limestone slab up against the gearshift and smeared four letters across the back. The yellow cross she'd painted hit her as reinforcement of a different kind. "I know you're ever with me, God. Still, I need you right now more than ever."

Rounding the curve, the farmhouse came into view, picture-perfect as painted in Old English Cottage. Tears began to mist her eyes thinking she might never see the humble dwelling again. With a toss of her hair, she refocused. The parking spot would be her next signal. Unwilling to pull into in her usual spot as directed, she remembered they had parked the department truck to the left of the drive by an old corral.

After scouting the features to the left, one stood out above the rest—the granary. Hake had been using the area as a turn-around zone, so the grass lay beaten down enough to fool Dane at casual glance. She slowed and turned her front bumper directly into the empty silo. With her foot, she slid the flat rock under the floor mat until it barely made a bump.

Dane turned the bike to head north and stopped outside her window. "Come on out and get on the back of my bike. If you try anything tricky, you'll live long enough to regret it."

Aley held up her hands so he could see them, and then realized she had to open the door. When she lowered her left hand, he moved the gun closer. She tripped the handle and let the door float open. Her seatbelt hindered her exit until she released the tether, a real plunge into high-risk behavior. Her mouth went dry as she straddled the motorcycle seat and tried not to touch the driver. That recoil lasted all of two seconds.

Dane revved the throttle so hard, the front tire left the ground, causing Aley to grope for a handhold to stay on. Dane laughed like a demon-possessed maniac at her plight and steered them toward a northern destination.

Between the tension and the sudden movement, nausea overwhelmed her caution. By the time they passed the corner of the front porch, she truly had a fight on her hands to quell the uprising. The tabby cat sprang from the barn, expecting to greet the new arrivals.

The familiar behavior pricked Aley's heart, a forfeiture which soon leaked from her tear ducts. All the elements she had grown to hold dear now fell like a shadow behind her, a foreboding of undeniable separation. Ahead she had only grass, so she determined to make it count. *What a humble ally.* The wind tore the droplets of regret from her eyes, creating a modern-day trail of tears marking the pasture road.

Chapter 23

The abandoned truck along the roadside put Hake on high alert as he turned down the entrance drive. His powers of observation sharp, he continued toward home. If he hadn't stayed at the office creating the message to Chief Mike tying the arson act with his suspect, he might have been home fifteen minutes earlier to enjoy Aley's warm smile. A staple of his daily greeting entourage, the meadowlark typically calling from the second fence post had gone missing, which only increased his wariness. Maybe Aley had flushed the bird—or not.

He took the midway curve with less speed than usual, which lent him more time to study the barnyard as he approached. Odd, Aley had parked to the left, using the old granary as a parking header. He pulled behind her car, intent to have a look inside. In a crouch, he slid out of the driver's seat and looked through the window. The car sat empty.

He opened the driver's door and took a quick survey inside. The scattered contents of her bag looked like she'd been raided. The threat drove his anxiety deeper. He almost missed the bump under the floor mat, making him open the door wider for more light. As he drew out the field stone, he examined the hand-painted cross and started to put it back.

Only when he stood did he notice the glossy smear on

the base of his thumb. He flipped the flat rock over and read the message printed in faint lipstick. "Okay Dane, you've beaten me home. Welcome to the only place on earth I have the true advantage—my own land." His teeth gnashed together as he slipped behind the wheel to approach the barn where he parked.

He scanned the scene, taking note of everything. The cat failed to run out of the barn upon his arrival. After checking, Honey wasn't on the back steps that led into the kitchen either. He killed the ignition as the realization seeped into his consciousness. *Dane has Aley.* He dashed into the house with two things teetering on his mind—grab the gun and get her back.

~

Aley knelt behind the water tank as instructed. The herd had moved between the farmhouse and their location, making it impossible to watch for Hake. She jerked around as the wildlife ladder scraped the tank rim. For some lunatic reason, Dane had it out for that ladder. Not threatened in the least, her brother could make her forty more where that one came from.

Gunshot rang out. She clamped her hands over her ears and squeezed her eyes closed. She had accompanied a madman out to the prairie, and didn't have a clue how to break away from him. Two shots later, the flare-up died back.

"Let's go," Dane demanded, his wrist flapping to wave the gun.

Aley slid on the seat, cooperative for the moment. She now had grass and cattle to work with, while Dane had three fewer bullets. She had to stay rational. More importantly, she couldn't provoke his volatile anger. Hake seemed to be an expert at that trick, so she'd leave overcoming a lunatic to her savvy lawyer friend.

~

Hake scrambled into the Jeep, laying Reece's rifle

across the passenger seat. Aley usually sat there, which added to his motivation to get underway. Old Betsy gave her signature salute and reversed out of the barn. He'd have been lost for direction if he hadn't spotted the barn cat trotting down the pasture road. Like a good hunting dog, Honey followed her prey. That made north his next direction.

Short of the Rails to Trails boundary beyond his fence, he began to assess the various components at his disposal. He scanned the horizon and only saw cattle. If he drove to the first rise, he could see further. No other strategy trumped that one, so he headed northeast to pick the highest spot on the ridge.

Thankful that this portion of the tract remained virtually treeless, he commended the former owner for his diligence against hardwood encroachment over the years. Aley had once mentioned that some landowners let the grassland waste away with tree and shrub growth to enhance the hunting quality. That struck him as counterintuitive, since he was on a hunt. Wide open served his purposes, but likely proved less advantageous for his quarry.

Four steers stood clear of a water tank. Odd, they didn't seem too interested in his passage. Sidetracked, Hake drove closer to inspect the situation. Water spurted from a hole on one side of the tank. Of course the wildlife ladder had been removed. He'd find it later and bolt it on next time. That hole in the tank would require a patch, a minor challenge he'd undertake another day. He revved the engine, and the Jeep clawed at the prairie grass to gain the ridge.

~

Dane knew his risky press to the north would pay dividends. He nosed the motorcycle into a rock-lined channel that seemed perfect for an ambush. Tall bluffs flanked each side, making the rock walls extend almost twenty feet high. Euphoric that he'd found the narrow hideout, he skidded to a halt and jerked his elbow into his passenger to signal her dismount. He eased the bike further in to better camouflage their presence and parked along the southern wall.

"Isn't this channel dandy?" He motioned for Aley to follow. "Seems useless now, but I bet it was top-notch in its day." At the far end, some kind of circular foundation remained. In the center, a rusted anchor block provided the perfect tether for his prisoner. "Come get acquainted with your new latch-hold."

Though her eyes shone with fear, Aley did what she was told.

He slid off his belt and used it to secure her to the spot, tying her wrists to the anchor. Part of his pending pleasure, she would witness the hapless landowner being shot down when he stumbled into their ambush. A long shadow fell as the sun began to sink on the horizon, adding to his cover. With premeditated care, he selected an ideal perch and began to keep watch. He knew that the lawyer would come out looking for them, because the creep always had to stick his nose in other people's business. Predictable behavior could become a flaw, one he intended to avoid. He crouched like a wary coyote, poised for lethal attack.

~

Calmer than she should have been, Aley surveyed her predicament. Loose enough, she'd already worked the belt down an inch off her wrist. Being free proved only a matter of time. A quarter-sized chip of flint lent itself as her only convenient weaponry. The cattle stood closer to the rise, but seemed to be shifting their way. When the Jeep cleared the ridge, she saw what had caused their movement. "Be smart about it, Hake," she pled under her breath. Using her left foot, she scooted the rock closer. With only one shot to deliver, she'd have to make the most of it.

~

From where Hake stood, the entire pasture sat exposed—except for the far side of the railroad spur and its carved-out cattle crossing. Analytical, he decided to drive across from the east so the Jeep's rollbar could help protect him. If Dane lurked down in the rock-lined passageway, he'd flush him out by providing a target too tempting to pass up. A plan laden with risk, he needed to flush his prey into a clearing, and then he'd bear down on him. Aley might become vulnerable in the process, but only for a split second.

He suspected the motorcycle might come into play, as he'd seen the grass bent in a linear track back at the tank. Though the bike might be agile, he'd pit his Jeep against it in a flat-out showdown on uneven terrain. Fortunately, the northern fence line prevented any race from proceeding further—unless Dane doubled back. He'd watch to force him north, if possible.

Hake accelerated and headed down slope. Precious seconds ticked by as he overshot to the east. Finally, he manhandled the steering wheel to bring the vehicle around for the sitting duck pass. As he assessed the draw's potential, he felt the need to heighten the attraction. He switched off the ignition and slid from the driver's seat, keeping a low profile. The rifle teetered in his clandestine grip, so he tightened his wrist. For five seconds, he fully exposed his body as bait, pretending trouble at the front grill. An eternity of time ticked by with no reaction from the madman.

~

Crazy like a fox. Aley watched Hake set his snare from her perch east of the cattle crossing. Dane had climbed higher up the rock wall and positioned the gun to fire from a two-handed grip. Ready to be shed of the restraint, she tugged the belt over her sweaty wrists, gritting her teeth against the pain. The rough buckle dug into the side of her thumb enough to make it bleed. That proved to be all the lubrication she needed to get unbound. In slow motion, she reached for the rock. *Come on, Hake. Start Old Betsy.* She crouched, ready to take her shot.

~

The urge to move forward goaded Hake. He shook off

his disappointment that open bait hadn't flushed his enemy into action. He slid back behind the wheel and propped the gun by the gearshift. "Trusting you, God, as I'm running out of options here." He cranked the ignition and hit first gear. The vehicle backfired in anger, letting half the county know his exact position.

~

At the sound of the backfire, Aley uncoiled and slung the rock, aiming at the wall near Dane's head. It smacked the hard surface and sent fragments ricocheting on him where he perched. "He's shooting at you," she screamed at a run, acting wild-eyed at the outcome. In a frenzied reach, she swiped the side of his temple and showed him the blood on her thumb.

Repulsed in the heat of the offensive, Dane waivered and grew antsy. He backtracked down the wall and jumped onto the bike. As he kick-started the engine, he glared back at her.

Aley stood her ground. "Save yourself through the north gate—or die today for no good reason." A spit of rocks came as his only reply as he accelerated out of the channel. The bike cleared the crossing and banked north. Aley drew a long breath. *He's all yours, Hake.* They now had Dane right where they wanted him—in the open and on the run.

~

Hake had to blink to clear his disbelief when the motorcycle shot out of the gap. He ramped the Jeep's speed and dropped off the slope in a dead run for due north. If it came down to it, he'd ram his reinforced front bumper up against the back tire of the bike and render it useless. He only hoped he didn't have to take out a section of his four-strand barbed wire fence to accomplish that feat. He repositioned the rifle between his knees to brace for a possible collision.

Dane dismounted at a run. He jerked at the chain that locked the gate to a sizeable post. Without a combination to remedy the locking hasp, he leapt right back onto the motorcycle.

Hake had a split second to decide what direction to cut off, so he chose to deny the western flank. Once Dane headed east, he stomped the gas pedal. Even from behind, he felt confident he could call the shots. The madman had nowhere left to go.

The dead-end railroad spur opened up ahead. He blinked when the motorcycle did the unthinkable by ascending its entry ramp. Hake's only decision now fell as to how fast to push the bike's driver over the brink. If he let Dane hang onto the rim, he'd likely force a point-blank shootout. Since Aley remained down in the cattle crossing channel, he couldn't let that happen. With his leg taut, he mashed the accelerator to the floor, watching for his regular braking cue in the form of a rock on the side of the rail line.

Dane looked back over his shoulder only once. In seconds, the motorcycle left the spur and went airborne. In a final release of traction, the rear tire misaligned the bike and then everything exploded in midair. Distorted, the chassis barely made the far stone-lined wall where it struck with a crash, its driver unable to dislodge.

Wrapped in a more immediate pending calamity, Hake slammed on the brakes, but had long since passed the fateful safety marker. Rocks flew everywhere as the Jeep cocked sideways and drifted on gravel, losing traction with every passing inch. In a heart-halting moment, he saw the channel open below his left shoulder. The distance to ground level shot terror through his chest as the old jalopy began to opt for relinquishment of its embrace of the prairie's upper deck.

~

Aley recovered from the startling loudness of the blast and covered her face when the motorcycle slammed Dane into the south rock wall mere feet from where he'd been perched ready to commit murder half a minute prior. By the awkward angle he'd landed, she had little hope for his survival. Even prior to impact, the rear portion of the bike had been shattered by an invisible force that arrived with the explosion. Turning, she saw Janie Rose approaching in a gimpy run, a shotgun teetering in her hands.

The aged woman began to shoo her with a full-armed gesture. "Land sakes, Aley. Go help Hake down."

In a cautious trot, she closed in where the Jeep hung precariously over the rock rim of Sunset Spur. One rear tire continued to spin in midair. The incredulous scene ended with two shoe soles dangling from the top rocks beyond the front grill. When Hake attempted a foothold up on the spur, the desperate move proved to no avail. A siren split the twilight, only to confuse the scene further.

"That's the sheriff," Janie Rose said. "I called him when I saw the man in the truck force you to go with him. I figured we had our poacher back, but I wasn't about ready to play that shoot-em-up game again."

"Ladies," Hake shouted. "A little help over here, please."

Aley spotted the sheriff's car headed toward them along the old railroad track. "Janie Rose, you go let the good sheriff in the gate. Put in Christmas Eve as the combination."

"Christmas Eve, December twenty-fourth," the old woman muttered as she passed. "Oh, I can sure appreciate the significance of that, all right."

Aley took a deep breath and relaxed, now alone with Hake in one of their favorite courtship spots. She lifted her hands and centered them right beneath his feet. "Fly to me, Rancher."

Hake's grip failed and down he came, dropping into her arms until they both tumbled to the ground with the momentum. Like the granary exit and the spot-over fire, he arrived with excessive force. Part respite, the channel's rock wall dampened the siren's constant wail.

She tugged him further away from the Jeep, in case Old Betsy decided to surrender her cliff-hanging theatrics. Then, she took a personal moment to wrap the landowner in her arms. "I knew you'd come for me, Hake. I tried to help lead you with clues as much as possible."

He snuggled closer. "Like I tell my clients, you can run but you cannot hide."

Aley brushed the gravel off his cheek. Nose to nose, she marveled at the resourceful man in her arms. "No, you can't hide from a rancher who truly knows his land. As for me, I wouldn't want to." Saved from her perch along the rim of Hades, she melted into his kiss. Lost in his tender embrace, she faintly overheard the sheriff request assistance.

Hake pulled back, his eyes wide. "I need to learn how to mend a leaky water tank before I burn out my solar pump."

"Well," she teased. "You just might have the right woman in your arms."

He arched one brow into his hairline. "I hoped you might say that, as I need a new conservation officer to partner with me out here."

"Come Monday, I promise to check and see if the job might be open." She gave his scuffed chin a quick peck.

Janie Rose crouched over them with a look of intense scrutiny. "Say, can Hake walk? The sheriff's called for the ambulance, but it won't do this motorcycle fella one bit of good." With a groan of reluctance, she handed her shotgun to the sheriff at his stern insistence.

Aley pulled to her knees and stood. Hake required more help than that, but between them they managed to get him upright. The sheriff took one look at the dangling Jeep and shook his head. Aley winked and held up her injured thumb, which Hake promptly covered with a healing kiss. Before the ambulance could arrive, part of the herd wandered down the slope, re-staking a claim for the cattle crossing in the ebbing light of dusk.

Epilogue

Aley swung Hake's arm as she skipped to the lakeside pavilion over Peter Pan Park's mowed lawn. Families enjoyed their leisure, celebrating the holiday at the playground and nearby picnic area by simply being together.

Hake fixed his gaze across the lake. "How about the irony of becoming a father on Father's Day?"

"Well, Candice tried to avoid the coincidence, but she needed that last round of pushes to complete the delivery, so the clock ticked past midnight. I can hardly wait to bring baby Elijah here to play in the park. Can we head for the hospital next? I'm downright giddy to see him."

"First things first, Ms. Halstead." He nodded toward the pavilion and nudged her beyond the playground's perimeter.

The sheer overlay on her yellow dress caught the breeze and floated out like the petals of a primrose. A puffy cloud decorated the sky above the lake, letting her enjoy seeing double. If not for the grass tickling her toes above the soles of her sandals, she might have been traveling lighter than air.

Hake clasped her hand tighter. "It's beautiful out here today, isn't it?" Like a gentleman, he stepped to one side and guided her up the single step of the pavilion.

"Yes, picture perfect. I admire how the pavilion seems to frame the park in a panorama of earth and sky right along the horizon." She inhaled the fresh air streaming over the lake to cool late June.

Hake took both of her hands and stepped closer, intent to focus her. "Remember our first kiss right here? I'd honestly begun to think that might never happen."

She smiled and nudged his shoulder with hers. "Look how far we've come since then."

He gave her a longing stare and then seemed to shrink away.

She gasped when he knelt on one knee. With her hands locked in his, she couldn't cover her shock. She wanted to say something, but no words would come. The lake lapped at the structure's foundation, lending the moment a natural rhythm.

"I told you that day, welcome to love everlasting," Hake said. "But I find that's not enough for me anymore. Today, I want to pose this abridgement for your consideration. Welcome to love-at-my-side everlasting." He released her hand a moment and produced a diamond ring that twinkled in the sunlight. "Would you marry me, Aley? I can't take another day not knowing."

She grabbed his hand in spite of the ring, needing to connect. "I wonder how you make the rest of the whole world go away like that, Hake." She gave her head a shake, attempting to understand his heady influence on her. "Yes, I want to marry you. In fact, I hope your love-at-my-side everlasting starts in the not-so-distant future, as I have two jobs and nowhere to live at the moment."

He worked the ring in place and stood to take her in his arms. "You mean three jobs," he teased, rubbing his lips across her cheek. "Today, you're agreeing to become a rancher's wife." He lifted her off the pavilion's planking and captured her in his embrace, slowly spinning as if to give her a panoramic view of their future.

Aley held the man who stood at the center of it all, elated at the promise of their togetherness. She ended his kiss and found an ear to whisper into. "How does the end of summer sound for an outdoor wedding?"

"As long as you plan it prior to Labor Day, because I'm incorporating that holiday into our honeymoon. I already have my closed sign ready to hang at the office."

Magnetic with his adept ability to balance business with pleasure, she tucked her face under his chin to remain close. "God above will have to show me how love everlasting can get any better."

"Oh, I'll show you," Hake pledged, landing a kiss on her ring finger.

Her world began to spin again, with a man at the hub who made life happen in a whole new way. Transported by the hope-filled promise, she vowed to let him lead down the future's path as long as the scenery came flanked by fields of grass that combed blue skies along a lengthy horizon.

Message to the reader:
Thank you for reading Book 2 in my Horizons of Hidden Promise series! Please read further for the beginning of Book 1, "Rekindled from Ashes" for another romance blooming on the horizon.

Rekindled from Ashes: Saga of Resiliency

Chapter 1

An irreverent wind rifled through the shortgrass prairie of western Kansas. The first week of March seldom reached eighty degrees, so Burk Crosby determined to make the most of his work day. He studied the sagging top wire that enclosed his largest pasture and opted to tighten the fence with a splice, a quick fix that would keep the herd contained.

When the wind gusted, he nearly lost his hat, an irksome hindrance. He grabbed a length of barbed wire and slid fence pliers into his back pocket. Having already taken the head count on the cattle, he gave the ailing fence his unbroken attention.

The south wind rushed past again, sending his hat rolling down the fence line. He quick-stepped in retrieval mode with a grumble locked under his lips. A faint hint of smoke rubbed against his devotion to the fencing task, but he ignored it to set the wire splice in place.

A glimpse of the southern horizon made venom rise in

his throat at the cantankerous bluster determined to mar the warm day. Under clear skies, he could see a good ten miles into Oklahoma from where his ranch sat southeast of Ashland. Today, a dark bush seemed to overgrow the horizon, making any distant outlook impossible. He blinked to better discern the blurred hindrance.

Unsettled, he dropped the wire splice and walked along a steady rise on the landscape. Further west of town, such a slope plunged into red dirt canyons that eventually framed the Big Basin. Cut by a creek, this pasture offered a more gradual transition, but he was grateful for the elevation nonetheless. As his boots kicked dust at the top of the rise, he paused and assessed the southern horizon.

First to the east, and then to the west—as far as his gaze roamed—the dark bush vented skyward. Plumes of smoke began to snake from the bush, licking the air. "Lord God above, not a grassfire…" By the looks of things, half of Oklahoma might be on fire. With the boisterous wind hailing from due south, his ranch sat in the direct line of advance.

He turned to locate the cattle. Surrounded by knee-deep grass—winter-bleached and crackle-dry—the terrain lay volatile as all get-out. Sweat tightened his hatband. He broke into a choppy run off the knoll, needing a survival plan and needing one fast.

~

Swamped with hollow satisfaction, Lyndie Leigh Sessoms accepted payment from the rodeo coordinator and handed the check over to her manager. "Here you go, Ernie. Thanks for coming over from Tulsa to catch the Oklahoma City show."

The coordinator tipped his hat and disappeared inside the arena.

Ernie Matthews kicked at some wood chips lining the chute area as he folded the plump check into his wallet. "You could still get on the playbill down in Enid the fifteenth of March—if you wanted to."

She held out an open palm to stop him. Goodness knows that man could draw out a two-word prayer, given the opportunity. "Look Ernie, we've already been over this. I need a break—some time off to think about my future. This rodeo circuit has grown wearisome lately."

"But folks adore you, Lyndie Leigh." He leaned in to give her a show biz wink while he tucked the wallet away. "You're a modern-day Dale Evans. The world needs a star like that."

She sniffed and squared her feet. "Maybe what the world really needs is a Roy Rogers figure—a hero on a palomino to ride in and save the day."

"Speaking of horses, would it be all right for me to loan out Tracer for sire duty during your sabbatical? We could cut the fee fifty-fifty."

Her gaze shifted to the horse trailer already hitched to Ernie's truck. The buckskin's muzzle appeared through the window. "Do whatever you think is best. At the end of three months, we'll reconsider where we stand."

He tapped the heels of his boots together. "That's a mighty long time off, Lyndie. You'll have to come back strong. Where you headed, anyway?"

"Someplace that needs me." She offered her hand in a parting gesture. "I'll be in touch."

"Don't forget your Friday night radio spot. That's still a go for Western Star duty."

"String around my finger to remember." She pretended to tie one on. "Hope you'll listen in, so you won't worry about me too much."

He shook his head and stepped back. "Try to find what you're lookin' for, little lady. Life ain't about foot-dragging, after all."

"Be well, Ernie. Time for me to head north."

"Watch that Kansas state line. I heard there's a wildfire out of control up that way."

She saluted and walked toward her rig. Maybe she

needed direct exposure to fire. The camper trailer didn't necessarily appear flameproof—but she sure felt that way.

~

Ironic that he'd come out to *mend* fences, Burk now clamped down on the pliers and snipped through the fourth strand. With a little cooperation, he could move the entire herd onto his winter wheat to buffer them from the intensity of the blaze. Over the last half hour, the dark line had crept considerably closer. If only the wind would lay back some, then the pressure might ease off a bit. Still, he couldn't trust what amounted to a lame wish.

He jumped into his four-wheeled ATV and threw it into reverse. Ill at ease from the smell of smoke, the cattle stood packed together along the far fence. He planned to herd them through the new break, optimistic that the lure of greening wheat would be too much to resist. For the second time that week, he flat-out needed a herding dog.

Once in position, he made some noise by tapping the vehicle's horn a couple of times. Those honks scattered the herd like an angry bust on racked billiard balls. None went straightway into the corner pocket of the fence cut—not one. He spat and checked the grassfire's progression over his shoulder. For the first time, he spotted orange flames where the sky met the land.

"Come on—cooperate for once." He swept an arc to the east around a majority of the cattle and drove them back toward the opening. A solitary steer wandered into the wheat field and began grazing. Like a roadside advertisement, the suggestion spread. Within minutes, three-fourths of the herd stood on fire-resistant ground cover.

Regret for not having a gate handy pinched his side. Another twenty-five head still stood in harm's way. He glanced south and saw that the fire had already engulfed the adjoining McMinimy spread. Sickened at the sight, he swiped a hand over his lips and headed north, determined to round up the remnant.

As a last resort, he could cut the northernmost fence and leave the cattle to fend for themselves up on the Guards' property. A double-sized pond up there would make the perfect refuge. Of course, the cattle would have to reason that out and wade into the water. Something sat on the broad edge of ain't-gonna-happen with that scenario.

Burk breathed in smoke and coughed. He shifted the bandana up over his nose and wiped watery eyes on his sleeve. The wildfire advanced on the devil's frictionless sled. Where he stood at the base of the knoll, he was about to get run over.

A square plot lined in spring green opened to the west. He'd completely forgotten about the old settlers' cemetery. Mowed last October, it held practically no fuel for the fire. Racing to the longer edge, he frantically worked the hinges loose from one wrought iron panel and rotated it open. Slowed by dread that accompanied the last-ditch effort, he trotted up behind the southernmost steer and began to wave his arms. "Hey-yah," he called, closing the distance.

The pried-open railing acted like a funnel to guide the animals inside. Once half the animals had passed through the portal, the vise-clamp on his chest eased off some. He walked the last of the steers into the cemetery compound and took the panel in his hand to close the pen.

For no apparent reason, the herd spooked from the rear. Fighting the smoke, Burk hastened to secure the closure and trap them inside. When he looked up, five hundred pounds of attitude bore down on the opening. He saw a white blaze that marked two flaring nostrils. A split-second decision, he spanned the gap with his body to thwart the skittish escape attempt. The panicked steer remained unfazed. A direct collision stole his breath. Reeling, he crumpled to a helpless embrace of the ground where his rescue turned motionless black.

~

Lyndie chided herself for thinking it would be easy to

ride the coattails of the wildfire. Halted, a herd of cattle now claimed the highway as its domain. The last information sign she'd passed stated Sitka was two miles ahead. A gravel road to the west represented her only option, so she pulled the steering wheel in a full rotation to avoid the wide-eyed cattle.

Knowing country roads intersected every mile, she'd head north again at her first opportunity. The fire had already raked through this section. Wooden fence posts smoldered like abandoned cigarette butts down both sides of the road. All points in between could be described, in no uncertain terms, as lifeless black. The prairie had gone from landscape to lunarscape.

An improved road soon bisected this east-west road, so she slowed for a right turn. The gusty crosswind buffeted the camper one last time and surrendered to become a beneficial tailwind. With north her preferred direction, her chosen destination of Ashland must remain somewhere up ahead.

The truck geared down to achieve the climb up a steady rise. The damage along the way left a searing impression. In the corner of a pasture, a lifeless lump turned out to be a trapped steer. The somber sight dug at her nurturing instincts, but nothing could be done at this point.

Once the truck leveled out, an ornate arch appeared up ahead. Intrigued, she eased off the gas to take a better look. It marked a cemetery. There in the ashes, a cowboy knelt outside a wrought iron fence. Braking to a stop, she watched him topple over onto the blackened ground.

After throwing the gearshift into park, she killed the ignition. *Right place at the right time.* Slinking between barbed wire strands, she made her way to the downed man. Twenty-odd steers continued to graze inside the cemetery, extremely lucky to be alive.

Lyndie dropped to her knees at the man's side. With his shirt torn in several places, dried blood caked several of the holes. She touched his neck. It felt clammy cool. "Hey there, cowboy. Great job saving the herd. Looks like you outsmarted the wildfire." When he tried to roll onto his back, she assisted him.

"No...no smart to it," he replied in a scratchy voice. His chin wore a black-and-blue scuff. Hazel eyes the color of cedars in winter glanced away.

When she leaned closer to shade his face, his pupils failed to respond to the light change. "Okay, cowboy. I'm taking you into town for medical treatment. Think you can walk to my rig?"

"Point to my feet, will you?" The corner of his mouth twitched up as his entrancing eyes fluttered closed.

She tapped the toe of his closest boot, willing to play the comeback game. Her frank assessment began to pay a bonus dividend as the hazel-eyed rancher had been chiseled from a solid rock. When she locked her arms around his shoulders to help him stand, the rock analogy played out into a six foot-two muscle-clad man only a little the worse for wear.

His arm soon slid around her waist. "You lead."

She took a series of burdened steps. Glancing ahead, she spotted the barbed wire fence. "Hey, are you up to straddling the roadside fence?"

He rested a heavy head on her shoulder. "No—too in and out of it. Roll me under."

"Okay. Sure wish the steer back there with the white blaze could have had that option. I'm afraid you lost that one." She paused at the fence and lowered him for the roll underneath.

The man tucked a thumb into a tear in his shirt. "The two of us locked heads earlier, but I couldn't persuade him to stay in the cemetery."

"Sometimes winning seems like losing in the moment. It's best to make your final choice when you can stand up straight in your own boots." With that nugget of wisdom, she shoved him into a rolling motion and cleared her last apparent obstacle. *Goodness, what a find.* Those cedar-shaded eyes were another matter.

Author Bio:

Cindy M. Amos writes about ranching life with "man on the land" fiction from the heartland of America. Dedicated to the family's ranchland in both the tallgrass and shortgrass prairies of Kansas, she enjoys mixing honest sweat equity and nature appreciation as she accomplishes her ranching chores in the Flint Hills surrounding Council Grove. A little bird watching on the side never hurt anyone in the grand scheme of life when the meadow stretches to the far horizon. A work of fiction, "Reconciled from Heartache" represents the author's 39th book with Winged Publications and owner/editor Cynthia Hickey, in the Forget Me Not Romances imprint.
Member: American Christian Fiction Writers and Heart of America Christian Writers Network.

The author's entire booklist with Winged Publications can be found on her website:
http://cindymamos.wixsite.com/natureink

Her author page on Amazon is found at:
https://www.amazon.com/Cindy-M.-Amos

~Writing romance onto nature's landscape~

OTHER BOOKS BY CINDY M. AMOS
Landscapes of Mercy Series
Redeeming River Rancher
Saving Bicycle Man
Justifying Sound Strider

Sanctifying Ace Aerialist
Lifting Lock Runner
Salvaging Doctor Junk

National Parks 100th Anniversary Romance Collection
Everglades Entanglement
Mesa Verde Meltdown

Holiday 3-in-1 Collection
Running Out of Christmastime

Taming the Cowboy's Heart Collection
Warming Stone Cold Lodge

50 States Collection
Secondhand Flower Stand (Kansas)
Red Cloud Retreat (Nebraska)
Tidewater Lowlands (North Carolina)
Canyon Country Courtship (Utah)

John Denver 20th Anniversary Collection
Calypso Reimagined

Loving the Town Hero Collection
Cascading Waterworks

Cowboy Brides Collection
Renegade Restoration

America's Fabulous Fifties Series
Oil Field Maven
Airfield Aptitude
Camp Field Capable

Small Town Christmas Collection 2018
Gift Tag Tree

Romancing the Rancher's Daughter Collection
Waylaying the Hauler

Romancing the Farmer Collection
Furrowed Hearts

Adventure Brides Collection
Ocean's Edge

Romancing the Bachelor Collection
Impasse to Springtime

Romancing the Boy Next Door Collection
Forty Acres on Loan

Romancing the Doctor Collection
X-Raying the Doctor

Vote for Love Collection
Ballot Box Rumors

A Secret Santa Romance Collection

Sweet Regrets from Sourwood

Christmas Cookie Brides Collection
Pizzelles for Elves

Romancing the Drifter Collection
Derailing the Drifter

A Family to Love Collection
Skinny Ranch Romance

Nonfiction Little Lift Gift Books
Signs of the Seasons: Hints from Nature

The Men of Mustang Pass Series
Silver Lining at Mustang Pass
Copper Halo at Mustang Pass
Sapphire Skies at Mustang Pass
Holiday Hitches at Mustang Pass

Horizons of Hidden Promise
Rekindled from Ashes

www.ingramcontent.com/pod-product-compliance
Lightning Source LLC
LaVergne TN
LVHW012037070526
838202LV00056B/5526